A Little Rebellion Is a Good Thing:
Troubles at Traymore College

A
LITTLE
REBELLION
IS A GOOD THING:

Troubles at Traymore College

a novel by Duncan L. Clarke

BELLE ISLE BOOKS
www.belleislebooks.com

Copyright © 2020 by Duncan L. Clarke

No part of this book may be reproduced in any form or by any electronic or mechanical means, or the facilitation thereof, including information storage and retrieval systems, without permission in writing from the publisher, except in the case of brief quotations published in articles and reviews. Any educational institution wishing to photocopy part or all of the work for classroom use, or individual researchers who would like to obtain permission to reprint the work for educational purposes, should contact the publisher.

ISBN: 978-1-951565-87-9
LCCN: 2020907274

Printed in the United States of America

Published by
Belle Isle Books (an imprint of Brandylane Publishers, Inc.)
5 S. 1st Street
Richmond, Virginia 23219

BELLE ISLE BOOKS
www.belleislebooks.com

belleislebooks.com | brandylanepublishers.com

For Ann

This is presented as a work of fiction.

Contents

"I hold that a little rebellion is a good thing."

—Thomas Jefferson

The social turbulence of the sixties reached a women's college in rural Virginia in 1969 when a headstrong young male professor was hired. Through alliances with a dean and two students, he challenged Traymore College's paternalistic culture. In confronting its corrupt president, he jeopardized his career and put his life in danger. I know this to be true. I was that young professor.

—David Pritchard

1

Memory Jarred

"Watch out, Lovey!" I shouted.

"Oh, my."

We nearly stepped on the rattlesnake. The late afternoon sunlight caught the diamond-shaped head and brown-yellow body as it coiled on the side of the dirt path. Its rattles buzzed their warning.

Our German shepherd had been the first to notice. Alarmed, Maggie backed away with a deep growl. If not for her reaction, one of us would have been bitten.

Lovey and I were hiking near the Appalachian Trail along Jeremy's Run in Shenandoah National Park. We had been making our way back to Elkwallow Wayside, where we'd left our car, when we encountered the snake. The hike had been strenuous, and the day was an uncommon one that locked itself into my memory.

We talked very little on our hikes, especially the more challenging ones. We touched, smiled, and exchanged knowing glances as we walked, freeing our minds to think their own thoughts as we, each in our own way, absorbed the sights, sounds, and feel of the forest.

My wife of twenty years took up hiking only after we were married. Lovey had a preternatural intimacy with nature that

I envied but never could quite match. She was comfortable in the mountains and accustomed to the risks hikers face from weather, wildlife, falls, and other hazards. We had hiked all of Shenandoah's many trails together, and finished the entire Appalachian Trail in 1976. We came across timber rattlesnakes from time to time. Though uncommon, they are among North America's most venomous snakes, but thankfully, they're relatively mild-tempered.

On that brilliant spring day, we skirted the snake and continued up a trail that was soon adorned on both sides with sweetly scented bell-shaped lilies-of-the-valley in their translucent, porcelain whiteness.

Before long, less than half a mile from our car, a hiker approached us as he descended from Skyline Drive. He looked to be perhaps thirty and in good shape. His well-worn boots suggested some experience in the outdoors.

"Watch out for a rattlesnake," I warned. "It's on the trail. You'll encounter it soon."

"Thanks," the man said. "Don't see too many anymore. They're now pretty rare in Virginia." He leaned lightly against a large oak sapling with springtime soft yellow-green leaves. "People kill them. Cut off their rattles. It's sad."

"It is." I stared at my feet, took a deep breath, and recalled with real regret that I had done that very thing as a teenager. "You seem pretty knowledgeable about wildlife."

"I'm a park ranger. Today is my rare day off."

While I chatted with Ranger Howard Thornton ("call me Howie"), he revealed, among other things, that he was a graduate of Traymore University in Traymore, Virginia.

"Wow!" said Lovey, looking at me. "I'm an alumna of Traymore. Dave taught there for a year."

I scuffed my boots in the dirt and said, "That was well before you would have attended. It was Traymore College then, exclusively for women. You're looking at someone who, along with others, compelled that state college to accept men as students." I smiled and added, "Guess you owe your degree to me."

"How 'bout that," said Ranger Howie. "What did you do?"

"Long story," I said, leaning forward on my bamboo hiking stick. "In short, I got supremely pissed off about the college's willful violation of the law on this and many other matters. The college president at the time, Elzic Barton, was a rigid hard-ass who fiercely defended the *status quo*. He couldn't care less about the law—that is, until we whacked him over the head with it." I swung my hiking stick hard, mowing down some nearby stinging nettles.

"You must be a lawyer."

"Well . . ." I cracked my knuckles and smiled. "Maybe I sometimes acted in that capacity."

Ranger Howie tipped his baseball cap and stepped toward me. "Thank you."

With that, Lovey and I exchanged warm handshakes with him, and we headed off in opposite directions.

Just before Ranger Howie trekked out of sight, he turned and shouted: "Say, what's your name?"

"Dave Pritchard."

"Think I've heard that name . . . somewhere."

For two decades, I had given virtually no thought to my conflict-ridden, life-changing nine months at Traymore College. If not for the rattlesnake, Lovey and I wouldn't have spoken with the ranger. Snakes have symbolized everything from death to healing since before the Book of Genesis, but I didn't reflect on that at the time. I should have. A rattlesnake probably saved my life in the spring of 1970, when I was still at Traymore.

When we met Ranger Howie Thornton in May 1991, life was good. I was a tenured professor at American University with two young daughters. When I had left Traymore for Washington D.C. in 1970, it didn't take long for me and Lovey to get back together because she was a new graduate student at nearby Johns Hopkins University in Baltimore. Our relationship was an exceptional blend of love and lust. Within weeks, we were engaged. Three months later, on the campus of my alma mater, the University of Virginia, we were married in a nineteenth-century gothic revival chapel.

I had no way of knowing on that day in 1991, with the snake and Ranger Howie, that in just two years, Lovey would be diagnosed with stage 4-C ovarian cancer. She died seven years later, on July 7, 2000, at 9:35 P.M. at Georgetown University Hospital.

A funeral service was held in Washington at St. Columba's Episcopal Church. For three months, her ashes rested atop my fireplace mantle in a small, waxed cardboard box. Twice daily, first thing in the morning and before I turned in at night, I placed my hand on the box and whispered, "I love you." Then in October, my two teenage daughters, an elderly white-muzzled Maggie, and I fulfilled Lovey's express wish, and drove her ashes south into Shenandoah National Park. We parked at Beahm's Gap Overlook and hiked about a mile on a side trail up to the Appalachian Trail. There, on a golden autumn day along a high ridge, we spread her ashes amidst red leafed blueberry bushes. I recited lines from *The Book of Common Prayer*, changing "he" to "she": "I am the resurrection and the life, saith the Lord; she that believeth in me, though she were dead, yet shall she live; and whosoever liveth and believeth in me shall never die."

Descending back down to our car at Beahm's Gap, I again encountered a snake. The blacksnake was the largest I'd ever seen, and it immediately brought to mind my childhood pet, Cecil, a five-foot-long black rat snake with a blueish sheen. Cecil often sought the warmth of my chest and arms by slowly slithering up inside my t-shirt to pop his head out under my chin and "listen" with his tongue. Because of Cecil, I never feared snakes.

I needed both hands to gently lift all seven feet of the black-snake that was stretched out across the trail. Her tongue flicked rapidly as she wound around my waist and right arm. Her cool pressure was caressing, not constricting. Lovey? Cecil? Death and rebirth. I tenderly returned the blacksnake to the forest floor. We watched as she glided silently away into the underbrush. My daughters had no idea why a snake would move me to tears. But in a caring gesture, each girl took one of my hands as we resumed our descent to the car.

The blacksnake called up memories of the episode in 1991 with Ranger Howie. My mind was flooded with fragmented images of my long-ago connection with Traymore. Some were painful and frightening; others were erotic and exhilarating. If not for Traymore, I would never have met my sweet wife of thirty years. But the experience had almost ended my professional career and, more than once, my life. The Vietnam War, the civil rights movement, and the sexual revolution—all of which were pulsating through the country and at major universities—had just begun to affect this women's college in remote Southwest Virginia. When I challenged the policies of an entrenched and vengeful college president, I became his principal target.

2

Shipped

My PhD dissertation on the National Security Act of 1947 had just been accepted by all members of my doctoral committee at the University of Virginia. I still had to defend it orally before the full committee, and, more importantly, my fellowship would expire in two weeks. I had an urgent need for income.

My department's career office notified me of a faculty opening for a political scientist at Traymore College in Southwest Virginia.

"Never heard of the place," I said.

"State teacher's college, all women," said the office staffer. She added, "Traymore always seems to be hiring faculty. A little strange."

Unusual also, and possibly illegal under the Civil Rights Act, was Traymore's status as a state-supported single-sex college. But I needed *immediate* employment. At any rate, I was determined to be there for only one academic year before securing a job at a more reputable institution. So, I asked UVA to forward my resume to Traymore. Four days later, President Elzic Barton's executive assistant, Carla Pogue, called to invite me to Traymore for an interview with President Barton the following week.

On that August day, I left Charlottesville in the early morning in my rust-spotted 1961 white Chevy Bel Air.

A few hours later, I exited Interstate 81, turned down the volume of Tammy Wynette's "Stand by Your Man" on the car radio, and read the road sign: WELCOME TO TRAYMORE, THE NEW RIVER CITY. POP. 11,596. It was a hot, muggy day in 1969. Just outside of town was Traymore's largest employer, the Traymore Arsenal, which operated twenty-four hours a day producing artillery shells, bombs, and other military ordnance for the war in Vietnam. In front of this sprawling complex, two American flags flanked a large red, white, and blue signboard that declared, IN SERVICE TO AMERICA: 247 DAYS WITHOUT AN ACCIDENT. Three months later, a thunderous blast rocked the town. The next morning, the signboard was changed to, IN SERVICE TO AMERICA: 0 DAYS WITHOUT AN ACCIDENT.

The town's unremarkable main street was called Main Street. The Traymore College campus, however, was surprisingly spacious and attractive. Most of the school's buildings were brick, and several appeared to be fairly new. I pulled my car into a visitor parking space where a small maroon sign announced: OFFICE OF THE PRESIDENT.

When I walked through the door, a tiny woman with horn-rimmed glasses and a Lady Bird Johnson bouffant hairdo skittered up to me. With an air of supreme confidence, she said, "You must be David Pritchard. I'm Carla Pogue."

We shook hands.

I said, "Afraid I'm early for my eleven o'clock appointment with President Barton."

"That's fine," she said. "This gives me an opportunity to tell you a little about the distinguished Virginian you'll be meeting." Carla, who wore a battleship gray jacket with a matching skirt, sat down at her desk and pointed me to a nearby chair. "I must apologize. The president's office is being renovated, so you two will talk in the small conference room to my left."

"Oh, yeah," I said. "I noticed that many of the buildings on campus look pretty new."

"That's because of President Barton," Carla said with obvious pride. "He's the Old Dominion's longest serving college president, and he has grown Traymore College into the second largest public women's college in the country."

"Quite an accomplishment," I agreed.

"Indeed, and that's not all," said Carla, her eyes lighting up. "The college is stable and peaceful—no Vietnam demonstrations, no faculty senates or student activist groups, and very few bearded professors."

Swallowing hard and rubbing my chin, I forced a smile.

"You're clean-cut, and you wear a tasteful tie and jacket. The president will like that."

I cocked my head to one side and spoke carefully. "That's good to hear. I certainly would not want to offend anyone."

"What I especially admire about President Barton is that he's a devoted Christian and a proud patriot who was decorated in World War II for bravery during the Battle of the Coral Sea." Carla's paean to her boss was escalating to such heights that I thought she might soon break out in song. "He was a Navy captain who often says that 'it's imperative to do things the Right Way.'"

I crossed my legs and fiddled with my tie. "Sounds like Captain Barton runs a pretty tight ship at Traymore."

Carla jumped up, headed for the coffee maker. "Oh, yes!

He's resolved to act in the Right Way, and resolve begets discipline. . . . Can I get you some coffee?"

"No, but thank you." Taking some liberty, I quipped, "It is sometimes said that the U.S. Navy is two hundred years of tradition untainted by progress."

Carla wrinkled her forehead. "Never heard that before, but the president is a proud traditionalist and defender of traditional values for our girls. He personally drafted the college's social rules that instruct young women on the right way to dress, speak, and conduct themselves."

Bizarre, I thought. *Have I slipped back into the nineteenth century?*

At precisely eleven o'clock, a short, muscular man with a bulbous, mostly bald, deeply creased head opened the office door, walked past me, and snapped at Carla. "Tell Professor Tromblay that he'd better be in my office at two o'clock sharp, or else." He turned to me and extended his hand. "Elzic Barton. Come on in, son."

We moved to the conference room and sat down facing one another across an oval table. President Barton, who wore a dark blue pin-striped suit, did all the talking. His direct, almost brusque, manner and tone made it clear that he expected deference.

Without any preliminary niceties, he said: "I have two questions. Both are fairly personal. I'll understand if you don't want to answer." In other words, I'd better answer, and do so in the right way. "Do you attend a church?"

"Yes, but not as often as I should."

President Barton nodded. Anchoring both elbows onto the table and bending toward me, he said, "At Traymore, as in the military services, we believe that loyalty to one's superiors and to the institution is essential. Wouldn't you agree?"

"Of course." I knew full well that academe's culture—where individual liberty and freedom of expression generally trump notions of loyalty—was the antithesis of the military's emphasis on chain of command. But, once again, I gave him the response he wanted. Some might say I was being disingenuous or even dishonest. However, my answer to Barton's query was pragmatic. Moreover, unless overridden by higher values, I had no problem with the presumption of loyalty to the president and college.

Other than to remark that my CIA experience really stood out and that I was "well-qualified for the position," President Barton asked no questions about my professional background and qualifications. Fortunately, because of a referral from one of my professors at UVA, I had been able to spend two summers as a China military analyst at CIA headquarters in McLean, Virginia. I was surprised but heartened that Barton had noticed it.

"I'm offering you a position as associate professor of political science, tenure track. Salary is twelve thousand a year, the highest allowed by the state at this rank."

Recent recipients of the PhD degree who are hired for a tenure track college faculty position are customarily given the rank and salary of an assistant, not associate, professor. Without ever setting foot in a classroom at Traymore, I was getting a promotion. I nodded appreciatively but said nothing.

Barton stood, stepped over to a window, and only half looked in my direction as he scanned the campus. His face seemed to redden, and his hands were clenched tightly behind his back.

"There's Vietnam-related unrest at Virginia Tech," he said. "We don't want that at Traymore. Our girls must be shielded from leftists and anarchists. You know better than most about the pervasive, insidious threat from communism." Barton paused in his monologue and returned to his chair. He swiveled it around, stared directly at me, and asked, "Am I right?"

"Yes, sir." Again, I responded instinctively. To question such zealotry meant losing the job.

Elzic Barton stood, walked around the table and came over to me. "I think you'll work out just fine, son." He'd clearly concluded that I was no rabble rouser.

"Sir," I asked, "when will I meet with the faculty search committee?"

He chuckled. "Now, don't you worry about that. You're hired." He ushered me out of the conference room, saying, "We will have a contract for you in the mail tomorrow."

We shook hands. There were none of the customary meetings with a search committee, the chairman of the political science department, or interested students. The buck stopped, and began, with Elzic Barton. *Pritchard,* I thought to myself, *you're not in Charlottesville anymore.*

I walked down the steps to my car. This academic year was going to be quite a ride. Two students walked by and smiled. *And how,* I wondered, *is a twenty-seven-year-old single guy going to navigate safely in a sea of 3,857 young women?*

———

The oral defense of my dissertation in late August went well, as I knew more about the National Security Act than any of the UVA faculty. I received warm handshakes and pats on the back. The degree could not be officially awarded until the June 1970 graduation, but Committee Chairman Ted Sopolsky and the other faculty members now cheerfully addressed me as *Dr. Pritchard.*

All was not merriment, however. I feared that my contract with Traymore might be sentencing me to nine months in higher education's equivalent of purgatory.

Never had I dreamt of teaching at a public women's college in rural Southwest Virginia, but here I was. After my interview with President Barton and the consequent firm assurance of employment, I opened a checking account at the Bank of Traymore. The bank's president, Malcom Todd, told me about some cottages he owned nine miles out of town on remote Claytor Lake. "Except in the summer," he said, "they're empty. I'd be happy to rent you one for the school year."

Such an isolated location might expose me to burglary and other risks, I thought, but I accepted Todd's offer. I was a hiker who loved the outdoors, and Claytor Lake State Park was a short walk from the cottages. Also, a place that was far removed from the college would provide a refuge for me; my Siamese cat, Cycles; and my eighteen-month-old German shepherd, Xena.

I was not a cat person. A long-time now ex-girlfriend had given Cycles to me as a kitten. He was a yowling irritant, but I couldn't bring myself to dump him off at an animal shelter.

Xena was special. The name I gave her was a female diminutive of Xenophon, the ancient Greek soldier and historian. Xena was well-trained and fiercely loyal, a gorgeous silver and black female with an attitude: "Freeze, or I'm on you." Xena, like Cycles, had been a gift. The dog was a *quid pro quo* for my minor role in bringing a friend and her new husband together.

———

Three months before starting my doctoral program at UVA, I'd graduated from the Cornell University Law School. I'd decided not to practice law because I found myself staying up late at Cornell, reading *Foreign Affairs*, *Political Science Quarterly*, and books by Hans Morgenthau and Henry Kissinger. My mind was engaged in both the law and international relations/political science, but my heart was in the latter.

However, less than two weeks after arriving at Traymore, word somehow got out about my legal background. Faculty and students poured into my office, which I shared with another new faculty member, lanky and easygoing sociologist Cob Maplewood from Texas. Everyone wanted advice on what they claimed to be glaring infringements of their academic freedom and civil liberties. Not knowing the facts and not wanting to be seen as practicing law in a state where I wasn't licensed, my responses to their queries were guarded and conditional. I was also still naive enough to presume that my primary obligation was to my employer, but I soon learned that the administration was well-aware of my conversations with students and faculty.

———

"Professor Pritchard, are you busy?"

"Are you a student?"

"Yes, I'm Mary Jo Shifflet. One of your students said you might be able to help me." Mary Jo was jittery and clearly upset.

Her tangled hair looked unwashed. Mary Jo stepped hesitantly into my office and said, "I'm about to be shipped."

"Shipped?"

Glancing down, Mary Jo stammered, "Expelled . . . from Traymore."

"Have a seat, Mary Jo. Why are you being shipped?"

Mary Jo sat down and rocked back and forth in the chair. As she rubbed her wrist, she said, "Professor, they have fake fire drills that are designed to empty the dorms."

"They?"

"Dean Evelyn Baird and her stooges. They ransack every room in the dorm searching for anything they can find, like beer or liquor. In my closet, at the bottom of a trunk, they found some Rebel Yell bourbon that I'd poured into an empty detergent bottle. That's why I'm being shipped." Holding back tears, Mary Jo blurted out, "The bourbon tasted like detergent. I couldn't even drink it." I bit my tongue to avoid laughing.

If true, I thought, *this might be a questionable search and seizure at a public college, something the administration should be warned about.* Evelyn Baird was Dean of Students and a force on campus—someone I needed get to know. "I've been meaning to meet Dean Baird, Mary Jo," I said. "Let me get back to you on this."

Mary Jo thanked me profusely and left the office. I figured it wouldn't do any harm to try to help this one student, so I picked up the phone and dialed the dean's number, which I'd found on a rolodex that had been on my desk when I arrived.

"Dean Baird, Dave Pritchard in Political Science."

"Oh. Oh, yes." The dean seemed startled by the call. "I

understand you've already made quite an impact here, speaking with students and faculty."

"Thank you," I said, knowing it had not been intended as a compliment. I replied in kind, "My students speak so highly of you, I thought it was important for us to get together. I know very little about Traymore's culture and history."

"Well . . . I . . ."

"Maybe lunch?" After an awkward pause, I said, "Perhaps Wednesday at the Faculty Club?"

Evelyn Baird hesitated, almost certainly because her instincts told her to first consult President Barton. But she relented, "Wednesday at noon."

———

Dean Baird was late for our Wednesday lunch, probably deliberately so. I waited patiently, sipping my water and watching students walk past on the sidewalk outside.

"Professor Pritchard," came a voice.

Startled, I spilled my water glass as I rose too abruptly to greet her. "So sorry," I said. "My mind was on tomorrow's lecture."

Evelyn waited for me to pull a chair out for her to sit down, which I did. Evelyn Baird wore a no-nonsense navy blue suit and white cotton blouse with a lace-edged Peter Pan collar that was buttoned at the neck and tied with a dark blue bow. Affixed to her lapel was a gold-edged brooch of pink dogwood blossoms. If her light brown hair had not been so tightly imprisoned in permed curls, she would have been quite appealing. I guessed her age to be in the mid-to-late thirties.

While dabbing spilled water with my napkin, I said, "It's good of you to see me. Afraid I need enlightenment on how *not* to spill water at Traymore."

A student waitress came to take our order and raised an eyebrow when she saw us together.

"Tell me about yourself," Evelyn said with a hint of a southern accent. This sounded more like an order than a request. For several minutes, I described living north of New York City, my education and avid interest in hiking, recent summer analytical positions at the CIA, and how I learned of the opening at Traymore.

As I spoke, Evelyn's demeanor softened dramatically. By the time I finished, her face had a warm, it's-nice-getting-to-know-you smile.

I sipped some water and asked, "And you?"

The waitress brought our lunch.

"Before I left for college," Evelyn began, "I grew up in a close-knit Methodist family in rural Virginia near Clifton Forge. I loved my folks, but I couldn't wait to leave home. After graduating from Longmont College, I taught English at a high school in suburban Richmond before coming to Traymore." Evelyn paused a moment, poked at her coleslaw, and pressed her lips together. "My Confederate kinfolk saw their Shenandoah Valley farms devastated by northern troops during the War Between the States." She frowned and looked directly at me. "You're from the north." This was not a question.

I nodded and refrained from disclosing that my great-great-grandfather fought with a Union cavalry unit in the Shenandoah Valley under General George Armstrong Custer.

"You're single," Evelyn said. "Tall, lean, and athletic-looking.

Not unattractive." She added with a half-smile, "This is a women's college. Caution is advisable."

"Indeed. I have a girlfriend. Samantha visits this weekend from New York." This was, at best, a half-truth. Sam was visiting for the weekend, but we'd stopped seeing one another on a regular basis three years ago when she, not unreasonably, expected a marriage proposal after I finished law school. Thereafter, Sam had come down to Charlottesville every so often, but we largely went our separate ways.

Evelyn hesitated before lowering her eyes and almost whispering, "Some years ago, before coming to Traymore, I was engaged." She rested two fingers on her cheek and looked away for a brief moment. It clearly still pained her. "But I enjoy my work here and try not to dwell on the past." She fixed her gaze on me. Leaning forward she said, "You're a troublemaker, Pritchard, albeit an engaging one. With a distant girlfriend and four thousand Traymore girls, you're vulnerable."

I hazarded a sensitive question. "Would an appealing, single, educated woman like yourself be happier at an institution with more men?"

Lowering her eyes once again before looking up, Evelyn was silent as she stared out the window at nothing in particular.

We continued talking, paying little attention to our food. We barely spoke of Traymore's culture and history, our ostensible reason for lunch, and we eased into addressing one another by our first names.

Now seemed the time to allude to Mary Jo Shifflet. "Evelyn, an odd thing happened the other day. A student—not one of mine—came to my office claiming that she was being 'shipped.'

I had no idea what she was referring to, something about alcohol and having to leave Traymore. I said that it was unfortunate, but I was unfamiliar with the college's practices."

"I know the case," said Evelyn, waving a hand. "President Barton requires periodic searches of all the dormitories for alcohol and other forbidden items, like salacious posters or radical anti-war material, that might corrupt our girls. More than once we've found marijuana. Such a vile, addictive narcotic! The president's policy has proven wonderfully effective."

"Apparently so," I said gravely. "Of course, President Barton has a green light from the college's legal counsel?"

"I don't know. Maybe."

Bingo! That's it! Mary Jo's story seemed to hold up: a likely illegal search and seizure at a public college where written policies were, at best, vague. There was no probable cause or even reasonable suspicion to justify sweeping, indiscriminate searches, and, of course, no search warrant.

We split the check. "Well, thank you, Evelyn. It's been a pleasure."

"Yes, David. I enjoyed it. Let's do it again soon."

———

After lunch, I called Barton's office to tell Carla Pogue I wanted to meet with the president. Without mentioning my lunch with Evelyn, I said, "Please tell him that it concerns the administration's searches of dormitory rooms."

"Oh." A toxic pause followed before Carla finally stuttered, "Well, I don't think . . . He'll probably, possibly get . . . get back to you." She hung up abruptly.

Minutes later, my office phone rang. "Professor Pritchard, Ned Thompson, college vice president. We haven't met. The president asked me to call you."

"Thanks for calling."

"Afraid you won't thank me when you hear what President Barton just directed me to say to you. I apologize, but these are his exact words: 'Tell that SOB to mind his own goddamn business.'"

I was appalled. This was hardly the response I'd expected in attempting to inform the president of a potentially serious problem, one that could be easily avoided.

"Ned," I said, "I only want to help the college. These dorm searches invite costly legal challenges. At the very least, the college's attorneys should be consulted. There must be a misunderstanding."

"Nope. I quoted the president word for word."

"This is ridiculous. Can I come over and chat with you for a few minutes?"

"Sure. Come to the office at five o'clock."

———

Ned Thompson appeared to be in his mid-forties. He wore a green and black tartan bowtie, and he had apparently forgotten the popular jingle's message that "a little dab'll do ya" by parting his hair down the middle and cementing it in place with what must have been a quart of Brylcreem.

"Glad to meet you, David," he said as we shook hands. "Heard a lot about you." We sat down in plush leather lounge chairs that invited relaxed conversation.

Ned was an easy-going guy and a UVA graduate. He treated me and others with respect, but he kept his head low when it came to President Barton's policies. When fireworks went off, Ned jumped into the nearest foxhole and stayed there until the smoke cleared.

"David," he said in the manner of an experienced older brother, "you should know that President Barton does not view himself as an academic, a word he considers pejorative. Rather, he's a disciplinarian whose overriding priority is the protection of our students from forces he sees as immoral, corrupting, or unpatriotic. Nor does he revel in the free and open exchange of ideas. The president was, and remains at heart, a navy captain. He insists on being in total command of the Good Ship Traymore."

I sat up straight in the chair and gave Ned a brisk military-style salute.

Ned smiled. "Salute the president, and you'll thrive here. President Barton ordered the dormitory searches years ago, and he sees no reason whatsoever to consult you, our legal counsel, or God Almighty about their advisability."

"Look, Ned," I said, standing up and walking over to the chair where he was sitting, "I have legal training. I'm dead serious. Sooner or later, and probably sooner than later, the Good Ship Traymore and Captain Barton *will* be sued."

"I agree, and this isn't the only area where we're vulnerable." Giving me a sympathetic look, Ned rose from his chair and said, "The president is what he is. I learned early on that it's pointless to urge him to do what he's dead set against."

My face tightened, and I rubbed the back of my neck in frustration before speaking. "I appreciate your honesty, Ned. You deserve the same from me. I *am* an Academic with a capital A, not a fucking crew member of the USS Barton. I'm pissed." Clenching and unclenching my teeth, I pulled the trigger. "Ned, I know that messengers must sometimes deliver unpleasant messages." Then, rephrasing what Mark Twain once said about school boards, I said, "Please deliver, *verbatim*, my message to the president: 'God first made imbeciles. This was for practice. Then He made college presidents.'"

Sure, I knew—indeed *hoped*—that my visceral inflammatory retort would rankle Barton, but I didn't give a hot damn. The gloves were off. Even before arriving at Traymore, I'd vowed to stay for just a year and then move on to a finer college. Moreover, while Ned Thompson survived by staying out of the line of fire, that was not my *modus operandi*. Mere survival was too low a bar and, at a place like Traymore, that standard was clearly unethical. Witnessing what was happening to Mary Jo and then being effectively slapped in the face by Barton for trying to bring a legitimate matter to his attention invited a vigorous response.

So much for loyalty to the institution. After leaving Ned's office, I took an unhurried stroll across campus on this warm September day to reflect on what at its core was a moral issue.

Once back in my office, it took thirty minutes to locate the name of the only American Civil Liberties Union attorney in Roanoke, Ronald Cohen. I called and identified myself, told him I was a member of the New York Bar, and summarized Mary Jo's situation. "Well," he said, "you and I should get together. I'd want to speak with Miss Shifflet and, if possible, Dean Baird and President Barton. Of course, our Richmond office would make the final decision of whether or not to proceed. Assuming everything holds up, it sounds like a blatant Fourth Amendment violation. A pretty easy case."

This was encouraging. Once committed, the ACLU's legal assistance would come at no cost to Mary Jo. I called her with the news. She was ecstatic: "I'll call my parents." Within an hour, she was in my office sobbing. "My folks are good people who never got past the eighth grade. Momma is supportive, but Daddy says I must've done something wrong, that I should fess up to it, leave Traymore, and beg the Lord's forgiveness."

"Mary Jo, the ACLU will probably soon decide to take your case. You won't have to pay a nickel. Traymore is in the wrong, not you."

Tears rolled down her cheeks. "Daddy is a simple man, a farmer. I love him."

Mary Jo hugged me and walked away.

"Damn!" I shouted, pounding a fist on my desk. "What a rat's ass place."

Mary Jo was "shipped" for the remainder of the academic year. My initial clash with the administration had ended in a dismal failure. However, this was only the first month of my nine-month contract. *Let's see what I can come up with.* I vowed to do my damnedest to "ship" Captain Elzic Barton.

3

Invitations

Shortly after Mary Jo walked away, Byon Joon-Ho, chairman of the political science department, slipped into my office so quietly that I was unaware of his presence. I was staring at my desk phone, concerned about Mary Jo and wondering how I'd fallen into this situation, when Cob Maplewood called out, "Dave, you have a visitor."

I looked up and smelled trouble.

Byon Joon-Ho, who identified as "Korean," wore a dark blue suit and was among the thirty-five percent of Traymore's faculty with a PhD. He boasted that his doctorate was from St. Igor's University of Antigua, which may have explained his near-total ignorance of the political science field.

He stood stiffly. "Da . . . Da . . . David," he said haltingly, "we might know one another better, maybe? Perhaps later in afternoon, you be my guest? My apartment near campus. You like bourbon, Wild Turkey?"

Byon Joon-Ho edged further into my office as he jiggled his car keys and gazed blankly at the wall. We'd spoken only sporadically during my brief time at Traymore. His demeanor had always given me the impression that he was, at the same time, both cowering and devious. From day one, it was clear that Brian (the Anglicized version of Byon that he preferred to be called) was powerless, despite his title of department chairman—a designation in which he took inordinate pride. Brian couldn't fire or hire anyone, and he had no control over the curriculum or budget. He was Barton's loyal minion.

"Maybe," Brian pleaded, "you come just one hour?"

The weasel never looked me in the eye, although I was well-aware that this could be a cultural trait. I relented, "Okay, Brian."

On first impression, Brian's apartment appeared to be exceptionally well-appointed. It had ornate teak furniture, and his china cabinet displayed fine, centuries-old Korean porcelain. The porcelain, about which I had some knowledge, was exceedingly rare and found only in museums and homes of the very wealthy.

A huge oil painting of a nude woman hung at the far end of his living room. It was stunningly out of character. It was *not* a Renoir or Goya. Nor was it even in the alluring, popular, and sensual style of an Alberto Vargas, the famed Peruvian painter of pin-up girls. Rather, it was a crude, amateurish rendering of a naked woman whose splayed legs left nothing to the imagination. The painting might have been found in a back room of one of the many roadside stands that dotted the rural south specializing in velvet Elvises, Confederate battle flags, pink flamingos, and boiled peanuts. It did not come close to meeting my generally tolerant conception of what constituted art.

Really bizarre, I said to myself.

"What do you drink?" asked Brian.

"Just a small glass of wine. I have to drive back to Claytor Lake to clean up my cottage. My friend, Samantha, arrives tomorrow from New York."

"You have girlfriend. Good. Much temptation at Traymore."

I said nothing.

Brian attempted small talk and told tasteless jokes: "What's the most common bird at Traymore? The Pink-Breasted Pushover."

He laughed at his attempts at humor and then finally got around to his real objective.

"Da-Da-David," he stammered, "President Barton wants that I speak frankly with you."

What a surprise, you spineless slug. Looking directly at Brian, I said, "Yeah, yesterday Ned Thompson also relayed a Barton message to me: 'Tell the SOB to mind his own goddamn business.'"

Brian spun his chair around so he faced the opposite wall, his back to me. He could not, or would not, look at me when he spoke. I almost pitied him. "Please, I have no choice. President Barton says you not meddle in things at Traymore. We prevent you otherwise to find any job. So sorry."

I rose to leave. "Thanks for the wine." Brian never turned to face me, nor did he stand to see me to the door. His head was bowed. I walked to the car and drove to my cottage.

Twice more over the next few days, Brian, working as Barton's mouthpiece, issued similar but more pointed threats. The first one I ignored. After his second and final threat to sabotage my future employment prospects, I told him to "stuff it." Lines were drawn. We rarely spoke again.

———

Turning off I-81 at the Claytor Lake State Park exit, I followed a narrow, winding, paved road through an oak and pine forest toward the cottage. Caretakers Mara and Caleb Heath had told me that from mid-May through Labor Day, all eight of the Piney Woods Lakeside Resort cottages were usually occupied. But now, I was the sole renter. Mara and Caleb were an older couple who kept an eye on anyone entering or exiting Piney Woods. I stopped to chat with them and handed Caleb a can of Red Man, his preferred chewing tobacco. I mentioned that Samantha would be with me for a few days. Mara winked and chuckled, "Honey, y'all have a good time." Mara and Caleb were fine folks.

Samantha had visited me in Charlottesville a few times, but I hadn't seen her in almost a year. She'd been living in Manhattan with some guy for the past two years. When I met Sam at the Roanoke Airport, however, it felt like we'd only been apart for a few days. We were comfortable together. But comfort was not love. Not marrying Sam had been the right decision.

As I opened my cottage door at Piney Woods, Xena—who loved women and young children, but not strange men—spun around three times, welcoming Sam. Cycles the cat peered down cautiously from his refuge atop of the refrigerator. Sam and I talked, held hands as we walked Xena along the shoreline of Claytor Lake, and caught up with one another.

The next day, Cob Maplewood and his wife, Polly, invited us to dinner. They lived about five miles west of Claytor Lake in an old farmhouse that dated from the 1870s. As Sam and I made our way up their dirt driveway past Cob's Harley Davidson, we were startled by what we saw. Nailed to the side of the Maplewood's barn was the flaming red pelt of a fox. We both touched it before walking up the front steps and knocking on the door. Cob said rather proudly that he'd shot and skinned it a week ago. Its luxurious tail, just as in D.H. Lawrence's novella, was feathery soft and white tipped. Sam's only response was one of disgust: "Why kill such a beautiful creature?"

While Polly showed Sam around the farm, pointing out the only three chickens to survive the fox's predations, Cob and I exchanged intelligence. Since we were together in our shared office only infrequently—and even then, students were often present—we had little time to talk at length about our Traymore trials.

I filled Cob in on Mary Jo Shifflet, Dean Evelyn Baird, Ned Thompson, and Byon Joon-Ho. Then Cob, who—like me, and for the same reasons—was determined to leave after the current academic year, confirmed my suspicion about the various departmental chairs. He'd learned that the chairmen (virtually all were men) of the sociology, political science, history, secondary education, foreign languages, chemistry, physics, and likely all other departments had been personally appointed by Barton, largely or solely because of their unquestioned loyalty to him. Most of these chairmen had dubious—or, at best, unremarkable—academic credentials.

Cob raised two additional matters, one of which I was already aware of. Several of our students had informed us that they had been threatened by their deans for writing letters to the editor of the school newspaper, *The Highlander*, that were critical of the college's policies and practices. Indeed, the paper's editor, Sue Ewal, was one of my best students. Sue told me that she had been summoned to her dean's office last spring and informed that she would lose her scholarship if she continued to publish articles that were "unfairly or improperly critical of Traymore."

Sue said, "Professor, I've kept on doing what I've been doing, but I'm worried."

"Sue," I replied, "unless an item is clearly libelous, you cannot be censored by the administration. Tell me immediately if you're threatened again or punished in any way."

The second matter that Cob related was news to me, yet very much in line with the strict, controlling character of the college. He leaned toward me, almost falling off his living room couch. "Get this. It's incredible what that asshole Barton will do." Cob whacked his hand on the warped, wide-board oak floor. "Guess what a member of the psych department, who is on the staff of the New River Mental Health Center, told me last week?"

"Don't know. Barton's a flasher?"

"Worse. Listen up. That bastard wrote to the Mental Health Center demanding access to the confidential information that Traymore students divulge to the Center's psychologists and psychiatrists." Cob reached over to his coffee table and picked up some printed material. "Here are copies of Barton's letter and the Center's fiery reply."

"Good Lord," I gasped.

"Yup, I've got the goods on him," he said as he handed them to me. "The Center's Board of Directors really kicked him in the nuts."

The board's response read, in part: "If students ever get the idea that the Mental Health Center is operating a Gestapo system for the benefit of Traymore College, it will destroy any confidence students have in the Center. *Should Traymore attempt to exact privileged information from the Center, we will sever all connections whatsoever with the College.*"

Said Cob, "Barton retreated, but it illustrates just how far he'll go."

We had a convivial dinner, or, as Polly put it, "the Last Supper before our Traymore crucifixion." With good scotch and cheap wine, we were all pretty soused. A well-lubricated Cob revealed that much of his life had been spent on the family ranch in West Texas, and that his father had served with legendary Texas Ranger, Frank Hamer. Of particular interest to me, however, was his interest in western diamondback rattlesnakes. Cob said that when he was a high school senior, he'd won three thousand dollars for catching the most rattlesnakes and another thousand for having the heaviest snake at the annual Sweetwater Rattlesnake Roundup.

"Cob," I said, "now it's clear why I like you—our shared perverse affinity for snakes. What better preparation for dealing with Barton?" While clearly not in Cob's league, I mentioned my youthful adventures with my old friend Cecil the blacksnake.

It was late when Sam and I said goodbye. We stumbled down the steps into a cool night with a winking yellow half-moon and a sky sprinkled with stars. We called out a slurred, "Hi, foxy," as we wobbled past the Maplewood's barn to our car. With great difficulty and even greater luck, I managed to drive to the cottage without slamming into a tree, although I almost hit a deer. We were much too plastered for intimacy, an uncommon omission we rectified the next morning, albeit with pounding headaches.

Two days later, I returned Sam to the Roanoke Airport. We kissed, she boarded the plane, and flew back to her lover in New York. Her visit had been a respite from Traymore's tensions, and in retrospect, a farewell gift.

———

The next day, I called Tom O'Keefe. Tom, who had received his PhD in history from UVA in 1968, was the only person at Traymore with whom I had even a slight acquaintance before I arrived at the college. We had chatted briefly during my first week on campus, when he had invited me to join a group of disgruntled faculty members, the "POF" (Pissed-Off Faculty). The POF met most Wednesday afternoons at a straw-on-the-floor beer joint several miles from campus near Blacksburg. The ARSE-N-ALL bar's blinking red, white, and blue neon sign announced both its principal patrons—Traymore Arsenal workers—and its Saturday night strip shows.

Tom introduced me to the pissed-off faculty members when I attended the group's late afternoon gathering on the last Wednesday of September. "Listen up, folks." Tom raised his voice above the chatter. "Dave Pritchard from political science is with us today."

"Hot damn," growled a brawny guy with a buzz cut who looked like a Marine Corps recruiter. "It's the Boat Rocker himself. We've all heard about you, Pritchard. You've cut quite a swath through this shit hole." He rose from his chair, smiled, and extended his hand.

"Glad to meet you," I said, shaking his hand.

"John Manikas, physics. My pleasure."

Manikas was not a Marine, but he had served in Vietnam with the 82nd Airborne. He loved teaching math and physics at Traymore, and, while he objected to some of Barton's actions, he was more content with the *status quo* than were most of his colleagues. Moreover, he happily self-identified as being "pretty conservative."

John's home was about a hundred miles west of Traymore near Beckley, West Virginia, where he drove most weekends to be with his wife and children. He attended POF meetings to drink, schmooze, and share in the latest gossip.

"You've got a strong grip," said John. "Ever wrestle?"

"In high school. 172-pound class. Went to the state championships in Syracuse but lost my second match."

"I wrestled unlimited weight class for the Mountaineers in Morgantown. Bet I'd whup ya . . . if I still had both legs." John hitched up his pants leg, revealing the prosthesis. "Friggin' Viet Cong grenade."

I rested my hand on John's shoulder. "Think we're going to get along." He nodded approvingly when I whispered, "And I voted for Goldwater in '64."

"Okay, Manikas," said Tom, "don't monopolize the Boat Rocker. Incidentally, do you know why the baby Jesus couldn't be born in West Virginia? Because they couldn't find three wise men or a virgin."

"Damn," said John, slamming his fist on the table. "When are you leftwing nut-balls going to stop running down the great state of West Virginia?"

The group's attention eventually drifted away from pummeling John as various POF members began telling me about their respective backgrounds and fields of expertise.

Over time, virtually all disciplines would be represented at POF meetings, although historians, economists, mathematicians, creative writers, and sociologists stood out. The number of attendees at any given meeting would range from eight to fifteen. While there were a few regulars, like John, faces would change every week.

Soon, empty Old Milwaukee cans littered the table. By five o'clock, the jukebox was pounding out the group's favorites, always including Merle Haggard's "Okie from Muskogee." We howled in unison, sloshing beer on the floor, when ole Merle sang, "We like livin' right and bein' free," and especially, "The kids here still respect the college dean." We also loved Mel Tillis's, "Ruby Don't Take Your Love to Town." We crooned, "Oh Ruuuuby . . ." But Tillis's best line was, "Who started this crazy Asian war?" which prompted John to leap up and hurl crushed beer cans across the room at the bar, where Arsenal employees sat. None of them dared mess with him.

I learned a lot from my first night with the POF. Above all, I learned that faculty members who openly criticized any significant college policy were punished.

Tom O'Keefe said, "Last year, Ned Thompson warned me that if I became an officer in the local chapter of the American Association of University Professors, I would 'fall into disfavor with President Barton.' I became an officer, and Barton's letter of reprimand went into my file."

The only woman present, and the sole female member of the economics faculty, fit right in with the men, and her beer consumption matched theirs. She shook her fist in frustration and raised her voice when she disclosed to me what everyone else already knew: "In one of my classes, I discussed the likely economic implications of admitting men to Traymore. Barton summoned me to his office and told me bluntly, 'If you ever express the view, in class, that coeducation might prove beneficial, that will constitute grounds for dismissal.'" These and similar tales were told.

I learned also that the AAUP had found that fifteen percent of Traymore's faculty had left last academic year, most of them because of dissatisfaction with the administration; and, like me, an astounding twenty percent were expected to leave after this academic year. Traymore's deteriorating reputation probably explained why significantly fewer women had applied to this year's freshman class, and why the median College Board verbal scores for incoming freshmen fell from a deplorably low 466 out of 800 last year to an even lower 444 this year. "Yes," said one of the math faculty, "and the Southern Association of Schools and Colleges makes an accreditation visit next year."

Armed with this information, I called Dean Baird to arrange another lunch date in the faculty dining room. Although the students saw her as Barton's enforcer, she was not the evil witch of the south. Indeed, at our initial meeting, we had quickly established a rapport, and she had proved to be a valuable source of information. I looked forward to seeing her again.

———

Evelyn smiled as she sat down at the table, this time without waiting for me to pull a chair out for her. Her attire, a violet-colored shirtwaist dress, was noticeably more relaxed.

We had a short, chatty Friday lunch. Evelyn confirmed, directly or indirectly, most of what I'd learned from Cob Maplewood and the POF. None of these matters seemed to concern her. Evelyn Baird had other things on her mind.

"How did Samantha's visit go?"

"You remember?"

"Oh yes. Claytor Lake is beautiful. I bet your cottage is nice."

"Sam liked it."

"Did she cook anything special?"

"Well, she isn't much of a cook. Mostly, we talked." I was getting a little uneasy and tried to change the subject. "How often do you get into Roanoke?"

Evelyn picked at her salad, ignored my question, and went silent for a while. Something was on her mind. Her index finger traced the rim of a water glass as she tilted her head to one side. She fingered her pearl necklace and rubbed her cheek.

Finally, Evelyn blurted out, "Have you ever had a dinner of Virginia country ham with red-eye gravy, baked beans in molasses, corn bread with wild honey, homemade pecan pie, and maybe some dark ale? I soak the ham in my bathtub for two days to reduce the salt, then slow boil it on the stove for four or five hours before serving. Delicious."

"Sounds great. No, don't think I've had country ham."

"I'm pretty good in the kitchen, but I usually cook only for myself. Perhaps—that is, possibly. . . . Well, if you ever want to take a break from being a loose cannon around here . . ."

"Dinner?"

Evelyn's face reddened. Her ears turned scarlet. She looked down and said nothing, but nodded.

"That'd be nice. Now, though, this loose cannon has a class to teach."

We got up from the table and shook hands.

"Maybe again next Friday, when we might have more time?" I suggested.

"See you here next Friday. That'll be October third."

———

An earnest, almost professional looking young woman stood in the hallway outside my office when I returned from my afternoon U.S. foreign policy class. I vaguely recalled seeing her waiting in line to see me during my morning office hours. She apparently had tired of waiting and left, as she'd never made it into the office.

"Professor Pritchard, do you have a minute?"

With her shoulder-length sandy-colored hair, this woman didn't look at all like a Traymore student. She appeared somewhat older, more mature and purposeful, and much better dressed in her short-sleeve navy blue shift, light gray cotton cardigan, and what appeared to be an amber necklace. No Traymore student carried such a distinctive hand-tooled brown leather briefcase.

"Sorry, miss, I don't have office hours now. They're posted here on my door. My next office hours will be on Monday morning."

Clearing her throat, she said, "I have a class then." Her eyes narrowed as she crossed her arms. "I've been trying to see you for almost two weeks. *Please.*"

"I only have a few minutes, but please come in."

We moved into the office but remained standing.

"I'm Valerie Tavernetti. I'm president of the honor society, the associate editor of the *Highlander*, and a senior. Sue Ewal is a close friend."

"Sue's an excellent student. She has chutzpah. Bet you know that word."

"My family is from Baltimore." Valerie leaned forward and looked me in the eye. "Sue and I *both* have chutzpah. In fact, that's why I'm here. Most Traymore students care only about their morning biscuits and gravy and their weekend dates. *I'm* outraged about the tragedy that's Vietnam." Her jaw tightened. "I'm trying to put together a faculty panel on Vietnam. I'd like you to be on it. Dr. Byon Joon-Ho refused to help."

"No surprise there," I said.

"Vice President Thompson told me to drop the idea because it encouraged 'disruptive behavior.'" Valerie's face tensed.

I taught the only course on United States foreign policy at Traymore, and the Vietnam War was the central international issue confronting the country. The war and the draft were roiling university campuses. So, why not agree to do it? A Vietnam panel would infuriate Barton, but I'd already crossed that bridge. I stretched both arms above my head.

"Miss Tavernetti, you're certainly tenacious. That's commendable. I'd be happy to be on a panel. I'm sure Professor O'Keefe could provide an historical perspective, and I know some good people at UVA, Virginia Tech, and William & Mary who would probably agree to come."

"Fantastic, professor—and, it's *Mrs.* Tavernetti. When can we do it?"

This woman's a bulldozer. "*Mrs.* Tavernetti, I'm so damn busy. Drop by Monday at noon, we'll figure something out."

We'd been standing in my office while talking, but Valerie now set her briefcase on the floor and, with a playful grin, sat down in the chair opposite my desk. I remained standing. *She won't even take "yes" for an answer. How am I going to get her out of here so I can leave?*

She raised an eyebrow, tossed her hair, and said with a smile, "What are you doing this weekend, Professor Pritchard?"

"Mrs. Tavernetti . . ."

"My husband and I would like to invite you to dinner this Sunday, if that would be convenient. We could talk then."

Valerie said she and her husband, Vincent, had an apartment in Blacksburg, where Vincent was a graduate student in electrical engineering at Virginia Tech, while Valerie majored in economics and political science at Traymore. Except for Elzic Barton, no one at Traymore had attempted to steamroll me so boldly.

"*Mrs.* Tavernetti, I'm very . . ."

"Do you like barbeque?"

"Sure, but . . ."

"Good. I'll ask one of my classmates, Marigold Dunfree, to join us. You'll like her. Sunday at seven."

Valerie plucked a scrap of paper from my wastepaper basket and scribbled on it. "Here's our address, but Marigold knows the way. You can pick her up at the corner of Jackson and Main at 6:30. She's tall, with dark hair."

Mrs. Tavernetti stood and grabbed her briefcase. Before leaving she said, "Please, call me Valerie."

4

Battered

Early Sunday evening, tall, dark-haired Marigold Dunfree stood at the corner of Jackson and Main, three blocks from campus. She sported a yellow baseball cap and flashed a broad smile as I pulled up to the curb.

"Marigold?"

"That's me." Like a Virginia filly clearing a split rail fence, she sprung into the front passenger seat.

"My name is-a Guido," I said, trying to be cute, "My game is-a fútbol."

"Baloney, professor."

Marigold, a junior in jeans, was a no-nonsense business major from Virginia's Eastern Shore. And, as her flying leap into the car suggested, I soon discovered she was an athlete—the hundred-yard dash and the 440.

"So, Marigold, how did you get stuck with me tonight?"

"Val's a good friend. We're in an econ class together. She asked if I'd like a blind date with a faculty member. I said, 'If he's a he, he doesn't have warts on his nose, and he's under thirty-five, I'm in.'" Marigold flashed a smile.

"Hmm," I said, grinning, "that's a pretty low bar. Guess I qualify. I don't really know Mrs. Tavernetti—Valerie—at all. Indeed, I'm not sure I should be doing this."

Marigold slid across the car seat until she almost touched me. "Don't you worry none, professor. I can tell that you and I will get along. Val's a good person, extremely bright. Did she mention that she's president of the honor society?"

"She did, and that she wants me to be on a Vietnam panel."

Marigold was a talker whose strengths did not include discretion. She revealed that Valerie was seeing "a shrink" in Roanoke because of marital problems. Her husband, who Marigold called That Asshole, "doesn't come home some nights, drinks like a fish, and treats her like a medieval serf. I go over there fairly often to get between Val and That Asshole."

"Great," I said, gripping the steering wheel. "Should be a fun evening."

When we pulled up to the Tavernettis' drab, three-story, postwar-era apartment building, I opened the car door for Marigold.

"Jeez. No boy ever does that for me."

"My mother's influence."

"That's nice," said Marigold as we walked up the steps to the apartment.

"Mom always says that 'respecting women is respecting yourself.' It's simply the right thing to do."

"Respect is fine; reverence is not." Winking at me, she said, "I'm not Saint Marigold. We can have a *really good* time." She bumped me with her hip and laughed.

Valerie came to the door in a white blouse, green cotton skirt, and blue calico apron. Marigold and Valerie hugged. Pointing her finger at me and winking, Marigold said with a broad smile, "He's okay."

The smell of barbequed ribs wafted through the room we entered.

A folding table with four exquisitely arranged place settings had been set up in the living room of the cramped student apartment. When I complimented Valerie on the tasteful arrangement, she admitted to a long-time interest in interior decorating.

"I apologize that Vincent isn't here," said Valerie. "He should've arrived hours ago."

Marigold and I followed Valerie into the small kitchen, where she was fixing a salad. Hoping some good news might help to offset Valerie's unease about her husband's absence, I said, "Yesterday I called Professor O'Keefe and two others, one here at Virginia Tech and another at UVA. All three agreed to be on the panel. However, the third Saturday in October is the only day they could all make it."

Valerie whirled around, sending cucumber slices plopping onto the floor. "Fantastic! I'll book Barton Hall tomorrow."

Dinner was ready, but no Vincent. Valerie opened the bottle of wine I'd brought, and we learned a bit more about one another. Valerie said she'd gone to Catholic schools in Baltimore and still attended Mass fairly often, and her father was some big pooh-bah in the Knights of Columbus.

"Are you religious, Professor Pritchard?" Valerie asked.

"Well, perhaps, but I've been remiss on that front for a while. Christ urged us to love our enemies and pray for our persecutors. Traymore's administration makes it especially challenging to follow the Golden Rule."

"We Baptists know the Good Book," Marigold chimed in. "That's Matthew 5:43." Marigold was tickled pink to demonstrate her knowledge, or at least her memorization, of the New Testament, but after just two small glasses of wine she was beginning to slur her words. Resting her hand lightly on my shoulder as if patiently instructing a young child in Sunday school, Marigold continued, "Matthew also says, 'Blessed are those who hunger after righteousness.'" She chuckled, "So David, you're probably saved."

"Praise the Lord," I said, raising my wine glass.

The front door swung open and slammed against the wall. Vincent was red-faced and stocky, but not too tall. Probably about my age. He'd clearly been drinking and appeared somewhat disoriented. That is, until he focused on Marigold. "Marigold," he growled in a voice drenched with sarcasm, "*So* good to see you . . . *again.*" Turning to me, he said, "This guy must be the liberal academic."

Although Vincent's intonation made "liberal academic" sound like "toxic waste," I stood and held out my hand. "David Pritchard, liberal academic."

Vincent ignored me and stormed past his wife toward the kitchen. With a flushed face and clenched fists, he shouted, "What's for dinner?"

Valerie was shaken, embarrassed. "Vincent . . . I . . . We . . ." She couldn't finish her sentence.

Marigold leapt up and wrapped her arms around Valerie.

"For Christ's sake," said Vincent, "leave her alone. She's too damn fragile. Let her fight her own battles."

With both hands planted firmly on her hips, Marigold anchored herself in front of Valerie. Her posture said, "Fuck off, asshole."

"Marigold," said Vincent, "this is not your damn home away from home." He reached for my half empty wine bottle and poured all of it into a large Virginia Tech Hokies beer mug as Valerie and Marigold slipped into the kitchen.

Vincent chug-a-lugged the wine, blending a few drops of cabernet into his already well-stained and rumpled shirt. "Val speaks highly of you," he said, "That's a red flag for me. She's too damn liberal—like that traitor, Jane Fonda. And those drugged-out freaks who burn American flags."

"Vincent," I said, "I don't know your wife too well, but she doesn't look or act much like Jane Fonda. And I understand she burns flags only on alternate Tuesdays."

Vincent's bulging eyes glowered at me. His in-your-face belligerence sent an unmistakable message: *Don't mess with me.* He looked like a defensive lineman about to crash into the opposing team's offensive line. Vincent snarled, "Val's nowhere near as attractive as that Fonda bitch, and Good Sister Valerie is far more tight-assed."

"Valerie is one of our best students, Vincent. Her future is bright. You must be proud of her."

Vincent said nothing. His eyes narrowed as he slid his chair toward mine, like a predator stalking its prey. Trying to change the subject, I asked about his doctoral program. Once again, there was silence before he grunted, "It's okay."

If this scene had played out late at night at some seedy bar, I would have been in acute flight-or-fight mode. I was tense, didn't trust him as far as I could spit, and maintained constant eye contact. The situation was so bizarre that, at least subliminally, I anticipated an attack.

I opted for appeasement. "We may not be that far apart, Vincent. I voted for Barry Goldwater five years ago."

This unexpected and truthful admission seemed to calm him temporarily, at least until Valerie and Marigold brought dinner to the table a few minutes later. Then, he again denigrated his wife: "These placemats look stupid."

Valerie's eyes brimmed with tears, and she seemed frozen in place. Marigold and I glanced at one another across the table and grimaced. Vincent was a minefield who blew away all discussion, all civility. Conversation of any kind was out of the question. We ate dinner quickly for fear of further provoking him.

When Marigold and I rose to leave, Vincent remained seated as he gnawed on a sparerib. Valerie saw us to the door and walked outside with us to the front steps.

Marigold hugged her tightly.

"I'm so sorry, professor," Valerie said as rivulets of tears trickled down her face.

I took her hand and said, "Thank you. Dinner was delicious. Don't worry; our panel will happen."

Driving back to Traymore, Marigold and I said nothing at first, until she broke the silence. "Well, was I right about That Asshole?"

"On the button. I've never experienced anything like that."

Back in Traymore, at the corner of Jackson and Main, I jumped out and opened the car door for Marigold. She touched my arm as I gave her a peck on the cheek. She moved closer. I put an arm around her waist, and we kissed softly.

"Told you we'd get along," she said.

"Indeed." But I was thinking of Valerie.

———

Valerie was sitting cross-legged on the floor, leaning against the wall outside my office when I arrived Monday morning. Her long strawberry blonde hair was disheveled, and she wore the same green skirt and blouse I'd seen her in the night before. She braced her hand against the wall and winced as she stood up.

"Hi, professor."

Both eyes were blackened, and a purplish bruise ran along the left side of her face. It stood out starkly against her light skin.

"Good God, Valerie! What happened?"

"I moved out last night. A neighbor took me in when I returned from the hospital. Nothing was broken this time." Valerie looked down at the floor and wiped away tears with the back of her hand. We stepped into the office, and I closed the door.

I touched her arm. "Val, what can I do?"

"He struck me, hard, right after you and Marigold left. When I hit the floor, he . . . kicked me. My legs are bruised."

"Did you call the police?"

"No. He always apologized in the past. But this is too much, and I'm afraid. My father and brother are driving down today from Maryland to help me move out. They'll arrive early tonight. Dad's contacted an attorney in Roanoke. We meet with him tomorrow."

"Good, but it's important to report this to the Blacksburg police and file a complaint with campus security at Virginia Tech. You want it on the record."

"Okay."

"I've got to run to class, Val. I'm late."

"Can we have lunch?"

"Meet me in the lower faculty parking lot in an hour."

———

At noon, Valerie and I drove to Bessie's Place, a small family restaurant near Christiansburg, about eight miles east of Traymore. It smelled of burgers and fries, had a pressed tin ceiling, and each of its nine tables was covered with a red-checkered oilcloth.

Bessie introduced herself after she sat us at a rear table. Bessie infused Bessie's Place with Bessie. She was almost as wide as she was tall and exuded, in equal measure, warmth, and authority.

Looking at Valerie directly for the first time, Bessie said, "Sweet Jesus, honey. You all right?" She gave me an icy stare.

Grabbing my hand, Valerie assured her, "No, no. It has nothing to do with him."

"So sorry, honey," said Bessie as she patted my shoulder. "Apple pie is on me today." Valerie and I both ordered hamburgers.

I again stressed the importance of reporting the incident to the police. Valerie assured me she'd do so today when she returned to Blacksburg. She confirmed that Vincent had battered her repeatedly over the past year, and, as Marigold had told me, she'd been seeing a professional in Roanoke for months about her marital situation.

"Your safety is paramount," I said. "Don't make it easy for Vincent to find you. Relocate to where a male, almost any male, is nearby. Abusers don't want another man around. Your dad's attorney in Roanoke can help by getting a restraining order."

"Uh-huh," mumbled Valerie, staring at her water glass. "We've been married for two years. Vincent wasn't always like this. Something snapped about a year ago, when he began drinking heavily and hanging out with another engineering student. They listen to weirdo radio programs."

"Weirdo radio programs?"

"Yeah. Especially Cottonmouth, the Mouth of the South."

"You're pulling my chain."

"Oh no. It's real! Cottonmouth rails against 'man-eating feminists,' 'fellow traveling liberals,' 'parasitic welfare queens,' and 'outside agitators.' Vincent never misses Cottonmouth's program. He no longer attends Mass, but he's a true believer in Cottonmouth."

"Damn."

Changing the subject entirely, Valerie said, "Professor . . . David . . . could you possibly contact the school about securing Barton Hall for the Vietnam panel?"

"Of course. I'll do it this afternoon. You have more important things to do."

"You're so sweet." Then, looking at me intently, Valerie said, "Would you consider showing me your cottage sometime? Bet I can improve its design and decoration."

Caught completely off-guard, I replied, "Well, uh . . . let me chew on that."

We finished our lunch and got up to leave. "Y'all come on back, you hear," said Bessie as we left.

When I dropped Valerie off at her car in Traymore, we agreed to have lunch at Bessie's again on Wednesday. Valerie's parting words were sobering. "Vincent said vile things about you and Marigold. He has a gun. He made no direct threats, but I've never seen him this wild. Please be careful."

———

I brushed aside Valerie's warning and walked directly to Buildings & Grounds to reserve Barton Hall for the Vietnam panel. The hall was available for the afternoon of October eighteenth, but I needed an okay from the Office of the Vice President. Approval was usually *pro forma*. I filled out the requisite form.

Shortly after doing this, as I entered my office, the phone rang. "Professor Pritchard, it's Bud at Buildings and Grounds. Ned Thompson denied your request."

"Already? Any reason?"

"None given."

I hung up, then called Thompson. "Ned, what's going on?"

"President Barton thinks there might be a disruptive disturbance at your event."

"What the hell does that mean?"

"See page fifty-four of the *Student Handbook*."

The pink-covered *Traymore College Student Handbook, 1969-1970*, had been on my desk since Mary Jo Shifflet came to my office almost a month ago. "Just a second, Ned. Let's see. . . . 'Disruptive behavior: Students participating in or in attendance as a spectator at a disturbance disrupting the orderly function of the college . . . will be subject to disciplinary action.'" I laughed into the phone. Key words like "disruptive," "disturbance," and "participating" were undefined so as to give the administration maximum leverage.

"Ned," I said, "either the college has an idiot for an attorney, or, more likely, Barton never bothered to consult one." I pounded my fist on the desk, sending a pen skidding across the room. "Such vague language does not pass legal muster. Moreover, prohibition of the Vietnam panel almost certainly constitutes an unconstitutional prior restraint on the exercise of faculty and student First Amendment rights."

"Well . . ."

"Hey. Hot damn! Here's another prize provision on page fifty-four that's *prima facie* challengeable: 'Improper language: Students responsible for written or verbal public displays of profanity or obscenity will be subject to disciplinary action.' Maybe a protest sign on the day of the Vietnam event will read, 'Nixon, get the fuck out of Vietnam.'"

I leaned way back in my desk chair, reveling in the *Student Handbook's* rich pickings for civil liberties lawyers. "If this decision is not reversed very soon, Ned, Traymore will be sued, probably with ACLU backing. Of course, *The Roanoke Times* will also be contacted."

"Now, now. Don't go off half-cocked, David. I'll get right back to you."

Before leaving the college for my cottage late that afternoon, I found a handwritten note in my campus mailbox from President Barton:

> *Your request to hold a Vietnam Panel in Barton Hall on October 18 is approved. I will hold you personally responsible for any resulting disturbance.*

"Ha!" I yelled. This first victory was small, but I had Barton's attention.

5

Punished

Xena gave me her usual greeting when I opened the cottage door. She twirled around three times, leapt into the air, and then whizzed out the door to chase Canada geese into the lake. Cycles was hunched on his familiar perch on top of the fridge. Fortunately, Xena was usually able to hold it for many hours without peeing on the floor. She wasn't perfect, but neither was I. Sometimes I had to clean up the mess after she'd dined on a delicacy or two from Cycles's litter box. Because of Xena's taste for cat poop, face licks were not encouraged.

I poured a glass of wine, put two records on the stereo— Janis Joplin, and Mendelssohn's Symphony No. 5—then sank, exhausted, into the couch. "Hopefully," I said out loud, "there won't be many more days like this."

———

I'd met Bill Vaughn my first full day on campus and liked him immediately. Since then, we'd had lunch or some other get-to-gether every week. I felt that I knew him well.

He looked like the forty-one-year-old tenured history profes-sor he was, with longish salt and pepper hair, a Harris tweed jacket with a plaid wool tie, and a not-so-faint aroma of pipe tobacco. Bill's scuffed cordovan loafers and wrinkled khakis clashed with his gray jacket. He was frumpy, homely, and fatherly.

Bill Vaughn was among the three or four Traymore faculty members who could legitimately be called a scholar. He had published a well-received book and several peer-reviewed articles on Virginia's history, especially concerning the influential planter and congressman, John Randolph of Roanoke. More importantly, Bill was the most respected, even beloved, member of the faculty. Without exception, students and faculty alike spoke highly of him. He cared deeply for the college, its students, and his colleagues. Sometimes, he even had kind words for President Barton: "I think he probably means well."

There was another identity, one that was well-known, that he neither hid nor flaunted when he was on campus. Reverend Bill Vaughn was an ordained Methodist minister who assisted in Sunday services at nearby Forest Avenue Methodist Church, and he was active in its Wesley Foundation.

He did not wear religion on his sleeve, but his gentle words were matched by his selfless deeds. John Manikas told me how Bill had comforted him after his mother's death, and Tom O'Keefe said he and his wife were eternally grateful for Bill's constant presence in the hospital when their young son was gravely ill. Professor-Reverend Bill was a Good Man.

But this Tuesday afternoon, Bill was distraught. He paced back and forth in front of my desk, shaking his head. "David, I don't understand why it happened."

"What's that, Bill?"

"For the first time in my nine years here, I'm not getting a pay raise, although the college indicated otherwise last semester. And that's not all. My upper division classes are being taken away, as is summer teaching, and I'm being forced to teach an introductory course on Saturday mornings."

"Holy cow, Bill. Did you piss on Barton's beagle? Burn a draft card?"

"I'm clueless. Dave, you've become the go-to guy for many of us. The president's office won't tell me anything."

I rubbed my forehead, glanced at the desk calendar, and was reminded of my upcoming Friday lunch with Evelyn Baird. "Well," I said, "there is one possible source of information. Why don't we reconvene here on Friday at about four? There's a chance, just a chance, that I may have something for you."

"Thanks, Dave. Bless you."

"When the Bill Vaughns of the world are vulnerable," I said, "we're all vulnerable."

I walked with Bill down the empty hallway toward the front door with my arm around his shoulder.

As we stepped outside, Bill remarked, "Things will work out. God may give minimum protection, but He provides maximum support."

I returned to the office and picked up the phone. "Evelyn, David. Just calling to confirm our Friday lunch."

"I'm looking forward to it."

"Great; see you then."

———

The next day, I met Valerie at Bessie's Place for lunch. Her black eyes were blacker, and the facial bruise was still evident, if camouflaged somewhat with caked makeup. As we entered the restaurant, Bessie greeted us warmly.

"Bessie," I said, "I just had to return for lunch, and for another piece of your delicious apple pie."

"You're my kind of man," Bessie said. She took our order and went into the kitchen.

I asked Valerie, "How did it go yesterday?"

"Fine, I think. I'm filing for divorce. My attorney will seek a restraining order against Vincent, but, as you said, he warned that aggrieved spouses often flout them."

"That's right."

"My attorney also reiterated something else that you'd mentioned… Don't make it easy for Vincent to find me." Valerie said she'd found a small basement apartment not far from Bessie's in a house owned by Christiansburg's deputy fire chief.

"Excellent," I said. "Even if Vincent can locate you, he'll think twice about risking an encounter with that guy."

Valerie's attitude and demeanor were much improved. She smiled more easily and had cleaned herself up. She wore dark blue corduroy slacks and a cheerful pink cotton sweater. Her voice was almost sunny. "Dad and my brother, Bob, return to Baltimore early tomorrow morning. We still have plenty to do this afternoon and evening. Can you and I have lunch again, maybe tomorrow?"

I shifted uneasily in my chair as Bessie brought our food. She said, "You two look like you're made for one another."

"You're pretty observant," said Valerie, with a wink at me.

I smiled guardedly. "Val, you're really pleasant, but this may not be the best time for us to have frequent lunches."

Her brow wrinkled. "Why not?" She bit her lower lip.

"Well, this is a stressful time for you, and . . ."

"David, you and Marigold are my anchors. I'm *so* grateful for your support."

I said nothing as I chomped into my tuna sandwich and tried to change the subject. "We're on for the panel, Val. Ned Thompson balked at first because Barton feared there'd be a disturbance."

"That's ridiculous. This is Traymore, not Berkeley."

"Of course. I had to raise the specter of legal action and publicity before the administration capitulated."

"You're *good*, David." Then, changing the subject completely, she said, "Tell me about your cottage."

"It's unimpressive, one of eight identical, rather dull cabins on Claytor Lake. All of them are occupied in the summer, but now I'm alone. It's a quiet and safe harbor from the insanity of Traymore."

Valerie's eyes lit up as she leaned across the table. She took my hand in hers. "David, I'd *love* to see it. Being by the lake would be a welcome distraction from all that's going on."

"I guess . . . maybe someday."

"Not someday. Soon. Please." Valerie put her water glass down. "I'm a good Catholic, David. I'm still married. I *won't* commit a mortal sin."

I exhaled, probably too noticeably. "Alright, possibly after the Vietnam Panel."

"Promise."

"We'll see."

Valerie squeezed my hand. I left Bessie a generous tip. "Hurry back," said Bessie as we went out the door.

———

That afternoon, after class, I drove to the ARSE-N-ALL to touch base with the POF. As I walked through the bar's swinging double doors, I saw that empty Old Milwaukee beer cans were already accumulating on the faculty's table. Everyone called the beer "horse piss" or "Old Horsey," but this didn't seem to affect its rate of consumption.

"Heeere's Boat Rocker," announced John Manikas as I approached the group. "What Traymore cow pie did you step in this week?"

I sat down next to John, ordered an Old Horsey, and tried to keep my elbows off the sticky table. The place had a ripe odor, as if a squirrel had drowned in a bucket of stale beer last week and no one bothered to remove it. Turning to John, I said with a grin, "What makes you think I'm a troublemaker?"

"Ho!" John said, "you *have* been up to no good, you ole booger." Some of his beer dripped onto the table. "So, spill the beans."

Several of the thirteen faculty members who were present looked my way. "You know about Bill Vaughn?"

Tom O'Keefe and the two other historians in the group nodded. A mathematician piped up: "What . . . Bill Vaughn? If anyone walked on water, it's Reverend Bill." Pointing a finger at me, he continued, "Unlike Pritchard here, Bill's a peacemaker and above the fray."

"He was screwed by the administration and doesn't know why," said Tom. "No good person goes unpunished. Bill was denied a pay raise and forced to teach only freshman courses."

Gasps went up around the table.

"Afraid I have even more bad news," said Mel Tromblay of the anthropology department. "Three of us went to Case Western Reserve in July to help organize the forthcoming demonstration in Washington—the Moratorium to End the War in Vietnam. When our names appeared in the press, Barton placed letters of reprimand in our files."

Down came my hand on the surface of the table, rattling Old Horsey cans. "Bastard," I said. More beer dribbled onto the table and floor. "Mel, that's unconscionable. I won't be here next year, even if I can't find another job. But with colleagues like you and key students, we can go to court and work with the press. I'll do my damnedest to bring Barton down."

POF members pounded their fists on the table.

Tromblay's pasty white face dripped with perspiration as he slowly shook his head. He looked like a broken man. "Because of this, my two friends have submitted their letters of resignation, effective at the end of the academic year. I may join them."

A long, awkward silence finally came to a close when Manikas crunched a beer can and began softly singing nostalgic lines from "That Old Gang of Mine."

"The gang might get smaller yet after the eighteenth," I said. "I've organized a panel on Vietnam for that afternoon in Barton Hall, just three days after the demonstration in Washington. Tom and I are on it."

"Here, on campus? Barton will go bananas," said Mel Tromblay. "How'd you get his approval?"

Merle Haggard's "Okie from Muskogee" started up again on the jukebox. When Merle got to "We like livin' right and bein' free," I stood and sang along—loudly. Merle and I finished our duet. Then I replied to Mel, "My approach is more direct than Bill Vaughn's."

John slapped my back, causing even more beer to slosh, this time onto me. "Pritchard, you're cruisin' for a bruisin'. You won't last long."

"Got that right," I said.

It was only 5:30, but we'd all had enough depressing news for an afternoon. People were leaving when Manikas grabbed my wrist. "Dave, let's do something, take a break from chewing on Barton's ass."

I remembered that John had said he loved to hunt when he was back home in West Virginia. "Sure," I said. "A corn field near my place attracts doves. They taste great with wild rice and plum sauce. You must have a shotgun."

"Three."

"Let's skip the POF next Wednesday. Loan me one of your guns, and I'll reimburse you for all the shells we use."

"You're on."

———

I was about to leave my office for the Friday lunch with Dean Evelyn Baird when the phone rang.

"Dave?"

"Dan?"

My brother, Dan, would be celebrating his twenty-sixth birthday the following Wednesday. He was a man of few words, especially after he'd returned from Vietnam a year ago with a silver star, a promotion to army captain, and all of his body parts intact. I hadn't seen Dan in several months because he was a mining engineer who seemed always to be in places like Botswana or New Guinea.

"I have some time off. Could I bother you for a few days? I'd come down from D.C. on my birthday and return Sunday or Monday."

"That's fine," I said. "Another vet, a guy from West Virginia, will be with me that afternoon for some dove hunting."

"Sounds good. See you Wednesday."

———

Sitting down at our usual corner table in the faculty dining room, I apologized to Evelyn for being late. She'd been waiting. Evelyn looked up from some documents she'd been reviewing, and I noticed that her hairdo had a freer, more natural look. While it was a marked improvement over her permed curls, it still cried out for at least another four inches in length.

"You look *grand*," I said with a broad smile.

Evelyn returned my smile. "Thank you." Still smiling, she asked, "So, what mischief have *you* been up to this week?"

"You know, of course, about the upcoming Vietnam panel."

"President Barton is concerned about *your* panel. He said that it will attract 'subversives' and 'screwballs' to campus."

"Don't think the president likes me."

Evelyn gave an unladylike guffaw that drew glances from others in the dining room even though we were some distance from the nearest table.

"It'll be fine," I assured her. "Traymore students don't storm Bastilles."

"The president despises what he calls 'peaceniks.'"

"He prefers warmongers and spear-chuckers?" My eyes narrowed. "Look, I've just learned that he has severely sanctioned three faculty members for their opposition to the war."

Evelyn said nothing. After a long pause, she asked, "Why do people confide in you? You've only been at Traymore for a month."

"When I was twelve or thirteen, I had to memorize the Boy Scout Oath. It began with, 'A Boy Scout is trustworthy . . .' Maybe they trust me. Some think I can help them. Take Bill Vaughn."

Evelyn stiffened and put her fork down. She seemed surprised. "Professor Vaughn?"

"Bill told me what happened to him. The entire faculty is appalled. Why did Barton piss on the most esteemed person on campus?"

Evelyn fidgeted with her napkin and slid her chair back a few inches. She looked around the dining room and fussed with her purse strap.

"Evelyn," I said, "you and Reverend Bill are both good Methodists. Maybe you even attend Forest Avenue Methodist Church? Everyone knows that Bill is devoted to the college, its students, and the community."

"Yes. Probably I shouldn't . . ."

I cut her off. "I suspect that you agree to have lunch with me because I provide useful information about the faculty and, often, students. But . . ."

With a raised eyebrow, Evelyn interjected, "And I give you the administration's perspective."

"Yes, there is some mutuality, but we are both selective about what is revealed."

Grinning, Evelyn said, "That's because you're a troublemaker."

Returning her grin, I said, "I prefer boat rocker or muckraker."

"You have *something* on your mind," she said.

I leaned forward and asked in a low voice, "What happened to Bill Vaughn? I can offer a *quid pro quo*."

"Such as?"

"Likely lawsuits against the college."

Evelyn weighed this for a few seconds, cradling her chin in the palm of her hand. "You first." She giggled. "I'll show mine if you show yours."

"Well then," I said with a wry grin, "Mel Tromblay and possibly two other anthropology faculty members will probably bring suit, and Bill Vaughn will soon retain legal counsel."

Evelyn tapped her index finger on the table and looked up with a furrowed brow. She glanced furtively around the room. "Assure me" she whispered, "that what I say will be held in *strict* confidence."

Placing my hand over my heart, I replied, "Sources and methods are sacrosanct. I pledge *never* to reveal your identity, whether directly or indirectly."

Evelyn began her story with, "This came from President Barton."

As she told it, the strange episode began when Mildred Truse, wife of Traymore's eighty-seven-year-old chairman of its Board of Visitors, Millard Truse, thumbed through a copy of *Redbook* magazine as she stood in line at the Star Brite Grocery. She noticed a letter to the editor from Professor Bill Vaughn of Traymore College. Vaughn praised the physician who'd authored an article on premarital sex that had appeared in an earlier issue. Alarmed,

Mildred, who admitted to having read and been "shocked" by the original article, told her husband that she was "scandalized" by Vaughn's letter. Millard promptly called Elzic Barton and followed up this call with a written memorandum demanding that Professor Vaughn be denied a pay raise and incur additional penalties. Barton didn't hesitate to implement Truse's demands.

Said Evelyn, "Only I questioned the wisdom of these measures. My concerns were dismissed. I'm deeply troubled about what has happened to Professor Vaughn." Evelyn's voice broke, and her eyes reddened.

I shook my head in disbelief. "How stupid. The college *will* be sued for a blatant First Amendment violation."

Evelyn concurred. "David, I told them: 'Pritchard will be all over this one.' Nobody listened." She licked her lips and, with both elbows planted on the table, leaned toward me. With what appeared to be a mischievous grin, she asked, "Okay, what about that country ham dinner I offered? When can I expect you?"

I'd eluded her invitation before, but now I felt cornered and she knew it. At considerable risk, Evelyn had just divulged extremely sensitive information that effectively confirmed that our relationship was one of trust. She would be fired if I violated my assurance of confidentiality. For whatever reason, this dinner was important to her. *If we are to continue to meet,* I thought to myself, *I'd better accept.* I had grave reservations, however, especially if she harbored designs for an intimate relationship. Evelyn was pleasant enough, but there were lines I did not want to cross. Diddling a dean was certainly one such line.

I trolled for one last bit of information. "Dinner would be nice, maybe on Halloween? But why wasn't Bill Vaughn informed of the reason for the sanctions that were levied against him?"

"Millard Truse directed President Barton *not* to give Vaughn a reason. That's all I know."

Evelyn placed her napkin on the table and said, "Halloween works for me. What costume are you wearing?"

"Should I come as an angel or a devil? Trick or treat?"

"An angel would be *wholly* out of character, and devils must know that deans don't do tricks." She blushed.

"A forewarned devil it is."

————

Following my afternoon class, I stopped by Bill Vaughn's office. "Well, Dave, do you have anything? Even a William Faulkner couldn't make this stuff up, Bill." Without mentioning my source, I related everything Evelyn had told me.

"'I am merciful saith the Lord,'" said Bill, quoting Jeremiah. "Where and how did you get this information?"

"I gave my word to keep that confidential. Still, this is extremely good news. You *will* prevail in a legal action against the college. But what, might I ask, ever prompted you to write such a letter to the editor?"

Bill shook his head, leaned back in his chair, and related his story. It seems that after dinner one night, he opened a copy of *Redbook* magazine that his wife had bought at the grocery store. He read a two-page piece by a female M.D. who asserted that couples who were soon to be married might benefit from premarital intimacy. Bill recalled that the doctor had written that "there is no magic moment when sex changes from being nasty and dirty to becoming splendid and beautiful." Impressed by the doctor's "common sense insights," Bill wrote a short letter to the editor in which he disclosed that he was a happily married clergyman with three young daughters, and that he taught at a women's college. He then praised the author for her informed remarks.

"Sounds like common sense advice to me, too," I said, "but it's not surprising that your letter would be incendiary in Southwest Virginia."

"You're right," said Bill. His ears turned red, and he breathed heavily. "I should have known that there are a great many Mildred Truses."

"Bill, I'm virtually certain that either the National Education Association or the ACLU will provide free legal representation." I wrote down contact information for both organizations on a three-by-five card and handed it to Bill.

"Don't know how to thank you, Dave. God works wonders."

I rested my hand on his back. "You'll get through this, but Barton may not survive."

———

I spent the weekend walking Xena in the nearby state park, preparing for classes, and perfecting my resume. Finding a position at a respectable institution was imperative, but it wouldn't be easy. Networking in academe, as in most professions, is critical. Except for an awareness that many academic openings were advertised in *The Chronicle of Higher Education*, I had neither the experience nor any guidance in how to proceed. I was alone. But I knew I had to get out of this place.

My dissertation committee chair would normally have been instrumental in helping me locate a position, but Professor Ted

Sopolsky was in France on a Ford Foundation grant. Being isolated at a third-rate rural college that was unknown to most other colleges and universities didn't help. Peer-reviewed articles in respected journals would catch the attention of university faculty search committees, but a heavy teaching load, a mediocre library, and my self-appointed "boat rocker" activities ruled out research and writing. Moreover, my department chairman at Traymore, Byon Joon-Ho, had made it clear that he and Barton would attempt to undermine my job search.

A scattershot approach was the only option. So, I sent resumes with cover letters to the political science and international relations departments of thirty-two institutions of higher learning throughout the country, public and private, large and small. I could only wait for fish to bite.

6

Threatened

A short, thickset man appeared in the hallway as I was counseling a student during my morning office hours. Vincent Tavernetti meant trouble. He prowled outside my office, pacing back and forth. I reached for the phone, called campus security, gave them my room number, and said, "Come right away." The student, perhaps sensing my unease, excused herself and left.

Vincent stepped quickly into the office and closed the door.

"You can leave the door open," I said. "What brings you to Traymore, Vincent?"

Vincent said nothing and did not open the door. He sat down, uninvited, with a smirk on his face and his right hand buried in the pocket of a rumpled hunting jacket. The tension was palpable. He seemed ready to pounce at the slightest provocation. I rolled my desk chair back to increase the distance between us.

Edging his chair forward, Vincent slowly withdrew his hand from the coat pocket, revealing a chrome-plated pistol, probably a .32 caliber. His eyes glued onto mine. He smiled at my unease. The gun was not pointed at me. Rather, he laid it on his lap.

I stared directly at him and tried to remain calm, but my heart raced, and I tasted blood when I bit my tongue. The silence was heavy and ominous. Vincent's smirk morphed into amused hostility.

Where the hell is security? It felt like an hour had passed, but it couldn't have been more than a minute or two.

Just then, Cob Maplewood opened the door and nodded in Vincent's direction. Cob started to take off his leather jacket, but stopped. "What's up, Dave? You look like you've swallowed a friggin' armadillo. You okay?"

Vincent thrusted the pistol back into his pocket, leapt to his feet, and rushed out of the office.

"What the hell was that all about?" Cob asked.

I exhaled, rubbed sweaty palms on my pants, and kneaded my forehead. I told Cob about my dinner with the Tavernettis and Vincent's threats with the pistol. "I have no idea why he threatened me. Maybe he thinks I'm messing with his wife, which is crazy."

"Jesus H. Christ! You calling the authorities?"

Before I could reply, a heavyset middle-aged security officer appeared. "Professor Pritchard, you called security?"

"Thanks for coming over. Thought I might have a problem, but everything is fine. Sorry to bother you."

"Well," said the officer as he turned to leave, "just let us know if we can be of assistance."

"Thanks again."

Turning to Cob, I said, "Guess that answers your question. There are risks in reporting and not reporting. Barton would *love* to use this incident against me. He'd argue that this episode illustrates that much of what I do or say invites violent disturbances on campus. But the threat sure as hell felt real. Reporting it might deter future threats from Vincent Tavernetti."

I called Valerie to tell her what had happened and to warn her to be careful.

"I'm so sorry," she said.

"Does he know where you live, Val?"

"No, I don't think so, but *your* address is in the faculty directory. I'm worried about *you*. Can we get together somewhere?"

"Not for a while, I'm afraid. My brother arrives Wednesday. Too much is going on."

"Please be very careful. Vincent's volatile."

"You, too, Val."

With that, I hung up and walked down the hall to my class.

———

Returning to Claytor Lake, I stopped first at the entrance to Piney Woods to chat with caretakers Mara and Caleb Heath and to resupply Caleb with a pouch of Red Man chewing tobacco. Caleb's bib overalls were torn in one knee, smelled faintly of urine, and—judging from the smudges of red soil—hadn't been washed in weeks. His white t-shirt was stained with tobacco juice. Caleb and Mara lived on social security and what little they earned looking after the Piney Woods Lakeside Resort cottages.

"You take real good care of this old coal miner," said Caleb.

"It's nothing," I said. Turning to Mara—who wore a threadbare blue denim dress—I said, "I'm driving to New York for Thanksgiving. What can I bring back for you?"

"Honey," she chuckled, "ask the tooth fairy for the eleven teeth I'm missing."

"Afraid I don't have a hotline to the tooth fairy. Anything else?"

Mara fiddled with her dress and shook her head.

But Caleb spoke up. "David, years ago, when we were last in Roanoke—it was a Crusade for Christ in the civic center—Mara caught a whiff of something she's never forgotten."

"Your overalls?"

Mara playfully punched her husband's shoulder and bent over in laughter. "Hey," protested Caleb, "I save money on water and electricity." He continued, "No. A lady sitting next to us wore a perfume that Mara loved and has never forgotten." Caleb choked up and rubbed his eyes. "Right then and there in the civic center, the Lord spoke to Mara: 'I am the rose of Sharon, the lily of the valleys.' It was the Song of Solomon."

Mara kissed Caleb on the cheek and said, "It was called Bellodgia."

"Don't know much about perfumes," I said, "but nothing's too good for the Lady of the Lake."

Before leaving the Heaths, I asked about dove hunting in the nearby cornfield. "No problem," said Caleb. "It's owned by the same man who owns Piney Woods. He don't care none."

"I'll have guests on Wednesday. We'll likely try our luck. Oh, and should you notice any unfamiliar people or cars who do *not* appear to be my guests, could you let me know?"

"Of course," said Mara, looking concerned. "Any problem?"

"Hope not."

———

John Manikas arrived at the cottage late Wednesday afternoon wearing a burgundy Washington Redskins cap. "Spoke with Caleb Heath," said John. "Salt of the earth."

"Caleb and his wife are good people," I said.

It would be dark in about two hours, so we removed the shotguns from the gun racks in John's Ford pickup. We walked a short distance into the field with its wilted brown cornstalks. Xena, ever leery of strangers, trotted watchfully behind us, her eyes on John.

Not until the sun was setting did we see any birds. Four or five doves flew in low over the field. John fired, feathers puffed into the air, and two gray doves tumbled to the ground. "That's tomorrow's dinner," he said matter-of-factly.

When we returned to the cottage, Cycles, eager to be fed, dropped to the floor from his customary perch on the refrigerator. I offered John a dark English ale, a brew vastly superior to Old Horsey. I'd no sooner removed the bottle caps when the crunch of tires on gravel announced an approaching car. Dan had arrived.

Xena growled, pushed open the screen door with her nose, and rushed outside with raised fur. I raced after her, grabbed her collar none too soon, and patted her head. "Dan is friendly, girl. It's okay." Still on alert, Xena sniffed Dan cautiously.

At six-foot-two, Dan was a couple of inches taller than me and—although I'd never admit it—better looking. He handed me a bottle of Johnnie Walker Red. "You're not going to be surprised by anyone with *that* dog on the premises," said Dan, giving Xena a wary look.

"Good to see you," I said, patting him on the back. "Want you to meet a West Virginia dove hunter, John Manikas."

The two men, both tall and muscular, shook hands.

"It's dinnertime," I said. "From my vast repertoire of culinary classics, I offer my *piece de resistance*: homemade all (or mostly) beef hamburgers with canned sweet corn, followed by chocolate ice cream."

"I'm impressed," said Dan. "Good thing I had pizza along the way."

"In West Virginia," said John, "we'd consider that fine dining. Even better than roadkill."

It was now dark. We went inside, and, while I tended to dinner, Dan and John drank ale and talked. They had things in common: both had been college athletes, both were Vietnam vets and Republicans, and their professions overlapped somewhat, John the physicist-mathematician and Dan the engineer. Except for saying he'd served "south of Da Nang," Dan wouldn't discuss the war. Nonetheless, they got along well.

After dinner, we downed more ale, followed by the Johnnie Walker Red scotch. Well lubricated, I decided to tell them about Valerie's husband. I ended the story with, "Only my office mate knows about this. It's highly confidential."

"Holy shit!" exclaimed an inebriated Manikas. "You could get your head blown off. That Vincent guy is a nut case. Do you have any kind of gun?"

"No."

"Just a minute." John went out the door, followed closely by Xena.

"He's right, Dave," Dan said in a measured voice. "I understand why you didn't report the incident, but that might not have been a wise decision."

Dan stood and stared at a photo of our parents that hung on the wall. After a few moments, he asked, "Does this guy know where you live?"

"Probably."

John came through the door with Xena nipping at his boots.

"Hate to think what this dog would do to me if we hadn't been properly introduced," said John.

"Xena. Down! Stay!" I said. She twirled around three times and slid into a corner behind the phonograph.

John handed me a shotgun and some shells. "Return it any time. You need it."

"Doubt that," I said.

"Don't be a dumb-ass," said John.

Dan added, "Listen to him, Dave. Except for Xena, you're isolated and vulnerable out here." Xena's ears shot up when she heard her name. She stared intently at us from her corner.

I relented. "Okay. Thanks, John. Just lay the gun on the counter."

John yawned and staggered toward the door. "That was pretty good hooch. It's one o'clock, and I've got to get back to town."

"Drive *very* carefully," I said. Then, changing my mind: "You're plastered. Stay here for the night."

"Nope. See ya." He stumbled out the door. His truck twice swerved off into the field before he wrestled it back onto the driveway and out of Piney Woods.

7

Attacked

Dan and I had four more days together. We'd never been particularly close. Not that we didn't get along—we did. But we were different people, and we'd taken separate paths.

Dan had excelled in basketball; I had been a wrestler and baseball player. I loved music but had flunked Piano 101. Dan had been a trumpeter at the Latin Quarter in Manhattan. He had followed Dad into mining engineering, while I was the only Pritchard male in three generations *not* to go into engineering or medicine. We were both avid readers. Dan, in seeming contradiction to his pronounced pragmatic bent, went on for an M.A. in philosophy. He was a hard-right conservative, but I'd moved inexorably leftward since law school. We both enjoyed—indeed, reveled in—female companionship. But Dan viewed women as an inexhaustible box of Whitman samplers, while I was more selective and hoped to have a family someday. Finally, Dan hadn't been near a church in years. I had always been churchier and left my door open for the Holy Spirit, whatever that might be. Old, familiar hymns moved me deeply.

I had to be on campus for Thursday and Friday classes, but on Saturday Dan and I hiked with Xena at the Peaks of Otter, located near the Appalachian Trail north of Roanoke off the Blue Ridge Parkway. It was mid-October, and the cool air had a crisp leafy scent as we ascended the Sharp Top Trail. The fall foliage dressed the mountains with swatches of red and gold.

At the four-thousand-foot summit, we had a striking view of ridge after rolling ridge of the southern Appalachians in all their autumnal beauty. My worries fell away like the falling leaves as if to confirm that, where men and mountains meet, the spirit soars. The wild was my safe place.

Descending by a lesser-traveled path, we encountered a blacksnake. Xena sniffed it cautiously and walked away. Didn't smell interesting. The snake was unperturbed and calmly continued to sun itself on a rock ledge. It looked at us intently, flicking its tongue as if to tell us something.

Driving back to the cottage, Dan remarked, "That snake seemed to know us, like your pet snake, Cecil, when we were kids."

I thought of the unique—okay, *strange*—bond I'd had with Cecil, and my consequent fondness for snakes, particularly blacksnakes. Out of the blue, I said, "Here's a great title for a country and western song, 'I Rolled Snake Eyes in Life's Game of Craps.'"

Dan frowned. Then he shocked me with, "Could we go to church tomorrow?"

Our mother had raised us as Episcopalians. Dad was indifferent to religion, but he always acquiesced when Mom declared, "Dear, we *are* going to church."

I hadn't attended a church service since Easter. I said to Dan, "Now that's about the *last* thing I thought you'd want to do."

"Yeah. Lost a buddy in Nam. Can't get it out of my head. Maybe it'll help."

"We Episcopalians are a tiny, somewhat suspect minority in Southwest Virginia."

"Oh?"

"Evangelicals think we're liberal neo-Catholics. 'Liberal' and 'Catholic' are pejorative."

"And rich, too."

"Yup."

"George Washington and Robert E. Lee were Episcopalians."

"Yes, but few folks down here know this about their fellow Virginians. . . . I've heard good things about Christ Church Episcopal in Blacksburg. It dates from the mid-nineteenth century. We'll try it out."

———

We arrived at Christ Church on Sunday as the doors were closing for the eleven o'clock service. The congregation was singing the processional hymn, "Holy, Holy, Holy," which always choked me up. As we searched for a pew, I sang along from memory. "Early in the morning, our song shall rise to thee. . . ."

During the Prayers of the People, when a lay leader read, "Give to the departed eternal rest," and the congregation replied, "Let light perpetual shine upon them," Dan rubbed his eyes and muttered, "Frank." I took communion; Dan did not. Nor did he kneel during the service. He sat silently, head bowed.

The rector, Rev. Matthew Greenway, was about fifty, with graying hair parted down the middle, a coast-to-coast smile, and ample girth. He greeted us warmly after the service, as did several parishioners, some of whom were faculty members at Virginia Tech. We accepted Rev. Greenway's invitation to meet with him briefly in his office, although I suspected he'd try to rope me into his parish.

He *did* urge me to join Christ Church, but I was noncommittal. He made it clear that he was well aware of the "troubles" at Traymore College and offered whatever assistance he might be able to provide. When I mentioned that Dan had lost a close friend in Vietnam, Frank, and that this was what had brought us to Christ Church, Rev. Greenway rested his hand on Dan's shoulder and quoted from *The Book of Common Prayer*: "Grant to all who mourn a sure confidence in thy fatherly care, that, casting all their grief on thee, they may know the consolation of thy love. Amen." Guilt and grief seemed to subside as a warm serenity enveloped me. We all shook hands.

———

After church, Dan and I drove to Bessie's in Christiansburg for lunch, and then returned to Piney Woods at Claytor Lake. That night we retired early because Dan had a long drive to D.C. the next day to make a late afternoon flight. He again slept on the air mattress I'd inflated for him on the floor of the other bedroom, which I used as an office. Xena curled up, snout to tail, in her usual spot near the front door, and Cycles jumped down from the refrigerator and scooted into my bedroom to sleep, meatloaf-like, inches from my head. Honking geese glided over the cottage, splashing down in the nearby lake. A light breeze fluttered the curtains.

We had slept for several hours when I heard Xena's low guttural growl. I rolled over—probably another raccoon raiding the garbage can.

BLAM, BLAM—the unmistakable sound of gunfire from behind the cottage. Very close. Loud. The bedroom window shattered, and shards of glass sprayed the room. My face burned with pain, and I felt a warm, sticky wetness: blood—mine. The stench of cat urine filled the room. My mind raced: *geese, glass, raccoons. Focus, damn it.* Blackness, dust, pain. *Get down, fast.* I dropped off the bed to the floor, wearing only boxer shorts. I cut my hand, my chest. *Face really hurts. Blood, lots of blood.*

Get out of the bedroom, out! I crawled into the hallway. *Careful; keep low.* Where was Dan? *BLAM.* More splintering glass fell just feet away, this time onto the floor of the bathroom between my bedroom and Dan's. The hallway, at last. Glass splattered off the sink into the bathtub. I heard everything but saw nothing. *Don't turn on the lights.*

BLAM. BLAM. More shattering glass. That was Dan's room. "Dan, Dan," I cried out softly. No response.

Twenty feet from where I lay, Xena barked hysterically by the front door in the living room: *Let me out goddamnit; let me out.* She rushed over to where I was sprawled out on my stomach in the hallway outside the bathroom near Dan's room. Xena licked my bloody face, uttered a shrill whine, and raced back to the front door, where she spun around, barked wildly, and scratched at the door.

Her barks and whines drew another shot. *BLAM.* Xena yipped in pain. She was hit, but I couldn't see where or how badly. I heard the dog hurl herself against the front door with renewed ferocity. *So, maybe she's not injured too seriously?* I didn't know, but she wanted to *eat* the bastard. He'd never see Xena coming if I let her outside, but he'd sure try to kill her.

Darkness obscured everything—the assailant, the rooms, Dan, the pets. I stayed flat on the floor and slid silently, inch by inch. I winced as my chest, hands, and knees were cut. Heart and head pulsated with fear. No, *terror*. It tasted metallic. I was in a trance, trying to master my fear of death but not succeeding. Reality did not go away. This was no fuckin' dream. Dan's room was silent.

But I was not paralyzed by fear. *Yea though I walk through the valley of the shadow of death. . . .* Words from the twenty-third psalm ricocheted in my head—*I will fear no evil. . . .* There was hope, and rage. *Keep low.* Where was Dan? I crept into the doorway of Dan's cave dark room and whispered, "Dan?"

Silence. A muffled voice came from under the desk: "Quiet. Down. Keep lights off." The combat veteran had reacted instantaneously and instinctively.

BLAM. Another shot ripped through the cottage toward Xena's barks. No yips of pain that time; only her insistent growls.

My fingers touched Dan's shoulder, although we couldn't see one another clearly. "Shotgun?" he whispered.

"Living room."

We eased along the floor to the corner of the living room, where I had put John Manikas's gun. But *damn*—I'd neglected to load it, and I couldn't find the shells in the dark. I grabbed a flashlight from a low shelf but did not turn it on.

Then, very cautiously—while still lying on the floor, and with Xena scrambling to get out—I reached up and turned the doorknob. Xena sprang into the night. *BLAM.* A hush. The stillness was so electric it was audible. Then, panicky screams pierced the blackness.

Dan and I slowly got up off the floor. We stood, backs flush to the inside wall. Dan grabbed the unloaded shotgun; I held the unlit flashlight and peered tentatively out the front door into the darkness. Shrieks and growls emanated from the rear of the cottage. One helluva fracas.

"Let's go," I said.

Dan nodded, but warned, "Careful: he could shoot even with Xena attacking him."

We slipped out the door and edged along the side of the cottage. A brawl was raging. I turned on the flashlight to see Vincent Tavernetti rolling on his back, right arm badly torn up. A chrome-plated pistol lay on the ground ten feet away from him. A snarling Xena, teeth bared and hair raised, was inches from his face.

Tavernetti twitched. Xena chomped down on his face, shaking her head from side to side as if she was killing a rat. Blood spewed onto the ground, flowed down Tavernetti's neck and onto his chest, and painted Xena's coat red.

Tavernetti howled in pain, attempted to sit up, and raised his other arm to fend off the dog. Xena was unrelenting. Her jaws clamped onto his arm, dragged him back down, and drove him—head-first—into the dirt.

Tavernetti's cheeks were shredded flaps of flesh. A portion of blood-soaked scalp hung loose. And half of the SOB's nose was gone! He exhaled bloody bubbles, but nostrils and cartilage were torn away.

I shouted, "Xena! Down! Stay!" She backed off slowly and reluctantly, her eyes fixed on Vincent. I handed the flashlight to Dan, who held the shotgun in his other hand.

Despite severe injuries and considerable loss of blood,

Tavernetti did not quit. He struggled to his feet, staggered around, disoriented, and lunged toward the nearby pistol.

Dan quickly kicked it into the grass, out of reach.

I shouted, "Don't pick it up!" as I punched Tavernetti hard in the gut.

He buckled. I forced him down onto his stomach, my knee in his back. "Dan, go get Caleb Heath, the overseer."

I locked Tavernetti in a full nelson by placing both my hands under his arms from behind and exerting pressure with my palms on the back of his neck. My heart raced; the taste of revenge was exhilarating. I could have crippled him, and was sorely tempted to do so, when I heard Dan say, "Dave, Caleb's right here."

Caleb held a deer rifle, his finger on the trigger. "Mara and I heard gunfire," he said. "Sheriff's on his way. State police, too. You're bleeding pretty bad, David. Ambulance will be here soon."

"Am I *ever* glad to see you," I said to Caleb as I eased my hold on Vincent.

"What happened?"

I started to answer, "This guy tried to kill us . . ." when we heard sirens. Soon, flashing blue lights bobbed through the trees and down the driveway toward us.

Two state police cars screeched to a stop and four officers jumped out, guns drawn. Less than a minute later, Sheriff Harland Goetzke and his deputy pulled up. Headlights illuminated the scene, although by then the sun was beginning to peek over the mountains. That's about the last thing I remembered before blacking out.

———

As the ambulance sped toward Traymore Community Hospital, I regained partial consciousness. A paramedic and Dan, who had suffered several cuts, accompanied me.

"Where's Xena?" I asked.

"With Caleb and Mara."

"She likes them. How is she?"

"SOB shot off half of one of her ears. Caleb's taking her to a vet." Dan chuckled and patted my arm. "She gave him one helluva nose job."

"Wish it was his prick," I mumbled. "And Cycles?"

Dan hesitated. "I'm sorry, Dave. He just might have saved your life. You're covered with bits of Cycles." Dan picked a tuft of blood-soaked gray fur from my hair to show me, but I was too groggy to comprehend. I thought I heard the paramedic say, "He's lost a lot of blood. It doesn't look too good."

A bloody facial groove was carved along my jawline that ran almost to the chin. I'd been unaware of the glass shards and wood slivers in my neck and scalp until the surgeon later informed me that most of them had been removed. But my injuries were not as grave as the paramedic had feared. Indeed, after an IV of saline solution and three units of blood, I was pretty soon alert.

The twenty-one facial stitches promised a frightful scar, perhaps endowing my persona with an unwanted *gravitas*. However, it might also be seen as a "status scar" analogous to the dueling scar that nineteenth-century German university students sometimes inflicted on one another. Young women were supposedly drawn to men with such scars, an attractant I probably didn't need at a college where the ratio of single women to available young men was about four thousand to one. Still, I was afraid that I'd been disfigured for life.

The hospital released me on Tuesday afternoon, shortly before Dan left to return to Washington. As he opened his car door, we shook hands. "Let's go for a little less drama next time," he said. Then he drove away.

I resumed teaching the very next morning, but it was soon apparent that events had transformed an obscure junior faculty member at a backwater institution into a minor celebrity. The assault on my cottage, especially Xena's heroism, was quickly picked up by *The Roanoke Times*, *The Richmond Times Dispatch*, and Virginia radio and television stations. Even *The Washington Post* ran a blurb in its Metro section. My initial discomfort about the media coverage changed when I saw how much it helped focus public attention on Traymore's other troubles.

Xena was the star. Her photo, with half of a bandaged ear lopped off and tongue lolling out in a goofy shepherd smile, was everywhere. Headlines proclaimed: A REAL RIN TIN TIN, MAN'S BEST FRIEND SAVES TWO MEN, and DON'T MESS WITH XENA. I was deluged with calls from the German Shepherd Club of America, the ASPCA, and scores of pet magazines. One of the latter subsequently wrote under Xena's photo: "Dog gives new meaning to 'an eye for an eye.' Now, it's a nose for an ear."

With the notable exception of President Barton, the Traymore College community offered widespread support. Even Vice President Ned Thompson and my otherwise hostile department chairman, Byon Joon-Ho, communicated their concern.

No one was more distraught than Valerie Tavernetti. She left numerous messages for me at the college, one of which referred to the upcoming Vietnam panel on Saturday, the project she had initiated. Valerie actually drove out to Piney Woods on Tuesday but was denied entry by the police.

When I returned to class with bandages on my neck, the back of my head, and one side of the face, students stood and applauded. This enthusiastic welcome erupted into shrieks and rhythmic clapping when a red-haired senior rushed up and planted a loud smooch on my uninjured cheek. *Wow, maybe there is something to this scar thing.* Embarrassed, my flushed face stood out against the white bandages. The class loved it, and chanted: "Do it again, do it again." But I backed away.

Scores of faculty members, many of whom I'd never met, dropped by the office to express their support. The phone rang constantly, and the secretarial staff had written down at least two dozen messages on pink slips. One was from Marigold Dunfree, the blind date Valerie had arranged for me a couple of weeks ago: "Pritchard, CALL. You're safe with me. I'm a crack shot." Two others were particularly welcome. Christ Church's Rev. Matthew Greenway's message read: "David, bring Xena to church on Sunday for a blessing. We're celebrating St. Francis of Assisi." Of course, the patron saint of pets. The ACLU's Roanoke attorney, Ron Cohen, wrote: "Call anytime, Dave. I'm here to help."

Dean Evelyn Baird had come to the hospital Tuesday morning, but only medical staff, Dan, and the police had been permitted in my room. She'd left flowers and a note: "Halloween devil, please be well."

The immediate area around my cottage was taped off as a crime scene until Friday. The owner of Piney Woods Lakeside Resort, Malcom Todd, was most gracious. He offered me a fully furnished cottage until June, rent-free. It was about five hundred feet down the lakeshore from my former one. I could move in any time Saturday. Until then, Cob and Polly Maplewood invited me to stay at their place, not far from Piney Woods.

———

Vincent Tavernetti had been arrested at the scene, and, after medical treatment, he was arraigned and held without bond. It was later revealed that he had been scouting out the Piney Woods cottages. Then, before sunrise on Monday, October thirteenth, he had parked his car in Claytor Lake State Park, walked through a forested area to an open field that separated the park from Piney Woods, and crossed over to the cottage he had determined to be mine. At a distance of about sixty-five feet, he had fired seven rounds into the back of the structure from his .32 caliber pistol. Another round was fired when Xena attacked him. A police report stated: "David Pritchard's German shepherd tore off much of suspect's nose and inflicted other injuries."

Tavernetti was held in jail and charged with attempted murder, assault and battery, and other felonies. He faced at least twenty years in the state penitentiary.

8

Vietnam

I'd given little thought to the Vietnam panel since September, when I overcame President Barton's resistance and secured the individual panelists. But it was now October eighteenth, and the event was scheduled for four o'clock in Barton Hall. Valerie, Marigold, Sue Ewal from the *Highlander*, and several other students had posted notices about the panel on and around campus, and it was well-advertised at Virginia Tech. Barton Hall could seat twelve hundred people, and a large attendance was likely.

That morning, for the first time since the attack on my cottage, I returned to Piney Woods. I thanked Caleb and Mara for looking after Xena ("Any time, honey."), and I began to settle into the new cottage. I also gave some thought to what I might say that afternoon at the panel.

So-called "teach-ins" on Vietnam were cropping up like toadstools on campuses across the country. A teach-in was *not* what I wanted. Despite the name, very little teaching occurred at such events. Instead, they were one-sided affairs that, while understandably heated, often verged on the hysterical. I hoped for a genuine debate, some semblance of decorum, and a diversity of views from my panelists. That is, I wanted the panel not only to arouse, but to educate.

The Vietnam War was an intensely emotional subject. It

divided families, separated young from old, and tore much of the country apart. The war resonated at a personal level even with Traymore's all-female student body. Women students had no draft cards, but they had fathers, brothers, fiancées, boyfriends, and others who were serving, had served, or in the future could serve in the Vietnam quagmire. Some, a distinct minority, shared Valerie's moral repulsion to the war. Many more students, and President Barton, equated opposing the American war effort to being disloyal and unpatriotic.

My own views had evolved from uninformed support to informed opposition. After being exposed to scholarly studies of the conflict while in graduate school, and especially after reviewing top secret intelligence reports when I was an analyst at the CIA during the summers of 1968 and 1969, I had turned solidly against the war.

I arrived at Barton Hall forty-five minutes early. It was already filling up with people, including a substantial number of young men from Virginia Tech. Valerie greeted me with a warm and uncomfortably public hug; she whispered that she'd been "very scared" by the attack on my cottage. She, Sue Ewal, and the custodial staff had placed a dais on the stage. Each of the four panelists had a lectern, a chair, and a microphone. Campus security was present. So was the sheriff's department, including Sheriff Harland Goetzke, who was walking toward me. I vaguely recalled having seen him at the cottage shortly before I passed out, but only now did I notice his world-class potbelly. His paunch was so prominent as to raise a clear and present danger that at any moment every one of his shirt-buttons would pop off.

The sheriff shook my hand. "How ya doin', son? You're kinda hard to miss, what with all those bandages."

"A little sore, sheriff, but alive."

"You're damn lucky, young man. Caleb Heath filled me in about you. I've known Caleb since we were in first grade together." The sheriff leaned slightly to one side, unloosed a thunderous fart, and smiled broadly. "President Barton asked me to be here in case there's some kind of disturbance. That likely?"

I took a step backward. "No, not at all."

Sheriff Goetzke nodded approvingly. He and his deputies took seats on both sides of the hall.

By four o'clock, the hall was filled to capacity. Another one hundred people or so stood in the back and around the perimeter. Those who were seated in the front row included John Manikas, Rev. Bill Vaughn, Cob and Polly Maplewood, Valerie, Marigold, Sue Ewal, and—off to one side—Dean Baird. Traymore and Virginia Tech students comprised most of the audience, along with a significant number of faculty members from both schools, and a smattering of others I couldn't place. Finally, a cameraman from the leading Roanoke TV station was present, as were three reporters. They were probably attracted more by the recent highly publicized violence at Piney Woods than by a panel on Vietnam, but I was glad to see them.

"Ladies and gentlemen, welcome to our panel on Vietnam. I'm David Pritchard from Traymore's Political Science Department. I will *not* comment on my bandages." Scattered laughter and applause swept through the hall, all of it caught by the TV camera.

I introduced the other panelists. Traymore's Tom O'Keefe

was a close friend. Arnold Solomon, a young academic in blue jeans, was the only Marxist or neo-Marxist faculty member at UVA, at least outside of the Sociology Department. We were both New Yorkers and, while differing politically, got along well.

Virginia Tech's Henry Buchanan was only an acquaintance. I knew him mostly through his articles, which were supportive of the war. Buchanan, in his early fifties, wore a senior bureaucrat's gray striped suit. His demeanor was beyond serious, more like funereal. Buchanan was an "in and outer." That is, he'd serve two years in the Pentagon as a deputy assistant secretary, then he'd return to Virginia Tech.

"Each panelist," I explained to the audience, "will speak for only ten minutes so ample time is allotted for your questions. Professor O'Keefe will lead off with a condensed history of foreign intervention in the region from before the French colonial period through the Johnson administration. The other panelists will then assess the costs and benefits to the United States of American involvement in Vietnam. Professor O'Keefe will act as moderator."

Tom spoke for exactly ten minutes. Solomon then castigated "Washington's global imperialism and its *de facto* protectorates around the world." U.S. foreign policy, for Professor Solomon, was driven less by traditional geopolitical considerations than by "economic exploitation." Hence, "America is in Vietnam for the same reason it is in Saudi Arabia and Iran—to seize resources, especially oil."

Professor Buchanan rose from his chair. He gripped the lectern with white-knuckled fists and glowered at Solomon. With reddening face, Buchanan stammered something inaudible (but

I thought I heard "idiot") before blurting out, "What you just heard is bull . . . poppycock."

The audience stirred. Isolated clapping, whispers, and collective gasps were followed by a shout from somewhere in the back of the hall: "Love it or leave it, Solomon! Go back to Russia, you pinko!"

Tom O'Keefe's intervention was immediate. Stepping to the front of the dais, he declared in a loud voice: "Vigorous debate and free speech are hallmarks of respectable educational institutions, but I will not tolerate defamatory slurs directed at any of our distinguished panelists." This elicited loud applause.

Professor Buchanan responded to Arnold Solomon point by point, concluding with: "There is no substitute for victory. South Vietnam is the first of several dominos. If it falls to the communists, so will all of Southeast Asia. American credibility is on the line. If we do not honor our commitment to Saigon, irreparable harm will be done to our alliances worldwide." Buchanan moved away from his lectern, microphone in hand, and stepped to within two feet of where Solomon was seated. Staring at him like a hawk hovering above a rabbit, Buchanan said, "Finally, and I don't say this lightly, I question Professor Solomon's dedication to our country."

Solomon shot out of his seat and shouted, "Fascist bastard!"

Jumping between them, I pleaded, "Gentlemen, gentlemen, please sit down."

To my surprise and relief, they did, but the photographers and TV camera recorded it all. Audience whispers became edgy mutterings as slanderous insults now came from the panelists themselves. Campus security officers and two of Sheriff Goetzke's deputies stood up to make themselves more visible.

I placed my hand on Arnie's shoulder and whispered-, "You're right to be pissed. I'll handle this." Turning to Buchanan, I said in a low voice, "Henry, there are plenty of real issues to discuss. Let's not go for the balls."

Buchanan flashed a condescending grin and nodded, "Sure."

I kept my own remarks to ten minutes. Although critical of America's involvement in the war, I avoided casting aspersions on anyone's competence, patriotism, or parentage.

Tom O'Keefe then invited questions from the floor. A stunning young woman sprang up from her fourth-row seat. Blond hair cascaded all the way to San Jose. Her jeans were skin-tight, and her blouse was partially unbuttoned. This blatant disdain for Traymore's restrictive dress code screamed "Screw you, Barton."

Distracted by her striking beauty, I had to force myself to focus on her question. "Professor Pritchard, I heard that President Barton tried to stop you from holding this panel. Could you comment on this in light of Professor's O'Keefe's remark about the importance of free speech on college campuses?"

Oh-oh. Delicate question. Dean Baird tensed in the front row. She shot me a piercing gaze with an unmistakable message: *Careful, Pritchard.*

I paused for a moment before responding. "Well, miss, at the end of the day, the right decision was made." Evelyn exhaled, smiled, and even winked at me.

Dozens of hands shot up with questions on Vietnam. Professor Buchanan and I fielded virtually all of them, and we clashed with one another across the board. Buchanan was an informed provocateur. "Professor Pritchard," he sneered, "academics without real world experience are like plumbers without wrenches: not worth a damn." Muffled giggles rippled through the audience.

"Professor Buchanan," I replied, "war-mongering bureaucrats who blind themselves to facts on the ground could use academic plumbers to clean out their clogged mental pipes. If Kennedy and Johnson had listened to Asian area specialists at our great universities, we wouldn't be in this god-awful morass." Faculty, led by John Manikas, applauded. "Moreover, I've served in the CIA's Intelligence Directorate, where I followed North Vietnamese, Chinese, and Viet Cong military activities throughout the region."

"Well, you sure haven't learned anything."

"On the contrary, I've learned that our decision-makers know almost nothing about the history, language, or culture of Vietnam. Many senior officials, including Pentagon deputy assistant secretaries, don't even bother to *read* our finest national intelligence products, especially when they think they might disagree with them."

"Baloney."

"Oh? How many National Intelligence Estimates on Vietnam have you read in the last few years?"

Caught off-guard, Buchanan looked down. "Some."

"Then you'd know that the intelligence community and Director of Central Intelligence are today, and have been in the past, deeply pessimistic about our prospects for success. This is especially so after last year's TET offensive, which demonstrated just how unwinnable this war is. Why do you think otherwise?"

Buchanan coughed and ran a hand through his hair. "No ally will trust us if we run away from South Vietnam."

My pissing contest with Buchanan was interrupted by

another question from the audience. "What about that, Professor Pritchard? Won't U.S. credibility be hurt if we leave?"

"No. Most key U.S. allies, including Japan and Germany, think we're crazy for wasting blood and treasure in a rat hole that's of negligible importance to our national security. And we *have* honored our commitment to Saigon. We've honored it, and honored it, and honored it. The line between honoring this commitment and stupidity was crossed years ago."

Most of the audience erupted in applause. Some Virginia Tech guys began chanting, "Hell no, we won't go." This prompted Arnie Solomon, who hadn't uttered a word after Buchanan questioned his patriotism, to pump his fist in the air and join in the chant.

Tom O'Keefe entertained two more questions for the panel. I then brought the event to a close: "I thank our panelists for their time and insights, but I especially congratulate you, the audience, for your fine questions, your uncommon restraint, even when provoked, and above all, for your enthusiasm." Whoops and applause followed.

As the crowd dispersed, I chatted with faculty members and panelists (Henry Buchanan, despite our verbal tiff, was surprisingly cordial—"Call me anytime."). I shook hands with Sheriff Goetzke ("Well done, son. No disturbance."), and I exchanged waves with Evelyn Baird. I took particular note of the drop-dead beauty in the fourth row and hoped that she might look in my direction and maybe even smile. But she disappeared into the crowd.

It was almost seven when I started to leave. Only Valerie Tavernetti remained in the now empty Barton Hall. "We did it," she said, hooking her arm in mine as we walked toward the main door. We were alone, so I didn't object to her affectionate gesture. "I loved how you and Professor O'Keefe handled the really tense moments."

"The idea for the event was yours, Val. You deserve all the credit."

Valerie looked at me with wide eyes. She clasped her hands under her chin in a prayer-like gesture. "You agreed, I think, that I might be able to share my ideas for decorating your cottage. Maybe also rearrange some furniture. I'm pretty good at that. And you *did* promise that we'd go to your cottage after the panel tonight." She added with a coy smile, "After is now."

"I promised?"

She pulled my arm flush against her hip. "You did."

"Well," returning her smile, I said, "your husband shot the hell out of the cottage. It's being torn down."

She called my bluff. "The newspaper reported that you've been given another cottage."

I rolled my eyes. "Boxes are everywhere. It's a mess. Only began to move in this morning. And it's critical that we not be seen together too often. Vincent's criminal defense attorney would use and abuse this information. It could also jeopardize your divorce proceedings, and it would definitely cast me in an awkward light."

Val was not one of my students, but I was acutely aware of the risks in taking any student to the cottage. Yet, Val had become a vital ally in challenging Traymore's culture and, at any rate, I'd resolved several weeks ago not to remain at the college beyond the current academic year. Moreover, my other activities involved even greater risks: conspiring with Evelyn, giving informal legal advice to faculty and students, holding controversial panels, and speaking out on Barton's repressive practices. So, what the hell. If I fell off the tightrope, I fell off the damn tightrope. Barton was my target as I was his.

Val said, "No one at the college or elsewhere knows we spend time together, nor will they know. I live off-campus, my name has never appeared in the press, and I am very good at avoiding attention."

"Well," I replied with some trepidation, "extreme care is obligatory."

We were now outside Barton Hall. Valerie let go of my arm and turned toward me. "Extreme caution it is. Still, I really can help you at the cottage, and I'd love to do it. Please."

She gave me precious little wiggle room. "Tell you what. Xena was invited by the rector of Christ Church Episcopal to attend morning services tomorrow in Blacksburg for the celebration of St. Francis of Assisi."

Valerie raised an eyebrow. "You're joking."

"Not at all. Reverend Greenway called me personally. Why don't you meet me and Xena at the church a few minutes before eleven o'clock? We three can go in together."

She kissed my uninjured cheek. "Afterward, we go to the cottage?"

"I suppose."

9

Valerie

Valerie was waiting for me as I pulled into the church parking lot. She stood out, not only as a beautiful woman, but because she was impeccably dressed in a flowing light blue dress and pearl necklace. "Did you see last night's news?" she asked.

"No, never turned on the tube."

"What about this?" She held up the Sunday *Roanoke Times*. "You and the Vietnam panel are front and center."

"Were we praised or slammed?"

"Except for this front-page photo and Barton's grumblings, coverage was pretty positive, especially on the op-ed page."

The photo showed me interposed between a furious Arnie Solomon and a smug Henry Buchanan. The caption read, "Vietnam debate comes close to fisticuffs." Valerie read President Barton's remarks to me: "'The event brought discredit to Traymore College. It almost got out of hand. We should be supporting our troops, not tearing down the country.'"

When the church bell rang, we walked briskly toward the sanctuary with Xena on a leash. We'd agreed that under no circumstances would we reveal Valerie's last name to anyone.

Several parishioners met us at the door. "Wow, this must be Xena. Welcome, girl."

Xena tolerated the attention. Reverend Greenway must have

spread the word about Celebrity Dog's likely appearance. I told Xena to heel as we found a rear pew where she could lie down in the aisle.

The processional hymn, as so often happened, moved me deeply. "Amazing Grace! how sweet the sound. . . . Through many dangers, toils, and snares / I have already come. / 'Tis grace that brought me safe thus far / And grace will lead me home." Valerie slipped her hand into mine.

The thrust of Matt Greenway's sermon was that we are all imperfect in our thoughts and deeds; we are all sinners in need of giving and receiving forgiveness. I wasn't much into the notion of sin and its avoidance as a guidepost for life. Still, closing my eyes, I thought that, in church-speak, *I've sinned in the past; I'm entertaining sinful thoughts at this very moment about the married woman sitting next to me; and I may well sin before the day is out.* I gave Valerie's hand a quick squeeze.

The sermon was followed by the Prayer of St. Francis. "See," I whispered to Val, "I wasn't joking."

The congregation prayed in unison, "Grant that we may not so much seek to be loved as to love." Valerie slid closer to me in the pew.

Then came the Blessing of the Animals. Several dogs and cats, some critter a boy carried in a covered box, a goat, and a parrot accompanied their humans to the altar. I went forward with Celebrity Dog. Reverend Greenway blessed each animal. Xena seemed confused and uncharacteristically submissive. She pressed against me until we returned to the pew and Valerie.

When it came time for communion, people stood to go up to the altar for bread and wine. Valerie was uneasy. "Catholics can't take communion in a non-Catholic church."

I pointed to the program: "All are welcome to receive Holy Communion." Val shrugged.

I told Xena to stay. Val and I went up together. People nearby seemed impressed that Xena remained in place.

After the service, I wanted to hear the organ postlude, which that morning was J.S. Bach's rousing Toccata in D minor. But so many well-wishers surrounded us that we were swept up in the flow of parishioners moving toward the door.

"Pritchard, Peace of the Lord." Wearing black vestments, Henry Buchanan grabbed my hand. "I'm the verger here at Christ Church."

"Whoa," I said, "a lion in sheep's clothing, and fittingly it's a black sheep." Xena let out a low cautionary growl. Looking at Buchanan, I said, "She's a flawless judge of character."

"Like King Lear," said Buchanan, grinning, "I am a man more sinned against than sinning." He was genuinely friendly. "You gave as good as you got yesterday. I'm impressed." Then, turning to Valerie, "This must be your charming wife." She blushed, but neither of us corrected him. "Your husband has a promising future. That is, once he leaves Traymore." With a pat on my back, Henry Buchanan departed through a side door.

Once outside the church, Celebrity Dog got most of the attention. Matt Greenway greeted us warmly. He thanked me for bringing Xena ("It sure helped with attendance!") and welcomed Valerie to Christ Church. To my considerable relief, he was more discrete than Henry Buchanan.

I took Valerie's arm. "Let's go to Bessie's for lunch."

She said, "Let's call it *our* place."

As we walked toward the cars, a boy of about twelve approached us holding the same box he'd carried up to the altar for a blessing. "Can I pet your dog?"

"You sure can. She loves kids. What's in the box?"

"My snake. Her name is Cecelia." He removed the lid, revealing a well-fed blacksnake.

"Good Lord. When I was your age, my favorite pet was Cecil, the blacksnake. Are you certain Cecelia is a girl?"

The boy scratched his head. "No, just guessed. Think she's a girl 'cause she's a lot nicer than most boys. She doesn't fight; she doesn't bite; she's just right." Big toothy smile.

"Can I hold her?"

Still petting Xena, he nodded. "Yup."

With flicking tongue, the snake wound itself around my arm, but seemed to focus its gaze on Valerie. Valerie retreated. "Don't worry," I assured her. "When handled gently, they're very docile."

Valerie tugged at her dress.

After a minute or so of observing Cecelia on my arm, Valerie edged closer. "Val, just touch it with your fingers," I said.

With some hesitation, Valerie reached toward the blacksnake and ran the tips of her fingers along its midsection. "So smooth," she said.

Valerie probably wouldn't have agreed, nor would biblical scholars, but I sensed a meaning in the incident that, conceivably, alluded to the heart of Christianity, at least as expressed in the Gospel of John: "As Moses lifted the serpent in the wilderness, even so must the Son of Man be lifted up, that whoever believes in Him should . . . have eternal life."

We returned Cecelia to the boy, Xena hopped into my car, and

I followed Valerie to her house in Christiansburg. She dropped off her car and rode with me to Bessie's Place.

———

Bessie gave us a warmer welcome than usual. "Well, howdy, David. Some bear maul ya? I heared how that nut-loose guy shot up your place." Bessie almost knocked me off balance with her strangulation hug. "I've cooked a pot roast, and I have the apple pie ya like."

Valerie nodded our approval and said, "Did my nose detect onions, carrots, and potatoes?"

"That's how I do it, deary. And today's lunch is on me."

"Oh no, Bessie," I said, "we can't let you do that."

Bessie wagged both hands in the air, wiggled her ample butt, swiveled around, and vanished into the kitchen.

Valerie reached across the table and touched my arm. "Wonder how many people at Christ Church other than Henry Buchanan assumed we were married."

I shifted uneasily in my chair and scratched my neck before raising my left hand. "Who knows? Neither of us wears a ring. When did you take yours off?"

"The day after Vincent hit me. I never want to see him again."

Valerie's bruises had faded. With alabaster skin, Nefertiti-like sculpted features, long sandy hair, and ever-inquisitive green eyes, she was striking. We'd gone through so much together in such a short time that the combination of course preparation, searching for another academic position, coordinating challenges to Barton's administration, forging faculty-student alliances to confront the president, and the sheer stress of survival—mine and Valerie's—had distracted me from fully appreciating just how lovely she was. Valerie was strong, thoughtful, and deliberate. She did not, as a rule, act spontaneously. I don't mean this in a negative way; she was the antithesis of the provocative blonde who rocketed from her fourth-row seat yesterday with the question about Barton's attempt to ban the Vietnam panel.

Valerie took off her shoes. "In the eyes of the Church, Vincent and I remain married." She grimaced. Her toes rubbed my shin as she squeezed my arm.

"And," I said, looking directly at her, "you would *never* consider committing a mortal sin."

She licked her lips and looked down at the table with a faint smile. "What did Reverend Greenway say about how we are *all* sinners deserving of forgiveness?"

Bessie brought our lunch. "Hope y'all like it. Bet ya will." There was a sizeable crowd in the restaurant that Sunday, but before rushing off to serve others, Bessie leaned in to say, "Y'all 'bout the loveliest couple I seen in years."

Bessie walked away. Val and I laughed out loud when we both said, almost in unison, "Bessie's a good person."

Bessie never did bring us our check. She was in the kitchen when we got up to leave. I slipped two Andrew Jacksons under my plate, and we went out the door to the car. As I drove away, I turned to Val. "Well?"

"Uh-huh," she replied, and patted my knee.

"You *are* beautiful."

She snuggled close.

———

Anticipating a romp along the lakeshore, Xena panted in the backseat as we approached Piney Woods. The dog wasn't the only one panting in anticipation.

All of my intimate relationships with women involved shifting degrees of tension among the three Hs: head, heart, and hormones (HHH). The HHH balance is never, or very infrequently, perfect. And, of course, it's a continuous two-person interaction. *She* has her own HHH calculus. Hormones almost always dominate at the outset. Head (does it make sense?) and heart (love) come later or, commonly, not at all. By the time I'd graduated from law school, my head said, *Do not propose marriage to long-time girlfriend Samantha Smithson,* although hormones still hummed, and fondness, perhaps even some love, continued. When I subsequently attended the University of Virginia, Sam and I remained dear friends and still saw one another, albeit less often. But in Virginia, we never moved beyond the pleasurable playground of the bedroom. And couch, shower, beach, car, mountain lake, and—once, dangerously—a Ferris wheel. Hormones went "Whoopee." Head said, "Enjoy, short-term." Heart said, "No way." So it went with various women, love always being the rarest H.

Valerie and I pulled up in front of the cottage. Xena jumped out and tore after some geese. I opened the car door for Val. As she stepped out, her dress rode up to mid-thigh, revealing a garter belt. Hormones raged. Heart was unengaged, but Head flashed a bright green "go for it" as I jarred open the cottage door.

Cardboard boxes, furniture, and duffle bags were scattered around the living room and bedroom, and I'd piled more stuff on the couch and kitchen counter. Yesterday morning, before the session on Vietnam, I'd only had enough time to get the back office in reasonable shape. I'd paid little attention to the kitchen, living room, or—because I'd spent the night at the Maplewoods'—the bedroom. Nor had I anticipated having a female visitor, though, in retrospect, I should have.

"Looks like we have work to do," said Val, opening a window. "There's dust everywhere, and the place smells musty."

Except for purposes of functionality, I'd never given any thought to where furniture should go. Appearance was irrelevant. I just moved things around so as not to waste time. However, this was not Valerie's *modus operandi.* "The couch looks better at an angle," and, opening another window for fresh air, she announced, "Here's where the table goes." Val stepped to one side of the couch. "And a lamp belongs here."

"Whatever you say."

She smiled and continued arranging things, including my clothes, putting them "where they should be." Resigned to my irrelevance, I raised my hands, grunted, and fled to the office. She let a damp Xena into the cottage but ordered the dog to stay until she'd been dried off. I heard silverware clanking into a kitchen drawer. Glassware tinkled as Val found the right cabinet for it, and she put my CCR (Creedence Clearwater Revival) record— with its "Bad Moon Rising" —on the phonograph.

After an hour or so, the lady of the manor stuck her head into the office. "David, where's your vacuum cleaner?"

"What's that?" I said, which invited a playful punch to my shoulder. "Okay, okay. Think I noticed something in the bedroom closet, not that I'd ever use it."

Hands on her hips, Val blurted out, "What *is* the peculiar attraction men have to dirt?"

Soon, I was being driven from room to room by a roaring vacuum cleaner.

"David," she called from the bedroom, "could you help me for a minute?" She'd located my yellow flowered bed sheets. "Grab one side so we can get them on the bed."

I complied, now with some enthusiasm.

"These don't look like sheets a *man* would pick out." She tilted her head and looked across the bed at me.

"Oh, a former girlfriend got them for me at least five years ago."

Valerie shuffled to my side of the bed and wrapped her arms around my waist. "*How* 'former?'" she asked.

I replied truthfully (without mentioning Samantha's visit last month), "She's living in New York with her fiancé."

We kissed for the first time—that is, *really* kissed. Then we kissed again. This triggered a muzzy light-headedness. Val took my hand and led me to the kitchen. By then, I would've followed her anywhere.

"What's for dinner?" she asked.

"Dinner? Uh, what about spaghetti?"

"Bet you don't have fresh tomatoes, onions, garlic, or oil."

"Nope. Val, I'm only now moving in." I opened the refrigerator. It smelled of mold. "Ha. Here's an onion. Soft, but should be okay with the canned tomatoes and tomato paste."

She wiggled into the small kitchen and hugged me. "We'll make do," she said. "You should have known I'd be here. I wasn't subtle."

Feigning guilt, I dipped my chin to my chest and said submissively, "I *do* have wine, wherever you put it."

She turned, slipped in front of me, and extracted a Bordeaux from a corner cabinet. "Here." She handed me the corkscrew that she'd squirreled away in a "proper place" and said, "Let's drink to us."

The exquisite 1966 St. Julien Bordeaux had been earmarked for a fine meal. We downed it quickly as we sat and talked on the couch, now cleared of boxes. Despite her diligence, I found Val's energetic rearrangement of the furniture and placement of things to be disorienting, but I kept this to myself.

"Val, exactly a week ago, only a few hundred feet from here, your husband tried to blow my brains out."

With a pained expression, Valerie emptied her wine glass and poured another. "That's *good* wine." She shook her head. "Vincent was insanely jealous of other men—any other man."

"But you and I never did anything improper."

"Until now?" Val winked. She flicked a strand of hair from her face.

I smiled, then finished my wine and poured another glass, spilling a few drops on the floor with unsteady hands. "It's strange," I said, "almost fictional, that I'm here with his wife."

Valerie stood. "What about another bottle?" I persuaded her to wait until dinner, or what would have to pass for dinner. My uncle Jack had given me seven bottles of the St. Julien in anticipation of my completion of doctoral studies. St. Julien was not Boone's Farm apple wine.

"Fine, I'll hold off. What *is* strange," she said, "is that I'm here with you, yet I'm still conflicted." With a pensive expression, she took my hand in both of hers. "You must know how attracted I am to you."

Silence. I was well aware, of course, that Val had long been quite forward. How couldn't I be? I finally mumbled, "I've always thought, from the moment I first saw you, that you were simply lovely."

Valerie then repeated what she'd said before about her fear of committing adultery, not so much in fact, but in the eyes of the Church. I kissed her softly.

"And taking communion today at your church didn't help either, although I think the rule is stupid."

"Val," I said, holding her hands, "you have integrity and courage. You're reflective and you challenge authority, whether Barton's or the Pope's."

Her eyes widened. "David, you're sweet."

I smiled and said, "No one, including the Pope, has a hot line to the Lord."

Grinning broadly, Valerie said, "That's not what the sisters told me at St. Athanasia's School."

I laughed. "Probably not, but none of us are flawless, including the good sisters. It's okay, even human, to feel guilt. Just don't let it paralyze you."

We embraced.

"Let's get water boiling for our gourmet spaghetti," I said.

"Yes!" Val jumped from the couch. "And let's open that wine."

We ate less than half the pasta but downed most of the second bottle of Bordeaux. A tipsy Valerie then excused herself and stumbled off to the bathroom. I put Wes Montgomery on the record player, sat down on the couch, and wondered whether this was really happening. Here I was, about to go bed with the wife of a man who a week ago tried his best to kill me; he's in custody, charged with multiple felonies; and Valerie is a student at the college where I teach.

When Valerie returned, she swayed a bit, but seemed confident and completely at ease. She wore only a sheer pale pink half-slip. No bra. She sat on my lap as if she owned it. She did. "That was superb wine," she said.

I kissed her smallish, lovely breasts that gave off a musky, floral scent. "What's that fragrance?"

"Bellodgia," she said. "Like it?"

This was the perfume I'd promised to bring back from New York for Mara Heath. "Uh-huh. Lots." Bellodgia is honeysuckle, scotch whiskey, and perky breasts. It takes no prisoners. "Drives me crazy," I confessed.

We slid off the couch and wobbled toward the bedroom as Val sang, "Heigh ho, Heigh ho, it's off to bed we go. . . ." I pleaded with "Snow White" to be kind to my bandaged face.

The bedroom light was on as Val took off her slip and panties. "You are so beautiful," I said. I touched her cheekbone where there was still a slight bruise. "Bruises are almost gone," I said, "and so is the bastard who beat you."

We kissed. As we stood, she unbuttoned my shirt, loosened my pants, and kissed my bare chest. Running her fingers gently along my facial and neck bandages, Val said, "We've both been wounded by Vincent." She playfully kissed my cheek, then my nose. "I want all of you," she murmured, "bruise or no bruise, scar or no scar."

I rested my hands on her hips as she explored the exterior of my jockey shorts. Teasingly, she knelt down on her knees to plant firm kisses on me.

Val looked up. "Can I come in?" I nodded. Her fingers slipped inside the shorts, still not pulling them down.

"Much more of that," I sighed, "and the game's over." She pulled off my shorts, touched me once softly with her tongue, then leapt up pleading, "Don't come! Not yet."

We scrambled onto the bed. I came quickly. "Oh-oh," cried Val.

"Sorry, love," I said, kissing her forehead. "We'll try again in an hour or so. It'll be better."

Running her hand through my hair and breathing heavily, Val said, "We'll try again."

I fell fast asleep and was soon immersed in a dream that had recurred several times over the past decade. It was an amalgam of experience and fantasy. I was under a raft on Candlewood Lake with Laura—maybe it was Laurie or Laurel. Can't recall. We teenagers, wearing Speedo swimsuits, were alone on a warm August night. The organic smell of the lake and of the sodden wood raft wafted through the thick humid air. Crickets, peepers, and bullfrogs joined in a deafening chorus of sound. Their high-pitched buzz formed a protective barrier from the world. Moonlight and starlight filtered through the overhead boards. We kissed. I eased her one-piece suit down to her hips. She slipped her hand into my swimsuit as I kissed her breasts. Our universe was wet and warm.

I awoke with Bellodgia in my head and Valerie's hand between my legs. She whispered, "Again?" Her arms were outstretched like Jesus on the cross, but her legs wrapped tightly around me. "Sin, sin, glorious sin," she hummed to a tune in the musical *Oliver*: "Food, food, glorious food."

We moved easily, fluidly, as though we'd been fused together for ages. She shuddered, then shuddered again and again before letting out a sigh. Val flipped over onto her stomach, and we continued. Trembling, sparkles in the night. We kissed and fell into a deep sleep.

The alarm clock blasted off at six o'clock. I silenced it, kissed Val on the neck, and patted her bottom. "Awake?" I whispered.

"No." She pulled a pillow over her head, but I heard a muffled, "Coffee."

"Yes, m' lady." I stumbled into the kitchen with a slight headache.

When I returned with instant coffee, she'd inched to the edge of the bed. Without looking up, she said, "Shower."

"Yeah. Me too"

"Together?"

"Sure, but let me get a garbage bag to keep my bandages dry."

I'd just located a bag in the kitchen where Val had relocated them when a shrill scream came from the bathroom. Five leaps, and I was there. Valerie, stark naked, was bent over with arms crossed and legs together. "There! There!" she pointed. "Cockroaches! Shower stall."

"But Val, they're running away."

"Get them!"

Back to the kitchen, this time searching for the roach spray that I stored under the sink. It was there, but it had been moved to the back of the cabinet.

Returning to the bathroom, I opened a window and sprayed the offending bugs as Val retreated into the hallway, wrapped in a towel.

"That's it, Val. Most are dead, others have vamoosed."

She gritted her teeth, shook her head in disbelief, then returned to the bathroom, mumbling something unkind about men and cleanliness.

Valerie stepped gingerly into the warm shower. I joined her, the plastic bag draped loosely over my head and my chest to cover the bandages and still breathe. Laughing, she said, "I can only see half of you, the better half." She, helpfully, soaped and washed the better half as I reciprocated the favor as best I could, considering that I saw only her legs and feet.

As the bathroom steamed up, she said, "Do you love me? It's fine if you don't." She pressed me gently into the side of the shower stall as she continued to tend to my lower reaches.

"I do, do, do . . . I do love you," I stuttered.

"No, you don't."

My mind, such as it was, had just one overriding focus, but I managed to say, "Maybe not capital 'L' Love, but definitely lower case 'l' love."

When we turned the shower off and I lifted the plastic bag from my head, she said, "If this is lower case 'l' love, it's pretty nice." We kissed and got dressed. Valerie dried her hair with a towel since I had no hair dryer. "I'll bring one next time," she said.

Driving to her place in Christiansburg, we said little at first. She seemed to be in a haze. Before long, though, she slid over next to me. I was again captivated by the perfume she must have dabbed on before leaving the cottage. Val leaned her damp head on my shoulder and said, "We're a team, a solid little 'l' love team."

Resting my hand on her knee, I replied, "We are, indeed."

I pulled up in front of her house, got out and opened the car door, and kissed her. She hopped up the front steps and waved.

I waved back like a teenager in love.

10

Diddle a Dean?

I called Valerie late Monday afternoon when I returned after class to Piney Woods: "Hi, lower case 'l' love."

"I miss you already," said Val. "If you hadn't called, *I* would've shot up your cottage." We agreed to meet for lunch at Bessie's the next day, after my doctor's appointment.

———

That Tuesday, the doctor removed my bandages and stitches. The veterinarian had taken off Xena's bandage on Monday, and her stitches would come out on Wednesday. Tail wags and leaps in the air signaled her return to normal, but with half an ear missing.

I was less content than Xena. Although most of the wounds to the back of my neck and scalp were superficial, I had a fine, four-inch long pink scar along the jaw line and some mild redness. Dr. Clay Sadler, a tall, slender man in his late fifties, said, "Lady Luck was with you, son. Your facial wound was from a shard of glass. Had it been from a bullet, you probably would have muscle or nerve damage and some skin would have been burned."

I ran my fingers over the scar and stared at it in Dr. Sadler's office mirror. The disfigurement didn't shout Scarface, but it was certainly visible. "So Doc, what's it going to look like after a couple of months?"

"The scar will fade in time. After two or three weeks, the suture line will still be slightly raised, but the redness should be gone. In about two months, the scar line will be white and maybe a little depressed." He tilted his head as if waiting for my reaction.

"That's not great news, but it's better than what I feared." I thanked Dr. Sadler, shook his hand, and drove to the college to meet my class.

———

I was the first to arrive at Bessie's. Bessie beamed as she came over with two menus. "I figured *she'll* be here. When you two getting hitched?"

"Now Bessie, Valerie and I are just friends—really good friends."

"Just friends? Big mistake if you let that pretty bird fly away."

Valerie came in the door looking professional and sexy in a dark blue woolen miniskirt with matching top. I rose from my seat and kissed her on the cheek. From three tables over, Bessie waved and flashed an impish smile.

"The scar doesn't look bad at all," said Val as she fingered it lightly.

During lunch, our legs touched as we sat across from each other in a booth with sticky red vinyl seats. Val announced that she was applying to the graduate program in economics at Johns Hopkins beginning next fall. "Would you consider writing me a letter of recommendation?" she asked.

I took her hand. "It'll be a walk-on-water letter."

She thanked me and said, "I'm driving to Baltimore on Thursday to meet with the chairman of the economics department. Might stay the weekend with my folks. My mom isn't well."

We finished lunch, waved goodbye to Bessie, and went out to the parking lot. Before leaving, Val hopped into my front seat and put her hand on my thigh. My hand went under her skirt as we kissed. "Drive carefully, little 'l' love," I said.

"You, too," she replied, placing both of her hands gently on my cheeks. "I'm so happy being with you, David. In a few months, we'll probably find ourselves in different universes. Until then, well. . . . It's very nice."

———

It had been a while since I'd attended a meeting of the Pissed Off Faculty. So, after class on Wednesday, I stopped by the ARSE-N-ALL bar where, as usual, Old Horsey beer was flowing freely.

The instant I sat down at the faculty table, John Manikas boomed out, "Welcome, Scarface." Diplomacy was not John's strong suit.

"What's up, peg-leg?" I replied, referring to his prosthesis. His face tightened. "I have another West Virginia joke just for you, Manikas."

"Please, spare me," he said. But the faculty chanted, "Tell the joke, tell the joke, tell the joke."

"Why do geese fly over West Virginia upside down?" There was silence, except for a grunt from Manikas. "Because there's nothing worth crapping on."

Pushing back from the table, John capitulated. "Okay, I apologize. No more wisecracks about your beauty mark."

I threw an arm around his shoulders. "You're a great guy, Big Bad John, but tell me the truth: Did West Virginia's governor really marry his sister in a trailer park?"

Manikas excused himself to go to the men's room. He then walked behind me and poured a full can of cold Old Horsey down my back. The other ten or twelve faculty howled with laughter. The ARSE-N-ALL was not the Harvard Club.

We settled down somewhat and exchanged intelligence. Of particular note was the news that two First Amendment-related lawsuits had just been filed against the college and President Barton. I was familiar with both cases. Anthropologist Mel Tromblay had brought suit against the college after Barton formally reprimanded him for attending an off-campus gathering by critics of U.S. Vietnam policy. And Bill Vaughn's suit, with backing from the National Education Association, challenged Barton's severe sanctions against him for writing that letter to the editor of *Redbook* magazine. Professor Vaughn's case got immediate attention in the press, partly because of the legal community's consensus view (and mine, as well) that Bill would prevail.

Tom O'Keefe announced another important matter: "We will have our first-ever course evaluations this semester."

Someone pounded the table and grumbled, "But they'll be bullshit."

"Afraid so," responded Tom, rubbing his brow. "Many faculty members thought students should have a say in assessing the teaching effectiveness of their professors. Most colleges have student evaluations of faculty."

Knowing how Elzic Barton objected to students having a

meaningful say about anything, I said, "Bet Barton pissed all over that idea."

"Indeed," said Tom. "When this was proposed in the spring, Barton said, and I quote: 'Our students are too immature to judge teaching quality. However, *I* will *personally* evaluate each faculty member's teaching, beginning this fall semester.'" A collective groan went up around the table.

"Another wholly arbitrary lever for intimidation by someone with no first-hand knowledge of what actually goes on in a classroom," I grumbled. Heads nodded in agreement. With that, we chugged down our beer and headed for home.

———

Late Friday afternoon, as I left my office to head to the cottage, two students approached. "Professor Pritchard, do you have a minute?"

"Don't think you're in any of my classes. Do I know you?"

They giggled. "If you don't know us," said the shorter woman, "you should. We're BWOC—Big Women on Campus." I grinned. She continued, "We know *you*. You're a lawyer, right?"

"Well," I said guardedly, "I teach political science courses."

Pooky Loomis and Bea McNally introduced themselves as, respectively, presidents of the campus Young Republicans and Young Democrats. The two seniors differed politically, but both expressed anxious, even fearful, concerns about Traymore's academic climate. Pooky did most of the talking, with Bea adding "uh-huh," "yeah," and "you bet." No more than five feet tall and with smudged granny glasses, Pooky exuded a Napoleonic self-confidence. She was bothered—perhaps incensed—about something.

"Professor, I know you've heard stories from students—probably from faculty, too—of how President Barton and his minions regulate what we can say, what we can do, and even what clothes we can wear." Bea nodded.

"I've heard things."

Looking me in the eye and talking rapidly, Pooky continued: "Last spring, Bea and I contacted the American Civil Liberties Union in Richmond to see whether they might be willing to send a speaker to Traymore to talk about student rights at state colleges. That wasn't easy for me; my parents see the ACLU as radical troublemakers from New York. But things are desperate at Traymore, and we don't have to pay anything for an ACLU speaker." Pooky's hands were on her hips. "Students at Virginia Tech aren't hassled with the kind of rubbish Barton loads on us. The ACLU agreed to come, but not until this fall—that is, in two weeks, November seventh. We were hoping that you might introduce the ACLU's Arnold Thieleman." Pooky seemed to be holding her breath, and Bea clasped both hands together behind her back. "Please, please," they said.

This was a minefield, and an opportunity. Once I'd started to squeeze the president after the Mary Jo Shifflet incident in September, there was no going back. Nothing would infuriate and alarm Elzic Barton more than having the detested ACLU on his campus addressing a subject he believed firmly did not and should not even exist—student rights. Moreover, the press would be there. "Ladies, I'd be delighted to introduce Thieleman."

Pooky and Bea jumped in the air together and squealed, "Thank you, thank you, thank you."

"*Everyone* will be there," said Bea.

Indeed, posters announcing the event soon sprouted across campus. Fliers even appeared on Main Street and in the Winn Dixie grocery and Oddie's Café.

———

That weekend, walking with Xena beside Claytor Lake, I saw Caleb and Mara Heath up ahead. Caleb called, "David, do you have a minute?"

"What's up, Caleb?"

"There's stuff I've been wanting to tell you," said Caleb, leaning on his walking stick. "This goin' sound real strange to a professor—crazy even."

"You've got my attention," I said, stepping closer.

"The day before that guy shot up your place, I seen a huge raven on your roof." Caleb had a distant, watery gaze. "David," he continued gravely, "each time—before my brother died, before my momma died, and before our pastor died—a large raven appeared." Caleb wrinkled his brow and looked down at the ground.

Mara spoke. "But a raven also showed up when I met Caleb." She wrapped an arm around her husband. "And," Mara continued, "right after my daddy's heart attack, a big raven landed on our porch. Daddy survived."

I was not superstitious, but Mara and Caleb were so sincere that I nodded and thanked them. "Better keep my eyes open for ravens," I said.

———

I spent the rest of the weekend and much of the following

week preparing for class and, particularly, applying for positions at other colleges. None of the thirty-two letters I'd sent out had borne fruit. Seven colleges didn't even bother to send a letter of rejection; the other twenty-five replied with some variant of: "There were many highly qualified applicants. We regret to inform you . . ."

All I needed was a foot in the door, an interview. Applying at random from an obscure women's college in southern Virginia, without the active support of my senior academic patron—who was in Paris—meant the odds were long.

So, once again scanning the *Chronicle of Higher Education* for job openings, I mailed more letters and resumes, this time to thirty-four institutions, ranging from the University of California, Santa Cruz, to Lafayette in Pennsylvania, Sewanee in Tennessee, and Bemidji in Minnesota. I feared that no one would hire me after my experience at Traymore. My fallback option was the legal profession. That promised a job, but it was not my passion. I much preferred a modest salary at a respectable academic institution to a high salaried position with a New York law firm.

———

On Tuesday, I phoned Evelyn Baird to confirm our Halloween "date" that Friday. "You bet we're on," she said. "We'll have a classic Virginia dinner. Oh, and don't forget your devil horns and mask."

I purchased plastic horns and a black mask in Roanoke, along with a crimson cotton sweater, and loose-fitting red cotton sweatpants.

Evelyn's simple frame house was in a residential area about

two miles from campus. It differed from neighboring houses only in that it appeared to have an unusual turret-like upper floor. I pulled into her driveway at 7:30 P.M., walked up the steps with my St. Julien Bordeaux, and rang the doorbell.

An unmasked, barefoot angel with halo and wings appeared. She had wide, welcoming brown eyes and wore a revealing, floor length white satin gown. Her pleasant figure and especially her ample breasts were appealing.

Grinning, Evelyn welcomed me with, "It's the devilish boat rocker." We pecked one another on the cheek, taking care not to dislodge halo or horns.

"Wow!" I exclaimed truthfully. "What a heavenly angel."

"Thank you," she said with genuine warmth. "We'll see whether good vanquishes evil tonight."

As I entered the house, I replied, "I certainly hope so."

"You do? I was joking."

I smiled, touched her elbow, and stepped into a wood-paneled hallway.

Pointing to the kitchen, Evelyn said, "Dinner is almost ready. Help me get it on the table."

When we walked into the kitchen, I held up my bottle of wine and asked, "What should I do with this?"

Handing me a corkscrew, she gestured toward the dining room.

When I'd returned to the kitchen from opening the wine, Evelyn had made herself a cocktail. "On special occasions I have one with dinner, only one—a screwdriver. This is a special occasion." She offered to make me one, but I declined.

Someone who loved to cook had designed the kitchen. It had

an island in the middle which, like the counters, was covered with pink Formica laminate. The cabinets were maple; the gas range was new, as were the top-of-the-line fixtures; and it had a large stainless-steel double sink. But perhaps most impressive was the linoleum floor, with its modernistic pattern of alternating black and white squares.

The house was infused with inviting aromas from various dishes that we carried from the kitchen to the dining room table: salty Virginia country ham glazed with molasses and bourbon, a pot of bubbling baked beans with ham hocks, sweet potatoes with pecans, green peas and mushrooms with melted Gruyere cheese, hot yeasty biscuits with local honey, and small green salads with honey mustard dressing and blue cheese crumbles.

Given the peanut butter, pasta, and frozen dinners I'd been living on for the past two months, this was breathtaking. Evelyn even brought a large bottle of dark German Oktoberfest beer to the table. "We can share it."

The dim light from the dining room's simple overhead brass fixture was augmented by two tall white candles. The solid walnut dining table ("My grandparents', mid-nineteenth century.") and the fine Irish linen tablecloth were set with Oneida sterling silverware. The plates and serving dishes were Rose Chintz.

"Gosh, Evelyn, I'm overwhelmed." I pulled a chair out for her, and she smiled as she sat down.

"Thank you. Could you cut some of the ham? Thin slices are best."

I carved the ham and served her. Then, I reached over the plates for a biscuit. When my fingers were so close that I could feel their warmth, I was stopped in mid-air by Evelyn asking,

"Would you say grace?"

"Um . . . sure." I never said grace, but my grandfather invoked the Lord before every Sunday dinner. Grandad always repeated the same prayer, of which I recalled only fragments. The rest I created. "Almighty God, may your Holy Spirit so move the hearts of all those at Traymore College that suspicions disappear; divisions cease; and students, faculty, and administrators live in peace, justice, and love through Jesus Christ our Lord. Amen."

"Amen," said Evelyn, folding a napkin in her lap. "That was lovely."

I poured the Oktoberfest into two pewter mugs that she'd placed beside the beer. We toasted to Traymore's future and to All Hallows Eve. More importantly, I resumed my aborted mission to grab a biscuit.

"Evelyn, this is fantastic," I said after taking a second helping of everything.

"Glad you like it." Evelyn adjusted her angel wings. "I put a bit more time and thought into this meal than usual."

"If my former girlfriend, Samantha, cooked like this, I would've married her long ago." Then, looking at Evelyn, I said, "Your wings make it difficult for you to sit comfortably. Why not take them off?"

"Okay." A flush crept across her cheeks as she removed the wings. "Now," she asked sheepishly, "am I a fallen angel?"

"You're safe," I chuckled. "The halo is still in place." I reached up, removed my horns, and said, "No wings, no horns. We're neutered. Is there such a thing as a fallen devil, one who goes from being evil to being virtuous?"

Evelyn finished her screwdriver. "No, devils are always devils.

Please leave your mask on; even pseudo-anonymity is alluring and, somehow, comforting." Evelyn stood up, walked into the kitchen, and returned with another screwdriver.

"Whoa, thought you drank only *one* screwdriver with dinner?"

She raised her cocktail glass. "I'm feeling good."

I poured my second glass of Bordeaux.

"How is that wine?" she asked. "My cousin would buy his wine in gallon jugs. I hated it."

I held up the bottle for her inspection. "This is exquisite French Bordeaux. It has far less alcohol than your vodka."

Evelyn paused and tilted her head. "Can I try it?"

I leaned forward in my chair and passed my Waterford wine glass to Evelyn.

She sniffed the red wine cautiously, then took a sip. "That sure beats my cousin's stuff. Bring that bottle and let's go into the living room."

We sat across from one another, she on the love seat, me on an armchair. Evelyn rubbed the back of her neck and gave me an inquiring look. "Last month, you told me about Samantha's visit." Smiling, she said, "Her cooking couldn't be *that* bad."

I shook my head and chuckled. "Sam doesn't cook at all. Despite this shortcoming, she and her fiancé will be married in June."

Evelyn straightened her gown, raised an eyebrow, and swung her legs off the floor and onto the love seat. "Samantha must still like you if she'd leave her fiancé for a few days to be with an old boyfriend."

I sipped my wine. "We like one another. Even now, we sometimes travel together. It's easy being with Sam."

Evelyn grew quiet. She lowered her eyes and stared at her hands as if she might cry. Her shoulders drooped.

"I'm so sorry. Did I say something?"

"Oh, no." Her chin trembled and she cleared her throat. "I had a boyfriend when I taught in Chesterfield County. It still upsets me."

Leaning forward in my chair, I chanced a question. "May I ask what happened?"

She slid to one side of the love seat, sat up, and crossed and uncrossed her legs. "Where's that wine bottle?" she asked. I gave her half of what was left and took the remainder. "In the end, I'm convinced it came down to, well . . . sex."

"It wasn't good?"

There was another awkward moment. With a pained expression, she shook her head. In a weak voice, she murmured, "Not that. I refused him."

We both emptied our wine glasses.

"It was my strict rural Methodist upbringing," she said. "Today's church is changing, but when I was growing up in Clifton Forge, girls were told that sex outside of marriage was sinful, boys wanted only one thing, kissing led to pregnancy, and—scariest of all—I would go straight to hell."

I got up from my chair, squeezed in next to her on the love seat, and took her hand. "Evelyn, you know Reverend Bill Vaughn at least as well as I do. Bill told me what the theologian, Paul Tillich, once wrote: 'There is more mercy in God than there is sin in us.'"

Evelyn tucked her legs under her and leaned her head on my shoulder. I tilted toward her, and she nuzzled her cheek against my neck. Tickled by her soft hair, I detected a scent of lavender.

"Moreover," I said, "it sounds like you haven't done a helluva lot of sinning." I put my arm around her. Her tears dampened my face.

Evelyn suddenly jumped up, breaking the tension. "Okay, *Professor* Pritchard. What about pecan pie with whipped cream?"

"Sounds terrific, *Dean* Baird." Still wearing my mask, I followed her into the kitchen, then back to the dining room table.

The pie was sweet, rich, and delicious. After her first bite, Evelyn rested an elbow on the table and asked, "So, David, tell me about this Arnold Theileman who is speaking next Friday."

We seemed to be shifting into "business mode," so I wanted a *quid pro quo*. "First," I said, "fill me in about the so-called teaching evaluation Barton will conduct after this semester."

Evelyn wrinkled her brow, stared at me, and said, "I've already told you things that could get me fired."

Returning her gaze, I said, "We have a unique friendship. It's anchored in a deep mutual trust that I could never have imagined two months ago." I winked and smiled. "Dare I say that we sort of like one another?"

"True, sort of." We both laughed.

Evelyn confirmed what the faculty had suspected. The teaching evaluations would be used by Barton to reward supporters and punish boat rockers. "He mentioned you in particular. So, who's Thieleman?" she asked again.

"He heads the state's ACLU office in Richmond. The students who organized this, Pooky Loomis and Bea McNally, asked me to introduce him."

Evelyn shook her head and pushed pie crumbs around on

her plate. "President Barton is furious."

"I bet, but he wouldn't dare try to prevent it." Evelyn agreed, but she revealed that Barton had directed her to attend and take notes, especially on what I said and did.

"David, how old are you?"

"Twenty-seven." Then, guessing on the low side, I speculated, "You must be about thirty-two or, at most, thirty-three."

"Ha," said Evelyn. "Close. Try thirty-seven."

"You don't look a day over thirty-two."

"You're much too kind." Evelyn's crow's feet in the corners of her eyes hinted at long-term concerns. "Another few years," she lamented, "and . . ." She didn't finish the sentence. Smoothing and re-smoothing her white gown, she said, "Well, time flies. . . . I'm lonely sometimes." Evelyn clasped her hands together. "I am very grateful for your friendship."

"That's so nice of you to say. Of course, you have my friendship, and more: support, admiration, and—if I might say—affection."

I stood up, as it was getting late. When I started to take off my mask, which I'd never removed, Evelyn held up a hand. "Leave it on. Wouldn't you like a tour of the house?"

Downstairs, there were two bedrooms. One was hers; the other had been converted into an office. In a smaller room was a large loom. Evelyn acknowledged, "Weaving takes my mind off of . . . things." This room was filled with colorful, intricately textured wall hangings and throw rugs.

"Now," Evelyn stammered, "let's—let's go up to . . . the tower room." She opened an interior door, took a flashlight from a shelf, and directed its dim beam up a steep and narrow staircase. "There's a bedside lamp up there," she said in a low voice, "but the bulb is burned out, and I've never gotten around to buying a new one."

She went first. I followed with considerable trepidation and some difficulty, trying to maintain my grip on the hand she extended down to me. We ascended the creaking staircase with care to a circular bedroom with one small, shaded window where, she said, family visitors sometimes stayed.

Except for the flashlight and the faintest inkling of light from downstairs, the musty smelling tower room, where we were, was in total darkness. Still holding my hand, Evelyn turned off the flashlight and pulled me to the bed. "I feel safe in the dark," she said. "You can take off your mask."

I was uneasy and acutely alert. Evelyn had a good deal more to drink than I, but I'd promised myself some time ago that I would not diddle the dean. And I was growing fond of Valerie.

"Can I touch you?" Evelyn asked haltingly.

I said nothing, but my fingertips brushed her shoulder as an ember of desire invaded the prickle of silence.

"I'm a little nervous," she admitted. She asked again, "May I touch you?" Evelyn put a warm hand on my thigh, and I placed my hand over hers.

"That'd be nice," I finally mumbled.

"But, but . . ." she stuttered, "can I ask you, please, not to touch *me?*"

Evelyn took my silence as an assent. In the darkness, we saw nothing but the fuzziest outlines of one another. Unable to see, my sense of touch and smell, and—to a degree—of taste and sound, was intensified. What was probably a mere hint of lavender in the room now seemed pronounced.

Still touching her hand, I fell back onto the bed, listening in the dark as we breathed more heavily. We did not kiss. Evelyn moved her hand from mine and, with a mischievous giggle, slid it inside my sweatpants. Dean Evelyn was on a mission. Her hand continued its journey down the inside of my leg as her forearm pressed teasingly against me. She undid the drawstring of my pants with her other hand. Her fingers were like five, then ten, invisible feathers. She was purposeful and deliberate, but gentle. She was also inquisitive and exploratory, like a paleontologist who first handles a rare find.

Her grasp grew firmer, and so did I. "Make it last," she implored. She pressed one hand on my abdomen and stroked me with the other. My heart pounded as warmth flowed southward. This could not continue much longer.

Despite my implied promise not to touch her, I was sorely tempted. But before all restraint dissolved, Evelyn took my hand and tucked it under her gown, above the knee. "Higher," she murmured, "but not inside." I lifted her dress, ran a finger along the waistband of her panties, then descended. As I moved my fingers back and forth without entering forbidden territory, she rubbed me, and we kissed for the first time.

It may not have been "the shot heard around the world," but it felt like it at least reached West Virginia.

"Oh. . . . Incredible. . . . Thank you," sighed Evelyn.

"Thank *you*," I replied, panting heavily. After a few moments, I threw an arm around her waist and asked, "Well, my dear Dean Baird, did the Angel of Light vanquish the Agent of Darkness, or did she succumb to the devil?"

Evelyn reached down to where I was quite slippery, gave me a final squeeze, and whispered, "We both won."

Groping around in the dark, she located the flashlight. I got dressed, and we carefully made our way back down the stairs. We hugged in the hallway and kissed at the front door. It wasn't a passionate, "I'm going to drag you into the bushes" kind of kiss. Rather, it was a warm, sincere handshake of a kiss; one that read, "We're tight together, really tight." Indeed, we had solidified our relationship into an intimate friendship, as well as an informal alliance.

As I was about to go out the door, Evelyn held up a hand. "Wait." She vanished, but soon reappeared with a lovely purple-pink-orange woven wall hanging reminiscent of a sunset. "For you, David."

I thanked her profusely. We kissed once more.

Driving with care back to Piney Woods in the dark, my mind wrestled with how to characterize my changed link to Evelyn. We were not lovers in any classic sense. Were we semi-lovers? Conditional lovers? We enjoyed one another, but at its core our tie was functional. For Evelyn, I was a valued confidant who also provided useful information about students and faculty. And she now had a much desired, if self-constrained, sexual liaison with someone ten years her junior. For me, Evelyn was an invaluable, clandestine Traymore ally as well as an *ad hoc* dalliance and outstanding cook.

Arguably—although this was really stretching it—I'd kept my promise to myself. I did not diddle the dean. Fiddle with, yes; diddle, no. Turning into the cottages, I thought I could still detect a lingering scent of lavender and lovemaking—or was it only the rich loam and red clay soil of Virginia on a cool, humid autumn evening?

11

The Speech

Xena's cold nose poked under a blanket and into my armpit around seven o'clock. This, and her foul breath, roused me out of bed.

I wobbled into the bathroom. Then, only half awake, I made my way to the refrigerator to see if there was any unspoiled milk for my cereal. "Phew," I said after giving the bottle a whiff. "Damn. It's black coffee and toast this morning."

The phone rang. "Xena," I grumbled, rubbing the stubble on my chin, "who the hell calls at this hour?" With one erect ear and the other at half mast, she stared at me, thumped her tail on the floor, and tilted her head. All she heard, of course, was, "Xena, blah, blah, blah."

I picked up the receiver. "Hello?"

"David, Evelyn."

I scratched my back and yawned. "Why aren't you in bed?" Holding the phone in one hand, I put a pot of water on the stove with the other, then located the jar of instant coffee.

"I've been up thinking about last night."

"Plagued with guilt?"

"*Au contraire.* Joy. I've never been happier. I'm so grateful for our Halloween."

Xena spun around and whined, signaling an urgent need to

be let out. "Hold on a second; I've got to open the door for the dog."

When I picked up the phone again, Evelyn said, "Speaking of doors, you were adventurous to follow me through the door to the tower room."

My coffee was ready. Taking a sip, I said, "*You* were the daring one. Frisky, too."

"You're such a naughty devil." Evelyn was quiet for a moment. "I've been mulling over whether there might be other doors in the tower room that could be entered or at least explored."

I rolled my eyes and took another sip of coffee. "Seems like you've found your inner devil. From now on, and only between the two of us, you're *Develyn,* not Evelyn."

"You're a bad boy."

I needed to shave, shower, dress, eat breakfast, and get on with the day. So, I fibbed: "Develyn, you're a sweetheart, and I'd *love* to pursue this subject, but Xena's outside scratching at the door, insisting on her morning walk."

"I'll let you go, but if you scratch on *my* door it just might open."

Now I was fully awake. "Sounds like an invitation."

"Perhaps."

"See you Friday at the ACLU event."

"Yes, but I can't appear to be friendly, or even too sociable. I'll be there in an official capacity. President Barton directed me to sit in the front row and monitor you closely."

"Hope to give you something juicy to relay to the SOB. We'll be in touch."

I hung up the phone, went into the bathroom, and slapped

shaving cream on my face. The phone rang again. "Damn." I wiped off the foam and answered it.

"Good morning, little 'l' love."

"Hi, Val. Good to hear your voice. How'd the interview go?"

"Fabulous. The chairman of the economics department was gracious and encouraging. I have to finish my formal application soon because he indicated I might get an early and positive decision."

Still in my underwear, I sat down in a chair. "Wonderful. My letter of recommendation will be in the mail on Monday."

"I've *really* missed you. Did you miss me even a little?"

I confessed, truthfully, that I had. Both the escapade with Evelyn, and Evelyn herself, were *sui generis*. Neither diminished my fondness for Valerie. Indeed, I'd been chewing on Bessie's admonition: "Don't let that pretty bird fly away."

"So, did you and Xena sit alone in the cottage, sad and lonely, while I was in Baltimore?"

"Something like that."

"Poor baby. Let's wage war on loneliness after the ACLU event."

"Okay. We'll celebrate your likely admission to Johns Hopkins."

After getting off the phone, I was finally able to shave and choke down some dry toast. Then, I flopped down on the couch, rested my head on a cushion, and tried to sort out fast-moving developments.

Let's see. I had two ongoing female interests. One had real promise, the other one was, well, unusual. Plus, everything else—class preparations, teaching, searching for another job, and counseling both students and faculty. And, of course, spearheading a drive to oust Barton. Most nights I got less than six hours of sleep. I knew, or thought I knew, that all demands and challenges could be handled except for one.

As in the *Odyssey*, the sea I was sailing upon had treacherous shoals, and its isles were inhabited by hundreds of alluring sirens. An SOS flashed insistently across my bow: "Scores of Sirens. Beware!" Like Ulysses, I knew that resisting temptation was not my strong suit. I feared and, indeed, expected that a ravishing beauty would sooner or later present herself. She'd lack the discretion, maturity, and relative safety of Valerie and Evelyn. I'd likely take the bait, and Barton would have me for dinner.

I smacked my forehead, got off the couch, and went outside to fetch Evelyn's gorgeous multicolor weaving I'd left in the car the night before. Such a touching and personal gift. I draped it over the back of the couch, where Xena seemed ready to make it her own. On Monday, I hung it properly on the living room wall.

———

The speech on student legal rights by the ACLU's Arnold Thieleman had been widely advertised through the student newspaper, faculty announcements in class, and especially, the hard work of Pooky Loomis, Bea McNally, Sue Ewal, and dozens of other students. When I arrived at six-thirty, Barton Hall was already jammed with students and faculty. All seats were taken. Many people were standing in the back.

Pooky and Bea came up to me. "We knew there'd be a crowd, but nothing like this," Bea said.

After greeting them, I chatted with several faculty members, some of whom noted, as I already had, that Dean Evelyn Baird was sitting in the center of the front row. Evelyn nodded, but did not smile. Sadly, she stood out like a scarecrow in a field of daisies, an odd specter dressed in black academic regalia and mortarboard hat. The apparent, if misguided, intent was to intimidate students.

"Dean Baird is Barton's hatchet person," said Bea. "She's here to take names, especially yours, and kick ass."

Sitting next to Evelyn were Vice President Ned Thompson and Professor Byon Joon-Ho. Also in the first row was Sheriff Harland Goetzke, who waved at me. Several seats away from the sheriff, on an aisle, was a complete stranger and one of the few other men in the hall. He was a heavy-set muscular man with a crew cut who wore blue jeans, work boots, and a faded red plaid flannel shirt. He looked to be in his late thirties, sat with his legs wide apart, and stared intently at me. Clearly, he was not a member of the press, but he was photographing me with what appeared to be an expensive Nikon camera.

Most of the remaining front row seats were occupied by various student leaders, including Bea, Pooky, and Sue. Valerie sat to the far left in a sweater and bright pink skirt, not far from a reporter for *The Roanoke Times* whom I recognized.

As the start time neared, Pooky and Bea rushed up. They looked concerned.

"Thieleman's going to be forty minutes late," said Pooky. "His plane just landed in Roanoke."

I gazed out at the huge audience. "What do you propose?"

"People will leave if we don't do something to hold them until Thieleman arrives," Pooky said nervously. She pleaded, "Could *you* possibly say a few words before he gets here?"

"Let me first talk with Professors Vaughn and O'Keefe." After consulting with them, both of whom urged me to take charge, I agreed to make some extemporaneous remarks.

Pooky marched briskly to the lectern—which was almost as tall as she was—and tapped the microphone. "Welcome to our event on student legal rights. Our speaker, Arnold Thieleman, will be a little late. He is on his way to Traymore from Roanoke." She raised both arms in the air. "However, I am delighted to tell you that Professor David Pritchard has agreed to make a few remarks and take some questions from the audience before our guest arrives."

Evelyn glared at me. I could see her face reddening. For a moment, I feared she might leap up and say something, but she remained quiet.

Most of the audience applauded loudly. I was by now well-known across the campus. Even Sheriff Goetzke was clapping, but not Evelyn, Ned Thompson, Byon Joon-Hoo, or the stranger with a camera.

"Thank you, ladies." I paused, scanned the hall, and said, "A handful of men are present tonight, mostly faculty members. None of the men are students." I paused again and, with emphasis, said, "I predict that coeducation will be a major legal issue at Traymore in the near future." Scattered applause rippled through the audience. I noticed Sheriff Goetzke glance sideways at the stranger.

For fifteen minutes, I summarized some key holdings of state and federal courts that pertained to student legal rights at public colleges and universities. I then invited questions from the floor. Dozens of hands shot up. "Wow. I can't possibly respond to all of you. Let's take just a few."

Sue Ewal was standing in the front row, waving her arms.

"Professor, whenever I put anything in our student newspaper even mildly critical of college policies or practices, the administration censors it. Is this legal?"

An easy one. I took the microphone and stepped toward Sue. She was one of my own students. I knew her well. "Sue, the short answer is 'no.' Unless an item is patently libelous or clearly obscene—and courts define 'obscenity' broadly—it cannot be curtailed by the college."

Sue turned around to face her fellow students and, to thunderous applause, pumped her fist into the air.

I returned to the dais and recognized a student toward the back of the hall. "Why doesn't Traymore let us evaluate our professors and courses? My friends at other colleges do this every semester."

I raised my voice in order in order to be heard. "This isn't a legal issue. It's common sense. The consumer, you, should have a say in the quality of her education. Last spring, before I arrived at Traymore, the faculty urged that such student evaluations be implemented. President Barton objected. He said that *he* would evaluate professors and their courses."

Groans echoed throughout the hall. I stepped back and straightened my tie. (I always wore a tie and jacket to class and for public appearances.) "I'm told by my colleagues that President Barton said students were incapable of making wise evaluations."

"Bullshit! Ridiculous!" someone shouted. The hall erupted in chants of "Bullshit, bullshit, bullshit."

When things quieted down a bit, I said, "Incidentally, your *Traymore College Student Handbook, 1969-1970*, which I just happen to have with me." (I held up the pink-covered rule book.)

"States, under 'Improper Language,' that 'Students responsible for written or verbal public displays of profanity . . . will be subject to disciplinary action.'" Holding up the *Student Handbook* and stepping to the edge of the dais, I said: "This language is, on its face, unconstitutional. It is, if you will, bullshit." This brought down the house.

I was enjoying myself. Evelyn, however, went into orbit. She leapt up, hands on hips, and stared in my direction. Once again, I thought she might try to prevent me from speaking. Without saying a word, I stopped, flashed a forced smile, and returned her stare. The twelve-hundred-plus students in Barton Hall seemed to freeze. The hushed tension was palpable until Evelyn slowly sat back down.

I faced the audience. "You are all correct. It *is* ridiculous in 1969 that the outdated notion of *in loco parentis* is imposed on undergraduates, all of whom are eighteen years of age or older. A public women's college should not treat its students like children in need of parental guidance, especially male parental guidance. You are women, and you are adults."

I continued talking as rhythmic clapping resounded throughout the hall. "Concerning student evaluations of their courses, and other important issues, Traymore's administration demeans young women by assuming that you are incapable of making responsible decisions."

I knew that I was being direct and provocative. So, looking at Evelyn, I added, "Of course, I'm stating my personal views. I would welcome an open debate with anyone who has a different perspective."

Evelyn shook her head. Her expression, especially her arched eyebrow, seemed to say, "Fat chance, Pritchard" —or maybe it was, "Up yours, Pritchard." I couldn't tell which.

I was about to call on another student when Bea cried out, "He's here!"

As Thieleman entered Barton Hall and made his way to the podium, a student jumped up from the fifth row. She shouted, "Professor Pritchard, we want you, not Barton, for president."

Waves of laughter and sporadic applause swept through the place as virtually everyone—except for the administrators, the sheriff, and the mystery man in the front row—rose to their feet.

That's her, the head-spinning gorgeous blonde who asked a question at the Vietnam panel.

But there was no time to dwell on this. "So sorry I'm late." A surprisingly young, dark-haired man in a finely tailored gray flannel suit extended his hand. "Arnold Thieleman. My flight was delayed by the weather." We shook hands.

"That's fine. I've warmed them up for you." I stepped forward and introduced Thieleman. He came to the lectern.

Thieleman spoke for about thirty minutes. He said that his office was increasingly concerned about the situation at Traymore; that the ACLU was already representing one Traymore professor in a suit against the college, and he anticipated additional legal actions by faculty and students. He adeptly fielded several questions, expressing concern at what he heard from students about apparent infringements of civil liberties. Thieleman concluded his appearance with a statement that, while obvious to me, seemed to surprise many. "Students are citizens. They have constitutional rights. In the area of the First Amendment—the freedoms of speech, press, assembly, and religion—these rights are substantially the same as those possessed by any other person. This is especially so for students at a *public* college, like Traymore. This simple observation may shock many of you."

It did. A hush fell over the hall. It was soon followed by lively chatter. I took the podium to thank Thieleman. "Please accept our gratitude for your perceptive insights. We will take them to heart. You have reminded us that quality education is linked to freedom of expression in all of its forms. Twelve years ago, in *Sweezy v. New Hampshire,* the U.S. Supreme Court said, 'The essentiality of freedom in the community of American universities is self-evident.'" The event came to an end as Barton Hall shook with applause.

I again thanked Thieleman. He said, "Our guy in Roanoke, Ron Cohen, speaks highly of you. I can see why. Feel free to call me directly any time."

"Thanks. You will hear from me."

As the audience broke up, I saw Evelyn slip out a side door. The unidentified man with the camera melded into the crowd, and I noticed Sheriff Goetzke's eyes following him.

While I was speaking with the *Roanoke Times* reporter, I saw the sheriff waving his hand at me. I excused myself and walked over to him.

"David, there's something important you gotta know. Did you see the guy with the camera?"

"I did, Harley." The sheriff and I had interacted often enough that we were comfortable calling each other by our first names.

"He's a badass. His name's Aubrey Ray Blount. Spent time in the state pen some years ago for assault and battery. I'm pretty sure he's now involved with illicit drugs." The sheriff was dead serious as he adjusted his belt and holster.

"Why was he here, and in the first row?" I looked around for Valerie but couldn't locate her.

"Don't know. But when President Barton asked me to be here, he also wanted me to do something that crossed the line."

"How's that?"

Goetzke put on his wide brim hat and glanced down at his boots. "He asked me to assign one of my deputies to snoop into your personal life and generally keep track of you."

"Good Lord."

The sheriff looked up, narrowed his eyes, and swatted his hand in the air. "Told Elzic Barton—I've known him for years—that unless I had good reason to believe that you had committed a crime or were in the process of committing a crime, I would not and could not do it."

"This is disturbing, but hardly surprising. How does it relate to Aubrey Ray Blount?"

"Blount often works for a shady private investigation outfit in Roanoke called Dixie Dog Investigative Services. Knowing Elzic Barton as I do, I strongly suspect that he called Dixie after I turned him down." Then, looking directly at me while scratching his belly, Goetzke said, "Barton really despises you, David. He made it clear that, and I'm quoting, 'Pritchard threatens everything I've done for Traymore. It's my college, not his.'"

"Shit." I pounded a fist into a nearby seat.

"Blount's not too smart. Dangerous, I think, but not smart. If the SOB stalks or harasses you, or overtly threatens you, I'll haul his sorry ass into custody. You're a lawyer, David. Be alert. Good luck, son." Harley patted me on the shoulder and turned to leave.

He pointed up to the last row. "Think there's a little lady waiting for you way back there."

Valerie was in an aisle seat. As I walked toward her, I was somehow reminded of the adorable young raccoons I saw by the lake last month. But her brow was furrowed; something was bothering her.

Valerie stood as I approached. I glanced around to see if we were alone before wrapping my arm around her waist. "Why the frown?"

"What'd the sheriff want?"

"Tell you on the way to the cottage."

"Is it about the creepy guy with the camera?"

I nodded.

We dropped her car off in Christiansburg and headed for my Piney Woods cottage. I summarized what the sheriff had told me. She was unnaturally quiet before sliding over next to me and patting my knee. I held her hand until I turned south onto I-81. Except for the usual flow of eighteen wheelers, traffic was light.

Turning off at the Claytor Lake exit, I noticed that the only vehicle behind me also exited. Except in the summer, not many cars came this way, so I kept an eye on it. In a mile, the road forked. A paved road continued on to Claytor Lake State Park. The left fork was gravel and went to Piney Woods. When I veered off toward the cottage, the vehicle behind me suddenly stopped, did a quick U-turn, and sped away. It sounded like an old pickup truck with a defective muffler, but I couldn't be sure in the dark.

Xena was always happy to see me, but she adored Valerie. When we opened the cottage door, instead of rushing out as usual, Xena leapt up, wagging her tail furiously. She then pressed herself against Val. Her tongue lolled out as she begged for attention. Val kneeled down and gave her an affectionate hug. Xena reciprocated with licks and dog slobber.

"Well, girls, I hate to break this up." I gave Val a hand and helped her get up as Xena finally ran off to pee and harass the creatures of the night. I kissed Val on the cheek and lamented, "Xena never greets *me* that way."

"That's because you don't hug her enough, or sweet talk her. Girls need hugs and sweet talk."

We hugged. My fingers wandered under her sweater. Clothes were scattered across the living room floor from the front door to the couch. We never made it to the bedroom.

A roaring lust fueled the sex, and sex was a medium for sharing: "I've missed you," "We belong together," and, of course, "I love you." Sex was both lubricant and glue. It was also exhausting. We lay on the couch for some time afterward, breathing heavily, damp with perspiration. Only now was I aware of Val's Bellodgia perfume wafting up from my subconscious to once again capture me. "You smell *so* much better than Xena." I whispered, "That was *quite* a hug."

We showered, searched the floor for our clothes, and dressed. After a late dinner of hamburgers and salad, we finally made it to the bed, where we promptly fell asleep.

In the morning, we had a fine bacon and egg breakfast. When we were about to leave to drive Val back to Christiansburg, she pointed to the weaving on my wall. "Where did that come from?"

"Oh, I've had it awhile. Just recently got around to hanging it." *That was sure dumb of me.*

"It's lovely."

Driving out of Piney Woods, I stopped to take my Saturday *Roanoke Times* from the mailbox. On page two, above a photo of Arnold Thieleman, a headline read: "Multiple Civil Liberties Infringements at Traymore College."

I handed the paper to Val. "Great!"

We clung to one another as I drove north on I-81. "Crimson and Clover" played on the car radio . . . "over and over."

At her place, we got out and held each other tight. "See you soon, love," I said.

"Yes. See you soon, love."

———

Late Monday afternoon, shortly after I'd returned to Piney Woods following class, the phone rang. "David, Evelyn. Before you say anything, President Barton *directed* me to wear the formal academic attire to the ACLU event. I was *so* embarrassed."

"Well, that scarecrow outfit didn't deter critics, but it worked in one respect: I didn't see a single starling or blackbird."

"Please, be kind. It's bad enough. I need hand-holding and understanding."

"You have it."

"Thank you, but this is not why I called. Tomorrow, you'll receive a formal letter of reprimand for your words and actions last Friday. It's signed by me, but you should know that—while I do think you took undue license, and while I was annoyed—the letter was dictated to me by the president. It will go into your permanent file."

"Think I'll piss in my pants. Do you have any other good tidings for me? Maybe an impending attempt on my life?"

"David, I'm sorry."

"A real apparatchik." I immediately regretted what I'd said.

"What kind of a chick?"

"Sorry." I paced the floor. "It's my turn to apologize. You're a wonderful person and a dear friend, much more than an obedient functionary."

Silence. "That's nice of you to say. I think."

"Develyn, did you notice the big guy with a crew cut who photographed me?"

"Of course. Who was he?"

I hesitated to reveal everything Sheriff Goetzke had told me, but cleared my throat and said, "The sheriff is suspicious of him. Thinks he could be a threat, and Barton might be involved."

Evelyn gasped. "The president never said anything to me about this, and he tells me a lot."

I decided to go fishing. "Who might know?"

"Hmm." Evelyn paused. "His executive assistant, Carla Pogue, came to Traymore with him in 1952. They're inseparable. Carla knows everything, but she's very tight-lipped."

Inhaling deeply, and taking some liberties with what Harley Goetzke actually said, I spoke into the phone with a firm, steady voice. "Evelyn, the sheriff thinks the guy might harm me physically. Goetzke also thinks that if the president *is* involved, Barton's reputation could be sullied—or worse." While talking with Evelyn, and without realizing it, I'd assumed the posture of a wrestler at the start of a match: legs apart, slightly crouched, elbows tucked in, arms and hands at the ready, and eyes glued on the opponent (actually, I was staring at Evelyn's weaving). I took the leap. "Could you possibly try to coax some information from Carla? My safety and the president's standing could be on the line."

"Let me think. . . ." Silence. "This is sensitive. It'll be difficult. Carla's a momma bear who protects the president from threats, real and imagined. But we're close, and she knows the president confides in me. I'll take her to lunch, and we'll see how it goes."

I eased out of my wrestling stance. "Thanks a bundle, Evelyn—I mean Develyn."

"Well, Mr. Devil, if I succeed with Carla—and, of course, there's no assurance that she knows anything at all—Develyn will demand a pound of flesh. Yours."

"What about ours?"

"Okay."

"Very, very naughty." I shook my head and took a deep breath. "It's a deal, I guess. A Faustian bargain."

"I'll get on it tomorrow. It'll take more than one lunch."

"Before we get off the phone, I want to thank you again for the exquisite weaving." I looked at it as I spoke.

"I wanted you to have it. One of mine won first prize at the state fair last spring."

"I can see why."

———

Tuesday afternoon, I found Evelyn's (that is, Barton's) two-paragraph letter in my campus mailbox. It read, in part:

Dear Dr. Pritchard:

Your actions and remarks at the student-sponsored program on "student rights," held in Barton Hall on November 7, 1969, were inappropriate, distasteful, without prior authorization, and an intentional provocation. Your highly improper takeover, without an invitation from those in charge, seemed to have been due to your vested interest in the topic, or fear of losing an audience because of the delayed arrival of the scheduled speaker.

I chose not to embarrass you or myself by registering my objection during your presentation. A copy of this letter has been placed in your personnel file.

It was signed: Evelyn Baird, Dean of Students. Copies went to Dr. Byon Joon-Ho, Chairman, Political Science Department; Pooky Loomis, President, Young Republicans; Bea McNally, President, Young Democrats; and, Dr. Elzic Barton, President.

That evening, I wrote a three-page response which I delivered personally to Evelyn's office the following day. I expressed my "shock and surprise" at receiving such a reprimand; I emphasized that "those in charge" (Pooky and Bea) asked me to speak, and I did so only after consulting with other faculty members; that none of the dozens of students and faculty with whom I'd subsequently spoken considered my remarks "distasteful" or a "provocation;" and that Pooky, Bea, and I were legitimately concerned that a program so germane to Traymore not lose its audience while waiting for the speaker to arrive.

I added that Evelyn's failure to object to my actions at the time constituted an "implied consent—not that I needed your consent."

My letter concluded with: "Your formal, written admonishment of my actions and remarks might be interpreted as inappropriate retaliation, yet another imprudent attempt to punish and curb those who express views contrary to those of the administration." I sent copies to Pooky, Bea, Byon Joon-Ho, Elzic Barton, and—certain to catch the president's eye—the ACLU's Arnold Thieleman.

Never again did the administration mention the incident; it was as if nothing had ever happened. However, the speech lit a fire that inflamed most of the student body and much of the faculty.

12
RJ

It started out like any other Thursday. After my Constitutional Law course in the morning, I chatted briefly with a couple of students. I hadn't slept too well, and, after rushing back into the classroom to retrieve the jacket I'd left behind, I hurried down the hall toward my office. Several things were on my mind, especially the recent exchange of correspondence with Evelyn, when I collided head-on with someone. Her books and notebooks and my briefcase and lecture notes flew across the hallway. She tumbled backward, hitting her head on a wall before plunging to the floor. I careened off the opposite wall, also striking my head, but somehow remaining upright.

On the floor, and before looking in my direction, she screamed, "Damnit! Look where you're going, bitch." Holding her head, she tried to get up, but fell back down. Her disheveled long blonde hair spilled over her face.

Two nearby students offered their assistance, but I waved them away. "It's entirely my fault, miss. I apologize. My head was in the clouds."

That's when I saw that it was *her*, the beautiful girl I'd twice seen at a distance from the dais in Barton Hall. Here was the striking siren I had hoped, and feared, I would encounter. She was as volatile as she was alluring. But I knew, despite a pulsing red light, I couldn't just let her disappear again. Now, my head really was in the clouds.

I extended a hand. She took it, and I pulled her to her feet.

"Omigod! It's *you*. Please forgive me, Professor Pritchard. Are you hurt?"

"No, just a little bump on the head."

She rubbed her head and ran her fingers through her hair. "Me, too. I wasn't paying attention."

Straightening my tie and stumbling over my words, I stammered, "Why . . . why don't you step into my office? I mean, it's . . . ah . . . just down the hall."

"I know."

"You do?"

We were talking, but not really looking at one another as we retrieved the books, papers, notebooks, and pens that were scattered about.

"Yes—think I've got everything—everybody knows about you and where your office is located." She tossed some strands of golden hair from her forehead. "Let's go to your office."

My palms were sweaty, and my legs felt unsteady as we entered the office. I sat in my desk chair while this mini-skirted Venus eased into the chair across from me.

I paused for a moment, which felt like an hour, uncertain of what to say or how to say it. She was so stunning that I didn't know whether to look at or away from her. If I did the former, she may have thought I was leering; if I did the latter, she might have concluded that I found her uninteresting.

Finally, I blurted out, "What's your name?"

"Ruby Jean McKenna. Friends call me RJ."

"I remember you, RJ."

"Me?" She blushed and re-crossed her legs. I was lightheaded.

"The Vietnam panel and last Friday's program on student rights."

Leaning forward in a low-cut green chiffon blouse, she smiled broadly, her blue eyes sparkling. "And why would you remember *me?*" Traymore's dress code didn't mean anything to RJ.

I coughed, twiddled my pen, and struggled mightily, if unsuccessfully, to avert my gaze. "Because you have chutzpah."

"Hut's paw? What's that?

"Attitude. Damn the torpedoes. In your face. Brashness."

RJ nodded. "Yea, I suppose. Too many girls here keep their heads low and just go along with the crap Barton dishes out."

I could hear—really *hear*—my heart pounding. To relieve the mounting tension, I swiveled my chair at an angle to gaze out the window at the crisp, clear autumn day. Without looking at her, I said, "RJ, you're like my German shepherd, Xena. She loves some folks, but when she dislikes someone, Xena sure lets them know."

RJ leapt to her feet. "Xena! We all saw her on TV. I'd *love* to meet Xena. Can I see her?"

Now standing, RJ bent toward me in her revealing blouse, both hands on the desk. She acted as though she owned me, and she did. Crossing the Rubicon, I said, "Tomorrow afternoon might work, but Traymore's *Student Handbook* forbids students who live on campus—and I'm paraphrasing—from visiting a bachelor's place of residence unless she is a senior and another woman is present."

Pens and pencils bounced when RJ slammed her fist down on my desk. "What baloney. I see my boyfriend nearly every week in his dorm at Virginia Tech."

I stood, looked her in the eye, and capitulated completely, "It *must* be confidential."

"Whoopee! Our little secret." RJ flung her arms above her head and twirled around.

"Meet me tomorrow, two o'clock at Monroe and Main. We'll walk Xena in Claytor Lake State Park."

With an "I'll be there," RJ skipped out the door.

———

And there she was, leaning against a yellow street sign that read "CAUTION." RJ wore a brilliant orange top and snug jeans. She was as inconspicuous as a drag queen at a church social. With a "Hi, prof," she wriggled into the car.

I took the longer, more remote route to Piney Woods and checked my rearview mirror repeatedly to see if anyone was following. "RJ, tell me something about yourself. All I know is what I see."

"And what do you see, professor?" She smiled.

"Call me David."

"Okay, Davey."

I gripped the steering wheel tighter and turned toward her. "I see two things. First, you're an unrestrained bundle of energy, intensely independent, and open to whatever life may bring."

RJ pushed back in her seat. "You're one-for-one, prof—I mean Davey."

"Second." I now looked straight ahead, eyes on the road.

"You're far-and-away the world's most beautiful woman."

RJ swung her legs up and tucked them under her. She reached over and touched my arm. "Thank you. That's nice."

I turned and saw that her face was flushed. "I'm sorry, Ms. McKenna. I was too forward."

"No, you weren't, *professor*. And, it's *RJ*. I love that you say what you think."

"Guess we have that in common. But I still don't know much about you. How old are you? Where are you from? Why are you at Traymore?" We crossed under I-81 as we neared Piney Woods. No cars were behind us.

"I'm nineteen. From Columbus, Georgia. Told my parents— Daddy's a drill sergeant at Fort Benning—that if they sent me back to the damn Bible school in South Carolina, I'd run off to San Francisco. They relented, but only if I went to Traymore, which was cheaper than my first choice, Hollins College."

I chuckled. "So, your transfer was not from the frying pan into the fire, but from the fire into the frying pan." We both laughed.

As we approached the cottages, Caleb Heath, attired in his usual bib overalls and baseball cap, waved me over. I got out and we shook hands. "How you doing, Caleb?"

Caleb frowned. "A man was here this mornin' askin' 'bout ya. Big guy, crew cut. Didn't trust him any further than I can spit." Caleb lifted a leg and spat out a brown stream of tobacco juice; some dribbled down his chin. "Wanted to know which cabin was yours. Told him to git outta here."

"Would you do me a small favor, Caleb?"

"Sure."

"Call Harley Goetzke. He'll tell you that the guy, Aubrey Ray Blount, has a criminal record."

Caleb removed his cap and scratched his head. "I knew somethin' weren't right."

"What kind of car was he driving?"

"Ford F100 pickup, mid-fifties. Had more rust than red paint."

I inhaled deeply. "Would you let me know if you see him again? Sheriff says he'll arrest him for any misstep."

"Will do, David." I got back into the car, Caleb tipped his cap to RJ, and we continued on down the gravel road.

Xena and RJ hit it off as soon as we entered the cottage. RJ riled the dog with a tennis ball and teased her with, "Does Xena want to go for a W-A-L-K?" (letters Xena knew well). Holding the ball high, RJ called out, "Let's GO," and Xena jumped. This was repeated. "Let's GO" (jump); "Let's GO" (jump).

While they played, I changed into jeans and a heavy sweater. Soon, the three of us headed for the state park on this cool, sunny day. The air was still. Most of the leaves had fallen. We followed the lake shore before veering off on a trail I knew well. Dry leaves crinkled under our feet as we wound our way through a hardwood forest of mostly oak and ash.

In about forty minutes, we emerged at a boat rental facility, now closed for the season. We sat on the dock and drank water from a canteen I'd brought along in a day pack. Xena barked and plunged off the dock into the lake after some mallards.

"This is so nice," said RJ, although she was shivering.

"Here." I handed her the well-worn blue flannel shirt I'd stuffed into my pack.

"Perfect." The shirt was much too large, but she looked great in it.

RJ talked about her impermanent life as an army brat. As she spoke, she fondled a long lock of hair, caressed her face with it, looped it around a finger, and ran it along her lips. She was making things very difficult for me.

"It's getting late," I said. "Xena, come!" Xena swam to shore and, dripping wet, shook herself twice, showering us both. We headed back to the cottage on a more direct, if lesser traveled, path. As we walked through the woods, Aubrey Ray Blount came to mind. But we saw no one, and, at any rate, Xena would not have taken kindly to an encounter with a strange male.

The warmth of the cottage felt good, even with wet dog smell. I offered RJ my customary dinner of spaghetti and salad.

"Sounds good." She shed the flannel shirt and draped it over a chair but pleaded with me to let her keep it. "Oh, come on. It's cozy and smells of you. I'll sleep in it." She bounced up and down on her toes while holding her breath.

I laughed. "It's yours."

RJ grabbed my arm and kissed my cheek. She ran a finger gently along the length of my facial scar. "Sexy."

I felt my face redden, and I tried to concentrate on the demanding task of boiling water.

She located a *Blood, Sweat, and Tears* album and put it on the turntable. Squeezing into my small kitchen, she asked, "Do you smoke grass, Davey?"

"A few times in the past, but I don't have any. Makes me sleepy, and I'm not a hundred percent the next day."

RJ reached into her purse and extracted what appeared to be

a dime sized bag of marijuana. "After dinner?"

"No, thanks." I grabbed a bottle of wine. "I'll settle for this."

"Can I have a glass?" The drinking age was twenty-one. She snatched the bottle from my hand and poured herself a full glass of St. Julien Bordeaux.

During dinner, she was all talk. "I've lived in Germany and Japan. Speak German. Lived also in Texas, Arkansas, and Georgia. Why are you at Traymore? Have a girlfriend? My boyfriend at Tech is okay, but it probably won't last. I'm bored at Traymore. You're not at all boring. Why do you like me? I know you do. . . ."

She was ravenous, as if she hadn't eaten in weeks. Her orange top was soon flecked with splotches of marinara sauce.

"RJ, you've got marinara . . ."

"My older brother joined the Air Force. He never got along with Daddy. Neither did I." She gestured with her fork, sending a piece of spaghetti flying into the air and onto the floor where Xena, strategically located, snarfed it up.

"RJ, there's sauce . . ."

"Any more spaghetti?"

I rose to refill her plate. When I returned with the pasta, she was wiping her face with a napkin. The tips of her long hair touched the plate so that they, too, were saucy. Like RJ. She babbled on, hummed an unidentifiable tune, and every few minutes broke into a gleeful grin. "Answer my questions, Davey. Tell me you *don't* have a girlfriend." She reached across the table and took my hand. "Do you love her?"

"Well, she's . . ."

With a "Don't bullshit me" look, RJ announced confidently, "It's over. Right?"

I squeezed her hand. "I guess so."

RJ slurped down the last of her spaghetti and jumped up. She and Xena chased one another around in circles. Xena yipped, and RJ—hands on her hips and swaying to "You've Made Me So Very Happy"—chanted, "It's over, it's over, it's over."

Only then did she notice the spaghetti stains. "Damn." She winced and turned toward me with a strained smile. "Why didn't you tell me?"

"But RJ, I . . ."

"It needs to be soaked in cold water." RJ disappeared into the bathroom, and I heard water run in the sink.

I started to wash dishes. Concerned that my crumbling self-control would transform me into a moth headed for the flame, I considered returning this impulsive teenager to town. But then she came out of the bathroom and up behind me. "Got some in my hair, too. My blouse is soaking in your sink." She giggled. I dropped a fork and spun around.

Her bra, which was all she wore above the waist, was stained with a reddish marinara spot. My head jerked back, my heart raced, and I felt a euphoria bordering on disorientation.

"Should I soak the bra, too?"

Dazed, I took her hand, and we went into the living room. I wrapped an arm around her waist. My other hand unhooked the bra. I was awe-struck by the perfection and symmetry of her breasts, which surpassed even the realm of mythology. Or, maybe I'd just had too much wine.

RJ kissed my neck as I bent down reverentially to fondle her.

"I *knew* you liked me."

She smelled of autumn leaves, dry grass, and wet dog. We

kissed. Still standing, we pulled one another close. She tugged me over to the couch, where she sat down. "Don't sit," RJ commanded. "Just stand there." She unbuckled my belt, unzipped my jeans, and pulled them down to my knees. "*All* boys like this."

All boys, I thought, *suggests that she's had a pretty reliable statistical sample.*

"Wow! This won't take long," she said, as she wound her hair playfully around me and teased with her tongue. I ran my fingers through her fine yellow locks. My hands caressed both sides of her head as she proceeded. RJ's hair formed a canopy that largely obscured her skillful and clearly well-practiced attentions.

When she sensed that I was close, RJ pulled back, grinned mischievously, gazed up at me, and said, "Bedroom!"

It was then, as the train hurtled toward a precipice with a pounding, rhythmic *clickety clack, clickety clack, there's no turning back*, that I stepped away. Something—maybe fear, maybe guilt, maybe Valerie—compelled me to slam on the brakes. The locomotive steamed to a screeching stop, just barely.

"Oh, no. What's wrong?" RJ cried, still sitting on the couch and now subduing a rebellious strand of hair by taking it in her mouth.

I said nothing, pulled up my pants, sat down next to her, and gently extracted the wayward strand. Looking at her, I put it in my mouth. "Hmm. Marinara sauce."

I kissed her neck and stood up. "Got to get you back to the dorm before curfew, Miss Ruby Jean."

She pouted. "Phooey. I want to stay here with Xena. And maybe with you, too."

The ride back to Traymore was unremarkable, with one shocking exception. I rarely used condoms, partly because they killed spontaneity and desire, but primarily because my partners, whether Sam, Valerie, or whomever, were always—or virtually always—attentive to and responsible about birth control. So, belatedly, I asked, "Are you on the pill RJ, or maybe an IUD?

"Neither."

"What!" My eyes went wide.

"I've never had an IUD. And most doctors, at least in the south, won't prescribe the pill to unmarried women."

"God." I ground my teeth. Then I exhaled and thanked my lucky stars.

Seemingly unconcerned, RJ gazed out the window as she spoke. "It was fun, even if we never made it to bed. . . . I had sex at fifteen. Always been lucky."

"Luck runs out, RJ. Several doctors in Charlottesville wrote prescriptions for single women when I was there. I could put you in touch with one."

RJ reinserted her unruly wisp of hair between her lips and winked. "There's always withdrawal and what I was doing before you pulled away."

I shook my head and said nothing for a full minute. "RJ, you're a sweetheart." Then, raising an index finger for emphasis, I said in a measured voice, "This is serious. Don't ruin your life." I looked at her with a raised eyebrow. "If you're going to fuck around, don't fuck yourself." I instantly regretted having said this.

"You're angry at me." With a wrinkled brow and dejected look, RJ began to twist her hair.

"I'm sorry. Forgive me." I reached across the seat and touched her knee. "No, I'm not angry. You're a delight. Lord knows, I'm drawn to you. But I'm concerned. I want you to be happy *and* safe." She came over next to me. I took her hand and said, "Promise to be more careful. Bad stuff happens."

As we neared the town, I pulled over by a small park and kissed her. With her eyes locked on mine, she took my right hand, brought it to her lips, and ran the tip of her tongue along the full length of my index finger. "Okay, I'll be careful."

We drove into town and stopped at Monroe and Main. "See you soon, Davey." RJ winked, smiled, and hopped out, holding the blue flannel shirt.

13

Mustang Kimmy

Life's pace was accelerating. Over the next few days in mid-November, I saw or spoke with RJ, Valerie, and Evelyn. RJ called the following morning.

"Hi, Davey. Miss me?"

"Terribly."

"Really."

"Well, *pretty* terribly."

"Here's a test of *how* terribly you miss me. My boyfriend wants me to stay with him in Blacksburg tonight, but I want to be with you."

"That would be nice RJ, but I can't. I'm way behind in my preparations for class."

"Damn. You flunk the test. I'm leaving campus next week to go home for Thanksgiving. We might not see each other for a while."

I did miss RJ; that is, I desired her. But my life was hectic, too compressed, and being with her again was out of the question. Also, Valerie was on my mind. "RJ, maybe we'll get together when you return. If you see your boyfriend tonight, remember—be safe."

"Okay, Davey. I'll attack you when I return."

I plopped down on my couch where we'd so recently frolicked. "Remember, be careful."

Later in the week, I had lunch at Bessie's with Valerie, who spent that night with me. Things were going well for her, but it was my phone call to Evelyn that revealed potentially significant developments. As promised, Evelyn said that she had had lunch off-campus with Carla Pogue.

"We had a pleasant, light-hearted chat," Evelyn reported. "We've always gotten along. But when I raised the matter of that strange man who photographed you, she was startled. Carla mumbled something unintelligible and clammed up."

"That says a lot." I opened the fridge and extracted the last cold bottle of Heineken.

"Yes. She knows something, but I'm not there yet. So, I can't cash in on what you called our 'Faustian bargain,' but I'm working on it."

Ever the calculator, Evelyn outlined her "strategic plan." Carla's sixty-second birthday was coming up. Evelyn had invited Carla, two of their mutual friends, and Carla's sister, Angie, to a birthday dinner party at her home. Angie's niece, a senior at Traymore, was searching for a teaching job. And, said Evelyn, "I can get her an excellent position in Loudon County."

I thought it might assist Evelyn if I revealed what else Sheriff Goetzke had told me. "That's a great plan. It might help if Carla was aware that you knew something about the photographer. The sheriff said his name is Aubrey Ray Blount, a convicted felon." I took a swig of Heineken.

"That's alarming. I'm sure Carla doesn't know this. She sees herself as the guardian of the president's reputation. This might loosen her tongue, especially if I pretend to have additional information about Blount."

As we were ending our phone call, Evelyn said, "You are a clever devil, David."

"You're pretty shrewd yourself, Develyn."

————

On my way from the library to my office early that week, I saw Elzic Barton and Carla Pogue walking in my direction. They swerved away down a side path when they saw me. For whatever reason—out of fear, out of loathing, on advice of counsel—Barton always seemed to go out of his way to avoid encountering me.

When I entered my office building, I saw a new "ride-board" posting in the hallway where students and faculty seeking or offering rides to various destinations for Thanksgiving could post their names. Sue Ewal was there, scanning the board for a ride to New York. "Sue, you're welcome to come with me," I said. "I'm going up there."

"That's really nice of you, professor. There could be others who will need a ride."

So, I tacked up a 3x5 card:

> *Ride to New York City area. Leave Jubal Early Hall*
> *at 8:00 A.M., November 25; return November*
> *30. Can take three more passengers.*
> *Professor David Pritchard, x3974.*

The next day Kim Sherman, a first semester senior, called me at the office to see if I had room for four more passengers.

I told her, "My old Chevy has room if we can tolerate one another for several hours in tight quarters."

"Cozy is good," she said. "We'll be at Jubal Early Hall at 8 A.M.".

I later learned that Kim Sherman was the antithesis of a typical Traymore College undergraduate. At twenty-four, she was older. And she was a New Yorker in a school where eighty percent of the students were Virginians. She was a math-physics major who took some graduate-level science courses at Virginia Tech, and she was uninterested in teaching. Kim was a no-nonsense tornado of a woman. Her unconcealed hostility toward rural Virginia's social values and the repressive style of President Barton was unrelenting.

Kim and her younger sister, Rachel, had recently transferred to Traymore from the University of Illinois. This was remarkable. While many students transferred from Traymore, few transferred into the college. Those who did transfer in (like RJ) were not attracted to Traymore by its academic reputation. Indeed, the sisters had left Illinois because their father, a former University of Illinois faculty member, had accepted a position at the Brookhaven National Laboratory on Long Island, and coincidentally, the family's closest friends, two prominent physicists, had recently joined Virginia Tech's faculty and moved from Urbana-Champaign to Blacksburg. Traymore, of course, was near Tech and was a reasonable seven-hour drive from New York.

———

On Wednesday, my office mailbox had a letter from Miami of Ohio University, one of the schools to which I'd sent a resume. Fully expecting yet another, "We regret to inform you," it read instead: "We are impressed with your background and hope you will accept our invitation for an interview concerning the position in international law and organizations. Of course, your travel expenses will be covered." It was signed Professor Jacob Kraft, Chair, Department of Political Science.

Professor Kraft asked that I call soon, and I did. Except I first phoned a close friend at the University of Virginia. Phil Johnston was completing his doctoral studies in international law and, like me, was searching for a position. While I was aware that another opportunity might not present itself, and although I could easily teach international law and organizations, my interest and primary expertise was elsewhere: United States foreign policy and national security policy. Phil Johnston was ecstatic when I offered to call Jacob Kraft and suggest him, not me, for the position.

Later that day, driving home, I had a sinking feeling that I'd made a career-ending mistake. This was pressing on my mind as I stopped at the Heaths to see whether Caleb had any new information on Aubrey Blount.

Caleb was out, but I saw Mara. "Caleb called the sheriff," she said. "Harley Goetzke confirmed that that Blount fella's a bad apple, but thankfully we haven't seen him again."

"Thanks, Mara." I turned to get in my car.

"You're lookin' a little down, David. Everything okay?" Mara was concerned. She bit her lower lip.

I shrugged. "Things could be better, I suppose, but thanks for asking."

"David," she implored, now holding both my arms, "why don't you come to church with us on Sunday? When the Holy Spirit moves among us, the world lights up."

The invitation blindsided me. "It's really sweet of you to ask, but . . ."

"Pastor Grundy gets real personal with the Lord. I know you'll like him."

Mara was so sincere and unaffected. She'd be hurt if I turned her down. "Okay, Mara. What time?"

Her face brightened, and she clasped her hands tightly. "David, you'll love it. Come up here about six-thirty, after you've had dinner. We'll all go in Caleb's truck." Mara gazed up at the sky. "Praise the Lord," she exclaimed, and broke out in song: "*All hail the power of Jesus's name! Let angels prostrate fall.*" I'd sung this hymn myself since childhood, and we sang the last line together: "*Bring forth the royal diadem, and crown him Lord of all.*" We laughed and held hands.

On Sunday evening, we left for the Good News Church of God in nearby Dublin. The large, rectangular, white-framed church was packed with worshipers, and, although we arrived ten minutes early, we were fortunate to find seats in a back pew. Folks here differed from most of the parishioners at Christ Church Episcopal in Blacksburg. Dublin, with a population of about twenty-two hundred, was certainly not a university town. The liturgy of the Church of God—and "liturgy" may be an inappropriate word— was informal, and, as stated boldly in the program, worship was based squarely on "the inerrancy and infallibility of the Bible." The congregants were warm and welcoming. They wore their best Sunday-go-to-meeting clothes and appeared to be unpretentious people of integrity with firm beliefs and convictions.

Mara and Caleb knew everyone. They introduced me as their "brother in Christ." The service was lively, as was Pastor

Tyson Grundy. He was a tall, gangly man of about sixty with a pronounced Adam's apple; he wore a black three-piece suit that appeared to be a bit too small.

The music touched me deeply, especially the hymn "Blessed Assurance." It rekindled memories from the 1950s, when my Presbyterian friend, Wayne, and his dad took me multiple times to Madison Square Garden to hear Billy Graham preach.

We Episcopalians didn't usually sing this hymn, but because of George Beverly Shea's memorable, resonant bass voice that accompanied Rev. Graham at his Crusades for Christ, I recalled the words to the first stanza. People nearby turned and smiled when I raised my hands and sang it from memory. "*Blessed assurance, Jesus is mine! O What a foretaste of glory divine!*" Perhaps they concluded that I, too, was an evangelical Christian.

Rev. Grundy invited those who had not previously done so to "come forward for Christ." Two people made their way to the altar. Caleb and Mara stared expectantly at me, but I didn't budge. After the service, Pastor Grundy shook my hand vigorously at the door, saying, "Come back soon, son."

"You and I can return to Piney Woods now," said Caleb, looking at me. "A friend will take Mara home after her committee meeting with the Women of Good News."

On the drive back to the cottage, I turned to Caleb. "I enjoyed that. Good music, good preaching, good people." The sun had set. Trees were silhouetted against the lingering light.

Never a man of many words, Caleb grunted. He then cleared his throat and sighed deeply. "David, don't tell Mara what I'm 'bout to tell ya." This was out of character. The two of them were exceedingly close. "The Lord spoke to me. He said He'd call me home soon. When this happens, Mara will be upset and alone. Could you comfort her until others arrive?"

"Caleb, are you sure you hadn't downed a mason jar of that good Floyd County white lightening just before the Lord called?"

Caleb was silent and grim. A single tear ran slowly down his face. He trembled. I felt horrible. "I'm so sorry, Caleb. Of course, I'll be with Mara when the time comes. It's our secret."

He pulled the truck over to the side of the road and placed his hand on my shoulder. I, in turn, put my hand on his shoulder. We had an agreement.

"Thank you, David."

———

Our drive north to New York on the Monday before Thanksgiving turned out to be consequential. I knew only one of my passengers, Sue Ewal. I'd never met Kim Sherman, her sister, Rachel, or the other two students.

Kim exuded confidence in both her demeanor and appearance. She was at least five-foot-nine-inches tall, with shoulder length dark hair, olive skin, ample and unusually well-defined lips, and almond-shaped eyes that took in everything (and everyone). She had a fine, fine figure. *Here's someone who's been around the block a couple of times*, I concluded. She was certainly attractive, but "lasciviously frisky" is a more revealing description. Kim's faux rabbit fur vest, form fitting slacks, and leather riding boots declared, "Let's play." And play she did. Her left leg brushed my right thigh while I drove.

Rachel was, if anything, even more playful—and certainly bawdier—than her older sister. Indeed, she'd memorized a seemingly limitless number of off-color limericks. Her physical appearance was also different. Rachel was shorter, about five-foot-four, and had a fairer complexion and curly light brown hair. With her long wool dress and gray sweater, she dressed more conservatively than Kim. Rachel was what grandmothers mean by "cute."

The Sherman sisters were non-stop talkers. We hadn't driven beyond Roanoke before Kim and Rachel began to pepper us with their salty exchanges:

Kim: "There's been no Moses in my bulrushes in weeks."

Rachel: "Well, for weeks no one has parted my Red Sea."

This sisterly banter continued for much of the trip, and Rachel kept all of us in stitches with a seemingly inexhaustible supply of limericks and jokes.

Although humor was always in the air, most of the talk—or venting—touched on faculty legal actions against Traymore, the merits of the cafeteria's biscuits and gravy, and the universally despised dress code. I also learned for the first time that Barton had exploded when his daughter was supposedly "knocked up" by a Virginia Tech guy two years before I arrived. Sue remarked, "Everyone knows that Traymore's restrictive regulations became even more oppressive after this incident."

About the time we crossed the Delaware River into New Jersey, Kim—who had pressed herself against me in the front seat—blurted out, "I have a fantastic idea. Let's form a student chapter of the American Civil Liberties Union. Professor Pritchard can be our faculty adviser. Barton will wet his pants, he'll deny our request, and guess who will offer us free legal representation?"

"The ACLU," we shouted in unison. By now, late November 1969, I was in full combat mode against the Barton administration.

His regime was under siege with scathing press coverage, a mounting number of legal actions, and high-profile events on campus like the Vietnam panel and the large turnout for the ACLU speech on student rights. And, unknown to Barton, *de facto* alliances had formed among key students, faculty, and even a senior administrator (covertly, with Evelyn).

"Brilliant idea, Kim. Let's go for it," I said. Thanks to Kim, we now had yet another line of attack.

After crossing the George Washington Bridge into New York, I drove south on the Henry Hudson Parkway and dropped the students off in Manhattan at a subway stop near Columbia University. We agreed to meet there Sunday morning for the return trip.

I had a relaxing holiday break with my folks in Westchester and even found time to purchase a small bottle of Bellodgia perfume for Mara Heath. On Sunday, I met the students at the appointed time in Manhattan for our drive back to Traymore.

Kim insisted on again sitting next to me. "I sit next to Dave." No longer was I Professor Pritchard to Kim, although no one else took this liberty. "Oh yeah, big sis," giggled Rachel as she elbowed her sister and settled into the front seat by the window.

The drive back to Southwest Virginia was a slog. We were slowed by alternating patterns of rain and sleet. When we finally neared the Traymore exit from I-81, Kim's innate playfulness increased in intensity. Her hand rested lightly on my thigh as her leg pressed harder against me. I pretended not to notice. Kim smiled, bantered with Rachel, and generally feigned innocence.

As we approached the college in what was now the early evening, I said, "You've been such a convivial bunch that I'd be happy for all of you to meet my German shepherd and perhaps have some wine and cheese at my Claytor Lake cottage."

"Yes!" said Kim.

The others, no doubt attuned to Kim's not-so-subtle advances, politely declined the invitation. When we arrived at the college and Rachel stepped out of the car, she ribbed her sister, "Have fun in the bulrushes."

Well, Kim and I did frolic in the bulrushes, and the Red Sea was parted, but sex was somewhat tentative and awkward despite hours of escalating erotic tension in the front seat.

The following afternoon, Kim knocked on my open office door wearing a dress code-violating mini-skirt. She sauntered in, closed the door, and leapt onto my lap. She gave me a "Baby, I've got the hungries for yo love" kind of kiss. She then slid off my lap to straddle my left leg, rocking back and forth and circling a hand in the air as if lassoing cattle.

To the tune of Wilson Pickett's "Mustang Sally," she sang of Mustang Kimmy: "All you want to do is ride around Kimmy— ride, Kimmy, ride." Nibbling my ear, the over-perfumed Kim whispered, "Let's go back to the cottage. I'll fuck your balls off."

Caught off guard, *way* off guard, I stammered, "Isn't that a bit extreme?"

And, so, another crucial alliance was consummated, now with a student co-conspirator and soon-to-be plaintiff in the forthcoming ACLU suit against the college.

14

December

It was Tuesday, December second when I walked up the gravel driveway to deliver the promised Bellodgia perfume to Mara and some Red Man chewing tobacco for Caleb. As I neared their small house, I froze. Perched on the mailbox was a large, sooty black raven. The bird let out a deep, gurgling call and stretched its wings as I approached, but it did not fly away.

Although Edgar Allan Poe stayed for only a year, he and I attended the same university. Members of the University of Virginia's sixty-five-year old Raven Society were required to recite at least one verse of *The Raven* at their initiation. Fragments of this familiar poem flashed through my mind:

Ah, distinctly I remember it was in the bleak December. . . .

"Prophet!" said I, "thing of evil!—prophet still, if bird or devil!"

The Heaths, and many others over the ages, saw ravens as harbingers of momentous, often tragic, events. Given Caleb's conviction that the Lord would soon "call him home," I kept the bird's presence to myself when I knocked on their door.

Caleb shuffled his feet and said, "David, ya' shouldn't a done it," when I handed him the tobacco. Mara, however, was ecstatic about receiving something she'd only dreamed of. The Bellodgia earned me a warm hug and effusive, "Bless you, David."

Before I left my cottage for class on Wednesday morning, Valerie called. "Guess what, love?"

"You miss me desperately."

"Yes," she said with a lilt in her voice, "but it's something else. I've been accepted at Johns Hopkins, and with a fellowship."

I shot a fist into the air. "Fantastic! Let's celebrate. How about spending Saturday night at the Hotel Roanoke?"

"You're so sweet. I love you *almost* as much as I love Xena."

———

Later that day, I had lunch with Evelyn in the faculty dining room. We'd been lunching there about three times a month and, by now, no one thought much of it. Barton and Carla Pogue were aware that Evelyn was gathering information from me about forthcoming student and faculty machinations. Several of my trusted colleagues and some select student leaders (Valerie, Sue, and Kim) understood that I received intelligence from Evelyn about the administration. This backchannel was useful for all parties, but especially for me.

"David, there was a breakthrough Monday night at my birthday dinner party for Carla." Evelyn smiled smugly.

"Oh?" I said with muted enthusiasm and some trepidation. I was not particularly anxious to honor my half of our Faustian bargain.

Leaning in toward me, Evelyn said in a hushed voice, "President Barton *did* contract with that Roanoke investigation agency to keep track of you and your activities. However, Carla was horrified to learn of Aubrey Blount and his criminal background. She *wants* to think the president knows nothing about Blount, but she's uncertain."

"This is helpful information. Will Carla tell Barton about the conversation the two of you had?"

"No, and not because I offered to get her niece that teaching job. The loyal, tight-lipped, protective Carla Pogue that people see in the office is a different person when she's with trusted friends—especially after she's had wine and two of my screwdrivers."

"Really!"

"Yes. One obvious reason Carla won't reveal our conversation to the president is that this would invite serious retribution. She said that President Barton had directed her to tell no one and keep this matter strictly to herself. And there's a more fundamental reason. Carla is a devout, law-abiding Christian who fears that, in her words, 'there could be more.'"

"More?"

Evelyn cocked her head and rolled her eyes. "Only the budgeteers in Richmond know Traymore's budget as well as Carla, and they rarely audit the college. When she asked President Barton about how this private agency was being paid, he said only, 'Don't you worry about that. I'll take care of it.'" A triumphant smirk spread across Evelyn's face.

"Bingo! Misappropriation of public funds. What a gift." I threw a napkin up in the air, drawing stares from the next table.

"Hold on, cowboy. We don't *know* this yet. Carla is certain that the expenditure was not authorized by the Board of Visitors because she attends all board meetings. The president might have worked something out informally with the board chairman, or, much less likely, he paid for it out of his own pocket. At any rate,

Carla said to me: 'I'll tell you and only you what, if anything, I discover.'"

I was elated. All expenditures, especially one of such sensitivity, would have to come before the full board, and it was inconceivable that Barton would pay for this expensive surveillance himself. "I owe you big time, Develyn," I said.

She replied, "New Year's Eve in my tower room?"

"To resume and escalate our . . . um . . . activities?" I asked, though I knew the answer. I thought of Valerie. Whether consciously or not, my mind categorized Evelyn—and for that matter, Kim—as *sui generous*. These were two radically different women, yet each had depth and strength of character. I liked them immensely.

But as for love . . . it was only Val. Yes, this sounds contrived, self-serving, and certainly unethical. But that's not how I saw it then, and that's not how I saw it looking back over the years.

"Sounds devilish." Evelyn's shoe brushed against mine under the table. I now had a second, and very different, date with the dean.

We'd finished lunch, and Evelyn was about to get up from the table when I gave her a *quid pro quo* to relay to Barton. "Within days, and complying with college regulations for forming new clubs, some students will file a formal application to create a student chapter of the ACLU."

Evelyn gasped. "President Barton will have a stroke."

———

I'd been delinquent in attending POF meetings at the ARSE-N-ALL bar, so I stopped by late that afternoon. At twenty-one faculty members—including for the first time, Rev. Bill Vaughn—it was our largest gathering ever. I ordered an Old Horsey and waded into the banter.

"That scar doesn't look *too* ugly," said John Manikas, pointing at my face. "Want to trade it for this?" The former paratrooper pulled up his pants leg to show everyone his prosthesis. "What sacred Traymore tradition did you butt fuck this week?"

Laying my arm across the shoulders of my good friend, whose ripe odor suggested that he hadn't showered in at least a week, I replied, "Careful, Shit-on-a-Stick," referring, of course, to his prosthesis, "or I'll tell another West Virginia joke." And, so it went for the next couple of hours.

I told the group that Kim Sherman would head a student chapter of the ACLU.

"She's my best physics student," said John. Then, poking me in the ribs, he said, "I *wonder* who'll be the chapter's adviser?"

Another faculty member spoke up. "Barton will strangle that one before it's ever born."

Heads nodded.

"That's the idea," I said. "The ACLU will then sue his ass off."

"Clever, Pritchard, clever," said Tom O'Keefe. "What other constructive things have you been up to?"

"Well, after my speech last month—and I really appreciate several of you being there—I've occasionally been followed by someone." I crunched my beer can.

"Surprise, surprise," said Manikas, sweeping a hand across the table, sending several cans onto the floor. "Barton would love for someone to blow your brains out, to succeed where Vincent Tavernetti failed."

"Could all of you keep an eye out for a heavy-set man with a crew cut who . . ." Everyone laughed and pointed at Manikas. "No, no. The guy drives a mid-fifties red pickup. John's truck is newer, and, while it's hard to believe, Manikas is actually better looking."

John tousled my hair. "Pritchard, hang onto that shotgun I loaned you."

Before the group disbanded, Bill Vaughn—who hadn't said much—asked, "How many know about Hannah Carpenter?" I was the only one who nodded affirmatively because I happened to be in Bill's office when Hannah had tearfully related her story.

One of the relatively few women on the faculty outside of the large education department, Hannah was a geographer who had published in leading journals. An irate President Barton had summoned her to his office. "As I sat there," she'd sobbed, "he circled me and, red-faced, shouted, 'You're a lesbian! You're corrupting our girls. Resign or be fired.'" Hannah said she was in shock, had denied the accusation, and asked Barton for evidence.

According to Hannah, Barton had responded, "Where I got this information is none of your business. Have your resignation on my desk today."

Stunned silence followed. Reverend Bill, whose lawsuit was the first of several against the college, and whom everyone respected, spoke in a subdued voice. "Hannah submitted her resignation. We prayed together. I told her that Saint Luke provides assurance that 'The kingdom of God is within each of us.'"

We were all upset as we left the ARSE-N-ALL. I was livid. A very different biblical passage came to mind, one from Romans:

"Vengeance is mine; I will repay, saith the Lord." The Holy Spirit works in unpredictable ways.

———

Valerie and I hadn't driven more than five miles north toward Roanoke on I-81 before I noticed an old red pickup truck that kept about two hundred feet behind me. "Val," I said, "think we're being followed." When I slowed down, it slowed; when I sped up, so did the truck. After another few miles, I pulled into a rest stop. So did the pickup. It parked some distance behind me, off to the side and almost out of sight.

"I'm frightened," said Valerie.

Before going into the restroom, I instructed her, "Stay here and lock the doors. Don't worry. If that's Blount, he won't show his face."

"Where are you going?"

"To scare the bejesus out of someone. I'll be back soon."

The circular concrete block restroom had two entrances—one for travelers in passenger cars, another on the opposite side for truckers. I entered the closest door and exited on the other side, where several eighteen-wheelers were parked. With the large trucks as a shield, I began circling the perimeter of the parking area before crossing back over to the other (car) side, where I crouched behind some bushes. I crept cautiously toward my target, making sure not to be visible in a rearview mirror.

There it was, the rusty red Ford F100 that Caleb had described. I memorized the Virginia license plate, sprinted up to the passenger side, and glanced quickly at Aubrey Ray Blount. He was gazing straight ahead with sleepy eyes while working to dislodge a booger. I tapped on his window. His head jerked back as if he'd been punched, and he might have soiled his pants. Blount glared in my direction, but because of the angle of the sun, he may not have seen me clearly, or at all, even though I stood just four feet from his window. He gripped the steering wheel as if strangling a python and, white knuckled, started up his pickup, and peeled out of the parking area spewing black exhaust.

I returned to my car, where I assured Valerie, "We won't see Blount again, at least not on this trip."

––––––

The Hotel Roanoke was built in 1882 by the Norfolk and Western Railroad and had undergone many changes by 1969. But the imposing brick Tudor-style structure remained the region's most distinguished hotel, surpassed only by the Greenbrier— forty miles to the northwest near White Sulphur Springs, West Virginia.

We arrived at the hotel about three o'clock and delighted in our room's high ceiling and view to the west of the Blue Ridge Mountains. Our late afternoon lovemaking was unhurried and tender. Afterward, Val ran a finger along my scar, kissed it, and smiled.

At dinner in the hotel's Regency Room, after the waiter asked us both for proof of age, I ordered a bottle of champagne. I offered a toast, which to some might have seemed duplicitous. It was not. I did have things to sort out with Evelyn and Kim in my campaign to oust Barton, but I loved Valerie deeply and sincerely.

"Here's to my lovely Valerie," I said. "May we always be happy *together*." We both ordered prime rib and the hotel's signature peanut soup. Our hands touched across the table. That night we slept close to one another, cupped tightly like teaspoons in a drawer. We returned to Christiansburg the next morning.

———

Later that week, I made a rare breakfast visit before class to Oddie's Cafe in Traymore. I parked on the street across from the restaurant, but something caught my eye. I walked about a half a block and there it was, a rusty red pickup truck with the Virginia license plate number I'd committed to memory. Sheriff Goetzke had said that Blount was dangerous, but not smart.

On alert, I went to open the café's glass door as Blount was coming out. I stood directly in front of him, just five feet outside the door. I was tense and angry, fully prepared for a physical confrontation. Our eyes locked as he exited. "Mr. Blount," I said, "continue to hassle me, and you return to jail."

Blount stiffened, clearly surprised that I knew his name and criminal background. He lowered his shoulder and pushed hard against me. I stepped back, but still blocked his path. "Push harder, fucker," I threatened, "and it's another assault and battery for you."

Blount looked down and, like a fullback, bulled his way past me, growling, "Asshole." He got into his truck and drove away.

I stopped by the sheriff's office to report this and the past week's incident on I-81. "This is good and bad news, David," said Harland Goetzke, leaning back in his chair. "You may see less of Blount, and much less of his truck. If his surveillance of you continues, now that it's been detected, he'll have another vehicle. Or, someone else might take his place."

"Harley, I know for certain that Barton hired that Roanoke investigation agency."

"Told ya. Don't surprise me none, knowing Elzic Barton. Raises questions." Harley paused and scratched his chin. "Barton's rigid and angry. Once that coon dog is on a scent, he don't give up, even when the chase leads over a cliff."

I didn't mention my suspicion that the investigation agency was being paid with unauthorized state funds, but that could be what Harley meant by "raises questions." I turned to leave. "I'm late for class."

"Saw Mara Heath the other day," Harley said as he stood to see me out. "She sure *loves* that perfume. Oh, and I'll call over to Giles County and tell them about Blount. He lives in Pearisburg."

"Thanks, Harley."

———

Late that afternoon, before dinner and as the sun was setting, Xena and I walked by the lake. The temperature was dropping. A light breeze came up, carrying with it the distinctive piney, organic smell of Claytor Lake. But it was the sunset that stuck in my mind. It was not just the usual reds, pinks, and oranges on the horizon, but a psychedelic mélange of colors that infused and reflected off the water. Even Xena was transfixed as she pressed against me.

More extraordinary, and something I'd never witnessed before or since, was what occurred after the sun had set. A brilliant celestial blue haze hovered above and trembled around the oak trees that flanked the Heath's house. Luminescent flares, reminiscent of the glints given off by the sparklers we lit as kids, shot out from the shimmering blue mist.

It was difficult to fall asleep that night as the surreal bluish haze penetrated my window shades, painted the walls, and danced in every corner of the room. The aura had a sentient, even spiritual, quality.

Not long after I finally closed my eyes, the phone rang. Startled, I leapt out of bed, tripping over a rug before answering it.

"David! Come quickly. It's Caleb."

"I'm coming, Mara." I threw on a sweater, jeans, and shoes, then sprinted the five hundred feet up the driveway to the Heaths' and shouldered open their front door. Mara was sobbing on her knees next to Caleb. He was on his back in red pajama bottoms and tobacco-stained T-shirt on the floor just outside the bedroom. Caleb's eyes and mouth were open. His face was pale white. No pulse, no breathing. I pounded on his chest for five minutes, although I knew it was too late. The Lord had called him home.

I hugged Mara, then phoned the sheriff's office. The deputy on the graveyard shift answered.

"Dave Pritchard calling from the Heaths' place at Piney Woods Cottages. Caleb Heath just passed away. Send somebody quickly. I'm here with Mara. Harley would want to know."

"Yes, sir. I'll wake him. Someone will be there soon."

I returned to Mara, bent down, and put my arm around her. In a low voice, I asked whether there was anyone else she would like me to call.

"Reverend Tyson Grundy," she mumbled. Her hands covered her face. "Number is next to the phone."

It was not quite one in the morning when I dialed Rev. Grundy. The blue mist outside had dissipated. When he answered, I identified myself. "It's David Pritchard, pastor. Mara Heath asked that I call you. Caleb has died. I'm with her here at Piney Woods."

"I remember you, David. Tell Mara I'm on my way."

Within twenty minutes, Mara was being comforted by Rev. Grundy and his wife.

Soon the sheriff arrived with flashing blue lights. When Harley Goetzke saw his old friend on the floor, his shoulders drooped, and his eyes filled with tears. Harley knelt down on one knee, gently placed a hand on Caleb's chest, and said simply, "Ole buddy."

We all bowed our heads as Rev. Grundy offered a prayer: "Lord God, Brother Caleb prayed to you best because he loved you best. Caleb loved all men, the moneyed and moneyless, the powerful and powerless. Caleb *knew*, with faith unshakeable, that our dear Lord's love is eternal."

Rev. Grundy then prayed that Caleb's soul be committed to God. He turned to Mara. Placing both his hands lightly on Mara's still bowed head, he quoted St. Matthew. "Blessed are they that mourn: for they shall be comforted." Then, bending down to her, and with a voice that was scarcely audible, he assured her, "You will not be alone, sister. Christ will enfold you in his loving arms."

Harley Goetzke was preparing to leave, and the pastor's wife offered to spend the rest of the night with Mara. The Heaths' relatives would be arriving from around the state. Caleb's body would soon be taken to Yancy's New River Funeral Home. Time for me to leave. "Mara, my dear," I whispered, "you just let me know what I can do."

After glancing at the pastor, Mara took my hand. "David, I don't know how to thank you. Could I ask one more favor?"

"Anything."

"Reverend Grundy said he'll hold a funeral service for Caleb this Saturday. You're good with words. Could you say something about Caleb?"

"Of course." Because Mara knew and liked Valerie, I asked, "Could I bring someone with me?"

"Bring anyone and everyone—Matthew, Mark, and Isaiah, too."

———

After breakfast at Bessie's on Saturday, Valerie and I headed for the Good News Church of God in Dublin for what would be a new experience for her, a Roman Catholic. We had attended Christ Church Episcopal together, and the Catholic and Episcopal liturgies were similar. Services at the Good News Church were less structured.

Fortunately, the first three rows of pews were reserved for relatives and close friends of the deceased; otherwise, it was standing room only. The open casket service had Caleb, uncharacteristically, all gussied up in a suit and tie. He looked content, but I knew that he'd rather be wearing bib overalls when he met St. Peter.

Valerie and I were shown to seats in the second row, not far from Harley Goetzke. The opening hymn, selected by Mara, was "I Am the Bread of Life." Each of its five stanzas ended with, "And I will raise them up on the last day." The packed church resonated with the worshipers' full-throated singing.

The service moved right along as Rev. Grundy delivered a heartfelt homily about Caleb's selflessness and compassion for others. This was followed by a tearful remembrance by Caleb's younger brother, who'd come up from Bristol. Then it was my turn.

I walked to the pulpit and smiled at Mara, who was dressed in black and sat only a few feet from me. She nodded.

"The Good Book tells us to do justice, and to love kindness, and to walk humbly with your God. That defines a good man. Caleb, we all know, was a good man.

"Last month, when I first attended the Good News Church, I was overwhelmed by the warmth of your welcome, especially considering—albeit unbeknown to any of you—that there was an Episcopalian in your midst."

There was polite laughter.

"We are blessed today to be among fellow believers because I have a story, a true story, that all Christians will understand and treasure.

"Mara had to stay after the service in November, so Caleb and I drove back to Piney Woods together. On the way, he told me something in strict confidence, a confidence I have honored until now. He did not want to alarm Mara. 'David,' he said, 'the Lord is soon going to call me home.' I'm ashamed to confess that, at the time, I was a doubting Thomas. Then, the very night that he passed, a strange and beautiful blue haze enveloped the Heath's house."

Mara nodded her head vigorously and wiped away tears.

"I know now that it could only have been the Holy Spirit coming for Caleb.

"When I think of Caleb, I recall what a great Baptist preacher said a hundred years ago: 'A good character is the best tombstone. So, carve your name on hearts, not on marble.' Caleb carved on our hearts.

"Finally, next to God and his beloved Mara, there was something else that Caleb loved."

I pulled a red tin can out of my suit pocket and held it high. "Red Man tobacco." The congregation erupted in laughter as I placed the tin next to the casket.

The service ended with the Lord's Prayer, a benediction, and Caleb's favorite hymn, "Just as I Am." The congregation, hands in the air, stood and swayed to the music.

Just as I am, without one plea,

But that thy blood was shed for me,

And that thou bidd'st me come to thee,

O Lamb of God, I come, I come.

Mara, surrounded by relatives, stood at the church door with Pastor and Sarah Grundy. When Valerie and I finally made our way through the receiving line and hugged Mara, I whispered to her, "You were very strong, my dear." As Val and I turned to leave, we detected a familiar scent. Bellodgia, of course. Only the best for Caleb.

———

The campus emptied out during the long Christmas break, when I was to fly to Colorado for a family reunion. But, while many students had already left, including Valerie and RJ, a traditional holiday dance was always held on the last day of final exams. The feature event was a contest among the first ten couples to have registered. Marigold Dunfree, my first date at Traymore, had registered us way back in September after our traumatic dinner at Valerie's.

Marigold was an athletic and talented dancer. While I used to be pretty good with the lindy hop and rock and roll, I hadn't done much since the Ardsley High School dances that were held after every basketball game in the village "Chocolateria." Unsurprisingly, I was the sole faculty contestant, and the oldest.

Couples picked their own tunes in advance and were allotted only seven minutes on the dance floor. Unlike the other contestants, Marigold and I had had just one brief practice session. We chose "Sweet Little Sixteen" and "Devil with a Blue Dress On."

In my wrinkled khakis and orange cotton shirt, I was wholly out-classed by my partner's stunning magenta 1920s-style flapper dress. When it was our turn on the floor, the students and their dates let loose with raucous cheering and rhythmic clapping, especially when I twirled Marigold around and rolled her over my back. We didn't win, but to our surprise and delight, we landed in third place.

No sooner had we finished performing and congratulating one another than Kim Sherman, whom I hadn't noticed before, rushed up and kissed me on the cheek. "You two were fantastic." Kim then rejoined her date and blended into the crowd.

Marigold stiffened. "Who the hell was that?"

"Kim Sherman. She and I will likely soon be suing the college with help from the ACLU."

"Does Valerie know her?"

"Not sure; probably. They share a common passion for changing things around here."

Yenta-like, Marigold ventured into sensitive territory. "You and Valerie have gotten pretty chummy, I understand." She tilted her head to one side as a knowing smile spread across her face.

"I'm very fond of her."

"Do you love her?"

"You're pretty nosey, Ms. Marigold Dunfree. But, yes, I do."

Marigold wrapped me in a boa constrictor-like hug. "That's *exactly* what I wanted to hear."

I exhaled. "Whew, I was afraid you'd relieve me of my manhood if I gave the wrong answer."

———

Because of Carla Pogue's revelation, Evelyn had learned of President Barton's role in hiring a private agency to tail me. To my chagrin, Evelyn had now satisfied her part of our bargain. New Year's Eve was the agreed-upon time for me to honor my end of the deal. We confirmed this when I returned from Colorado.

While I was uneasy about our date, I hoped that it might be as personally and politically rewarding as our Halloween encounter. Hopefully, it wouldn't be quite as kinky.

When I arrived at Evelyn's, she came to the door dressed primly in a beige sweater with a matching mid-length wool skirt. She wore pearl earrings and a small gold cross on a delicate chain. "Come into my lair, Mr. Devil." I kissed her on the cheek.

Evelyn was a gifted cook, although considering what I usually ate, anything that didn't come out of a can impressed me. She'd prepared a savory dinner of southern fried chicken, baked potatoes with cheddar cheese, and collard greens with bacon.

Dessert was homemade chocolate cream pie. I contributed two bottles of my precious St. Julien Bordeaux, although by the time I arrived, Evelyn had already downed a screwdriver and was mixing a second.

"Want one?" she asked.

"No thanks. I'll stick with wine."

As before, her antique walnut dining table was set elegantly. Unlike the last time, however, I came prepared to say grace, having memorized a blessing sometimes said in church.

Life is short.
And we do not have too much time to gladden the hearts
of those who travel the way with us.
So be swift to love. . . .

(Here I paused and looked at Evelyn.)

Make haste to be kind.
And may the blessing of God, Father, Son, and Holy Spirit
be upon you and remain with you always.

"Amen," we said together.

"I do love that," said Evelyn, blushing. She unfolded her linen napkin, glanced over at me, and took a sip of wine. Seemingly gathering her thoughts, she paused and asked, "Do you really believe in the Holy Trinity?"

This triggered a lengthy, heart-felt response. For most of our dinnertime, I related my recent experience with Caleb. The raven, the Lord's calling him home, the other-worldly blue haze, Mara's late-night phone call, Caleb's death, and the church service.

"That gives me chills," said Evelyn, fingering her cross. "How did it affect you?"

"Well, after ten years of higher education, when I was awash in evidence-based research, my religious beliefs were diluted from convictions into hopes. This episode with Caleb, however, moved me profoundly. At its core, faith is fueled by feelings, emotions. Saying this is in *no way* a criticism of the faithful—quite the contrary. I must confess that I'm now much more open to the mysteries of the Holy Spirit. That is, to God as spiritually active."

As I spoke, Evelyn nodded in agreement. Her face retained its raspberry red flush and she unconsciously laid a hand on her heart. "You're devilish, but you're no devil, David. Come with me."

We stood and kissed warmly. She took my hand, and we climbed the creaky, narrow stairs to her tower room. There was no more light in that circular space than last time, but thankfully she no longer insisted that I wear a mask.

"You're a wonderful person," I whispered.

Evelyn's inhibitions had largely vanished. Our lovemaking was not constrained by odd sexual hang-ups. It was tender and trusting. Afterward, of course, she was no longer a thirty-seven-year-old virgin.

We lay together on our backs in the dark and talked openly, frankly. We'd kiss or touch each other, but mostly we just enjoyed a revelatory exchange of stories, ideas, fears, and values.

"Do . . . you love someone?" Evelyn asked hesitantly.

"Yes, I do."

There was a lengthy pause before Evelyn finally exhaled. "You are both very fortunate."

"We are. But you're special to me. You are *much* more than a friend." I reached over and took her hand.

"And you," said Evelyn, squeezing my hand, "are my best friend, the only person in the world in whom I can confide with complete trust. You've changed me."

"You *bet*, milady."

"No. Not *that*." She elbowed me. "I feel really awful about what I've done. I've truly hurt some students, especially those who were expelled because of what was found in their rooms during the trumped-up fire alarms I called."

I stroked her arm. "That's how we met," I said. "Mary Jo Shifflet. Back in September."

"Yes. I feel a nagging guilt about what I did to her. And others. I don't do those searches anymore, and you might have noticed my lax enforcement of the dress code."

I kissed her shoulder.

"So," Evelyn said, turning toward me and resting her hand on my chest, "what are *you* most guilty about? I bet you've been dating students, perhaps our probable *summa cum laude*, Valerie Tavernetti?"

"My dear, I keep the relationship between you and me, and all other personal matters, strictly confidential."

She kissed my cheek. "Good. So, what about guilt?"

"Only pathological narcissists and Stalinist-types are guilt free. Sure, I suppose there are aspects of my confrontation with Barton that might be faulted for allowing a worthy goal to justify employing peculiar means, but there's no guilt." I rolled toward her and rose up. I rested one hand on Evelyn's hip; with the other, I slowly ran my index finger between her breasts.

"You're *so* fresh," she said as she grabbed my wayward finger and brought it to her lips.

After some hesitation, I admitted, "I have been burdened by something that happened three years ago when I was a graduate student at UVA."

I told her about when I was elected as the sole student representative on my department's Rank and Tenure Committee. One of the eight faculty members on the committee was Professor Brady Shaffer, among the least accomplished of all our faculty. His publications were few, shoddy, and polemical, and he was a mediocre teacher who often didn't show up for class.

Yet, Brady had a big heart. He never mentioned it, but like Bill Vaughn, he was an ordained Methodist minister. There was no worthy cause that Brady didn't support . . . passionately, always passionately. He was kicked out of Brazil in 1964, not because he married a nun—although he *did* marry a nun—but because he organized peasant protests against exploitive landowners. The next year, Brady Shaffer was with Martin Luther King in Selma. The Reverends King and Shaffer were on a Martin and Brady first-name basis. Brady was a good person.

One day at a Rank and Tenure meeting, when I thought Brady was absent, I made a derogatory comment about this decent man whom I really liked. "Professor Shaffer, as we all know, is no scholar." He was sitting six feet away. Brady lowered his head but said nothing. He was hurt. I was ashamed. Of course, he graciously accepted my apology, but I wanted to crawl into a hole.

He retired that year and, within months, died in his native Texas hill country. I know that the heavenly welcome mat was out for Brady, but it might not be extended to a short-sighted dolt like me.

When I finished, Evelyn patted my butt, rolled over on her side, and kissed me. "You're human after all, Pritchard."

We spent the night together in her tower room. The next morning, I returned to my cottage. It was the first day of 1970. Our personal alliance was now set in concrete.

15

Evaluation

Classes were scheduled to resume on Monday, but the new year started off tensely. My cottage phone rang.

"Hi, Davey."

"RJ, how was your Christmas break?"

"Okay . . . but I should've listened to you. I missed my period last month."

I couldn't speak. Time stopped. *Thank God I pulled away*, I thought.

"Davey, you still there?"

"No. . . . Uh, yes." After a moment, I asked, "Are you pregnant?"

"Don't know. If so, it could only be my boyfriend at Tech. I'm afraid to see any of the local doctors. They can't be trusted. My friends say they tell the college."

I'd heard the same thing from other students and, months ago, from Cob Maplewood. However, the doc who treated my facial wound, Clay Sadler, seemed to be a sensible professional. "I'll make a call for you, RJ. Think I know a doctor with integrity."

"If I'm not pregnant, Davey, I'll be really nice to you. In fact, if I *am* pregnant, I'll have something really nice for you."

Fear now trumped temptation when it came to this

incendiary nineteen-year-old Lolita. I mumbled something incoherent and hung up the phone.

———

Dr. Sadler remembered me when I called him on Monday morning. He asked about my scar and readily agreed to see RJ when I informed him of her situation. "I'm afraid there are some older members of our medical community who don't respect the confidentiality of their student patients. Elzic Barton's insistence on controlling the personal lives of young women is disgraceful."

I called RJ. "You have an appointment with Dr. Sadler, Wednesday at nine."

———

That same afternoon I received another unexpected call, this time in my office. "Professor Pritchard, I'm Gladys McNally, Bea's mother."

"Oh, yes. Bea's a dedicated campus leader. What can I do for you?"

"Bea speaks so highly of you, professor." Mrs. McNally's voice was shaky. "She—she . . . says you might help." Cough. "Sorry, I shouldn't be bothering you." She blew her nose and took a deep breath. "I apologize. I don't know where to turn."

"It's no trouble at all, Mrs. McNally. Is Bea okay?"

"Well, she's . . ." Cough. "This is hard for me, professor. We're Catholic. Bea . . . is . . . pregnant."

I rolled my eyes. Pregnancy was in season.

"She's too young, and she doesn't want this," said Mrs. McNally. "Bea's the first in the family to go to college. The boy was a blind date. She's crushed and ashamed. I'd hoped you might suggest . . . something."

Mrs. McNally couldn't bring herself to say "abortion," which was illegal throughout the country. Moreover, I knew as much about that subject as I did about translating haiku from ancient Japanese tombstones: nothing. But if anyone might know something, it would be the free-spirited New Yorker, Kim Sherman.

Indeed, twenty minutes after I spoke with Kim on the phone, she called me back. "His name is Dr. Braco Ludomir." She read me his phone number. "He's from Yugoslavia, a real M.D., not a back-alley wire hanger type. He practices fairly openly in D.C. Apparently, Dr. Ludomir *wants* a legal challenge." She paused. "When am I going to see you, Dave?"

"Soon. Barton's stalling on our ACLU club application. He knows that an outright denial guarantees a lawsuit. Let's confer with Sue and others about this on the twenty-first, which happens to be my twenty-eighth birthday."

"Sounds good, birthday boy, but when are *we* getting together?"

"Maybe that night. Hey, by the way, does Rachel want a date with a handsome, young guy with a UVA PhD?"

Kim was tongue-tied for a moment. "You're mine, sweet cakes. If you have someone else in mind, Rachel is *always* in the market."

"My buddy, Phil Johnston in Charlottesville, will give Rachel a call."

I hung up and phoned Gladys McNally to give her Dr. Ludomir's number in Washington. Facilitating an illegal procedure did not disturb me at all. Bea's welfare came first, both morally and—as an ally—pragmatically. Indeed, my own deplorable behavior came within a whisker of making RJ one of Dr. Ludomir's patients.

———

The next day several students came to my office, led by Sue Ewal, who wore a white sweatshirt with "Liberate Traymore" in large red letters, and the tiny but feisty Pooky Loomis with her trademark granny glasses. They wanted my support for the first on-campus demonstration in the history of the college. Many of Traymore's best faculty members had announced their forthcoming departures, the student newspaper was severely censored by the administration, and the few women who spoke out about this and other offensive practices were being personally threatened by administrators.

"Professor," said Sue, "we're here to ask you to make a speech about our freedom to demonstrate and to openly express our views." Sue tilted her head as a sly smile crept across her face.

The others nodded.

Pooky laughed and added, "No more Ms. Nice Girl."

"The law is on your side," I reminded her.

Sue squinted her eyes. "But you know Barton will close us down unless we get you, other faculty members, and the press on-board *beforehand.*"

"Indeed. You're right."

We agreed that I'd speak in three weeks. Sue and Pooky would alert the press and reserve Barton Hall. The campus was to be plastered with posters announcing the speech, and in early February, a major demonstration would be held.

———

Two days later, a grenade landed in my campus mailbox: Barton's long-promised evaluation of the faculty's teaching during the fall semester. Unsurprisingly, only one of his criteria for assessing faculty competence could plausibly be seen as relating to teaching, an item labeled "effectiveness in the classroom." Most of the other measures were either patently ambiguous and open-ended ("judgment," "reliability," "attitude," "diplomacy"), or expressly designed to punish critics and reward supporters ("rapport with administration," "agreement with role and purpose of institution," "relations with department chairman").

There were three evaluators, none of whom had attended any of my classes: President Barton himself, his lackey Byon Joon-Ho, and Vice President Thompson. Each of the three assigned a grade ('A' to 'E') for each category.

Despite my thorough lack of respect for Byon Joon-Ho, his evaluation, while mediocre, was the best—all Cs, except for two Bs and two Ds. Ned Thompson assigned equal numbers of Cs, Ds, and Es, but did give me my only A—for "personal appearance." (Bearded faculty members received Es on this item.)

The only decisive evaluation, of course, was Barton's. He crucified me—nearly all Es, even for "personal appearance." His highest grade, a single D for "effectiveness in the classroom," was the sole category that seemed germane to professional competence. The president wrote on my evaluation form: "Your dislike with [sic] the traditions at Traymore College should make you very unhappy hear [sic] and interferes with your effectiveness."

Barton had promised the faculty that he would meet with anyone who wished to discuss his assessment. I called his office immediately, and Carla Pogue scheduled me for the following Tuesday. That night I prepared a three-page, point-by-point, single-spaced commentary and rebuttal to the evaluation, especially its form and procedure, which I provided to each evaluator. I was aware, of course, that my rejoinder would probably disappear into a dark hole, which it did.

I slept poorly for the next few nights, not out of fear, but because I couldn't contain my eagerness to personally confront Barton. The feeling was similar to the high I always experienced the day before a big high school wrestling match.

———

Shortly before my Tuesday session with Barton—the first face-to-face meeting between us since I'd been hired—there was some good news. RJ was *not* pregnant. She had promised to show me "a really good time," but in the perpetual struggle between passion and restraint, victory would now go to the latter. RJ would remain a close ally, but not an intimate one.

When I arrived for my meeting with President Barton, Carla's welcome was less formal than I'd anticipated. "Hi there, David." She offered me coffee and seemed almost friendly. At precisely four o'clock, Carla led me into Barton's office, which was configured for intimidation. The president sat behind a massive oak desk that was as imposing as a battleship. On the wall behind the desk was a photograph of newly elected Governor Linwood Holton, who, like Barton, was a World War II navy veteran. On one corner of the desk was a triad of three small flags: the stars and stripes was in the center, flanked by the blue Virginia state flag and the stars and bars of the Confederate battle flag.

Carla directed me to a plain, straight-backed, wooden chair that faced the president. It was a metaphoric electric chair for the condemned. This was a star-chamber proceeding, no niceties. I sat down slowly without taking my eyes off the president. I leaned forward, legs wide apart. I could almost smell the mistrust, as if something huge and festering had come inside to die. A sense of foreboding permeated the room.

Elzic Barton was short and muscular, a squat man whose rumpled wine-colored suit clashed with his green and gold paisley tie. His penetrating gray eyes were riveted on me, much as a cougar would regard a deer that had wandered into his lair. Barton had a bull neck and a balloon-like head. His demeanor was unambiguous: "I'm in charge. Don't mess with me." He did not greet me. Indeed, he said nothing at all. The silence was palpable.

I noticed that my chair was placed in the center of a circular carpet that featured a reddish-brown owl, Traymore's symbol. Woven into the circumference of the rug were four large words: Loyalty, Order, Reverence, and Duty. The acronym, LORD, could not have been accidental.

Some distance from Barton was Vice President Ned Thompson. Ned was also the provost. He managed most of the day-to-day affairs of the college. He was a reasonable, pragmatic administrator who, unlike his superior, had a credible academic background. He sat quietly, but when I said "Hi," he gave a nervous nod and a strained smile that said, unmistakably, "Sorry; there's nothing I can do." Thereafter, Ned avoided eye contact with me.

Directly across from Thompson, to my right, was a stranger

in a dark blue suit and red tie. I turned toward him. "Hello, I'm David Pritchard. And you're . . . ?"

The man snorted and peered at me contemptuously over the rims of his glasses. Blue Suit was a slight, fidgety man with bushy eyebrows who parted his dark hair down the middle. His Old Spice cologne filled the room. I also smelled an attorney.

"If you're counsel to the president," I said, "I want to know that. Who are you?" Blue Suit looked anxiously at Barton. Not getting a green light to disclose his identity, he remained silent.

Blue Suit then switched on a tape recorder without asking my permission. Seeing this, I removed a yellow legal pad from my briefcase and started taking notes.

"Put that away!" commanded Barton, slamming his fist on the desk.

"Turn off the tape recorder," I countered.

Barton's neck and bald head flushed as red as the fireplug he resembled. Blue Suit looked for a signal from Barton who grimaced and reluctantly nodded his assent. The device was turned off, and I put my yellow pad away.

Barton tapped his pen on the desk, scowled at me, and snarled, "Do you have something to say?"

"A great deal, but today I'm here to discuss your so-called teaching evaluation. It is a vague, patently ambiguous tool for intimidation. If used for anything of importance, like salaries or promotions, it is almost perfectly designed to be challenged in court."

Barton leaned forward. He was a ballistic missile, albeit a stubby one, in launch mode. He suddenly leapt to his feet, walked briskly around his desk, and started toward me.

I tensed and stood. *The SOB is not going to bully me.*

Blue Suit shot up from his chair, quick-stepped over to Barton, and whispered something to him. The president returned to his desk and sat down, after which Blue Suit and I both sat.

"President Barton," I said, raising an eyebrow (which Evelyn had told me really irked him), "why did you give me a 'D' for the category 'effectiveness in the classroom'? This is the only item I care about. All the others are bullshit."

Barton's nostrils flared. Beads of sweat appeared on his forehead. He yanked his tie loose and crossed his arms. "You've attempted to arrogate to yourself the Office of Dean of Students," he said.

Calling Evelyn to mind, I grinned. "What do you mean by 'arrogate to yourself?'"

The silence was stifling. Barton appeared to be hyperventilating. He finally spat out, "With a spanking new PhD, you believe you can change things at Traymore College."

You bet your ass I do. I chuckled, probably too condescendingly. Predictably, this sent Barton up the wall; his red face now acquired a purplish hue. I was enjoying this.

Elzic Barton was not the poised, intellectually sophisticated president of a Yale, Stanford, or virtually any other respectable institution of higher learning. No, this unrefined old navy captain headed a largely unknown public women's college in Virginia that was rapidly losing whatever academic respectability it had had, while hemorrhaging students and faculty.

Traymore's decline was evident to almost everyone, including the press and even some members of the state legislature. But Barton continued to cling to his rigid, outmoded, and frequently unconstitutional supervision of the college.

"President Barton," I said, "you have not answered my question. Why did you fault my 'effectiveness in the classroom?'"

Blue Suit jumped up and, looking at Barton, spoke audibly for the first time: "Careful what you say. Better yet, say nothing."

Ignoring this advice, Elzic Barton lobbed a pen across the room in my direction, and, as I'd hoped, let loose with, "I understand that you dealt with student legal rights in class. THAT WAS IMPROPER."

Blue Suit gritted his teeth, ran a hand through his hair, and sat down despondently. Ned Thompson shook his head.

I patiently explained that the course was Constitutional Law; that the Bill of Rights and its First Amendment were part of the Constitution; that the subject was directly relevant to the abuses of and legal actions by Traymore's faculty and students; and that the class had voted unanimously to spend time on the topic. Moreover, intense student interest in the matter had translated into excellent course grades on the final examination. I refrained from informing the president that throwing a pen at me could be construed as an assault.

"I don't give a damn," Barton said, shaking his head. "That's none of your business." Staring at me intensely as he opened and closed his fists, he mumbled something under his breath that I couldn't quite make out. Blue Suit suddenly raised both of his palms toward the president, signaling *stop*. Barton was a vengeful autocrat, and his muttering had sounded vaguely like, "You'll get yours, Pritchard," but I couldn't be sure.

"President Barton," I said, ignoring the words that he may or may not have uttered, "you have neither the legal right nor the professional standing to question the substance of what I teach. Moreover, I don't recall ever seeing you in any of my classes. Your understanding of what I said in class is, at best, pure hearsay."

Barton trembled with anger. "Pritchard, you're like the cow who swishes her shit-smeared tail through a pail of fresh milk."

"That's pretty good," I replied. "But I prefer a more accurate analogy—that of Hercules cleaning out the shit-filled Augean Stables."

We glared at one another in a lengthy, pulsating silence.

Barton finally stood, hands on his hips. I rose up from my chair. "In a few months, you won't have a job here. Have you found another one?"

"Not yet."

"I will see that you *never* secure another academic position in Virginia, or anywhere else."

As I turned to leave the office, Ned Thompson rose and shook my hand. "Good luck, David." This simple act took some courage.

"Thanks, Ned," I said.

Carla Pogue smiled as I exited.

Now I had confirmation of what I'd suspected. On some matters of great importance, Barton was incapable of conducting himself in a calm, deliberative manner. Thus, he was vulnerable. But his threat to deny me future employment, whether credible or not, was unsettling, especially because January was late in the academic hiring cycle and I had no job prospects.

16

Escalation

For two months, the administration sat upon the students' application to form an ACLU chapter on campus. The college usually approved proposals for new student groups in less than two weeks. Since I was listed as the faculty adviser to the club, and because it was an organization the president despised, the delay was clearly intended to kill the project.

Seven students crowded into my office in late January to discuss this matter. Two sat in chairs, one stood, and the remainder spread out on the floor. The group included Kim Sherman—the proposal's originator and the chapter's anticipated president; her sister, Rachel; and Sue Ewal.

"What would you like to do?" I asked, leaning back in my desk chair. "We can wait longer, which will please the administration. We can give up. Or, we can contact the ACLU in Richmond."

"Sue the bastards!" Rachel blurted out. The others all agreed.

I stood and stretched out my arms. "Well, ladies, I'll call Richmond this afternoon." They were pleased, even buoyant, as all but the two sisters filed out of my office.

Rachel came near, brushing my hand lightly. "I'll be quick, professor." Then, bumping mischievously against Kim, she purred, "I *know* you two want to be alone."

Kim wrinkled her brow and scolded her sister. "Rachel, say what you have to say, and get lost."

"Okay, big sis." Rachel gave me an impish look. "Many thanks for setting me up with your friend Phil from UVA. He's *great!*"

"Glad it worked out," I said.

With wide eyes and a coast-to-coast, rascally smile, the always randy Rachel said, "It not only worked out, it worked in and . . ."

"Gross! Get out of here," shouted Kim, shoving Rachel toward the door.

Rachel started to recite one of her countless limericks: "There once was a young girl named Rachel . . ."

"Out! Out!" yelled Kim, escorting her sister from my office and closing the door. Turning toward me, Kim apologized. "Sorry. She's been like that forever. . . . So, birthday boy, what about *us?*"

Several thoughts flashed through my mind. *Kim's a crucial ally and a likely plaintiff in an ACLU lawsuit against the college. Close coordination with her is essential. She is levelheaded, attractive, and—critically important—she can maintain strict confidentiality. Neither of us wants a long-term emotional relationship with the other, but she very much wants to play. So, why not roll the dice?*

"Third and Main," I said. "Pick you up at six o'clock."

Kim winked, gave me a peck on the cheek, and skipped out of the office.

———

Arnold Thieleman, who directed the state's ACLU out of its Richmond office and who had spoken at Traymore in early November, had invited me to call him directly "any time." I'd kept him and Ron Cohen of the ACLU's Roanoke office fully informed during the students' application process, so Thieleman wasn't surprised when I called in January.

"We will contact President Barton about the application this week," he said. "If there's no movement soon, we'll file suit."

———

Despite a heavy wool overcoat and scarf, Kim was shivering when I met her at Third and Main. She hopped into my car and snuggled close, holding two cardboard containers. "Chinese food and a surprise," she said.

We arrived at the cottage at dusk. Xena gave Kim a perfunctory sniff, wagged her tail, and ran outside. The phone rang.

"Professor, Sue Ewal. There's a crisis. Dean Baird just called me. She said that President Barton has canceled your speech in Barton Hall."

Three weeks ago, I'd promised Sue and other student leaders that I would deliver an address that was designed to support their plan to hold the first on-campus demonstration in Traymore's history. "Damn, and just forty-eight hours before the event," I said. "Let me try to reach Dean Baird." Kim was listening intently.

"That's not all," said Sue. "Campus security tore down all our posters this afternoon."

"Hang in there, Sue. I'll get back to you."

Seeing the expression on my face, Kim asked, "What's wrong?"

I slipped an arm around her waist, related what Sue had told me, and asked her to put the food in the fridge while I called Dean Baird.

Kim frowned. "That's a waste of time. She's a bitch, Barton's puppet."

I dialed Evelyn's home phone.

"Evelyn, what's this I hear . . . ?"

Evelyn cut me off in mid-sentence. "I was about to call you. President Barton is adamant about denying you access to Barton Hall." Evelyn proceeded to confirm what Sue had said.

"That's stupid. It'll inflame the students and give the press a heyday."

"Yes. An attorney for the college, Ned Thompson, and I all objected."

"So, what motivated Barton to do this at the last minute? He's known about my speech for weeks."

"Not sure," said Evelyn, "but the president's loathing of you and his professed, if unfounded, fear of an unruly disturbance appeared to drive his decision."

"It's probably too late to ask a court for relief." I paced back and forth. "I'm stuck."

"Not necessarily," said Evelyn. "The Wesley Foundation, which is closely affiliated with the Forest Avenue Methodist Church, often has speakers. It's across the street from the college. Forest Avenue is my church, and Bill Vaughn is an associate pastor there. Call Bill."

"Great idea. Evelyn, you're a sweetheart." With that, I hung up the phone.

"*Sweetheart!*" said Kim snidely. "What kind of bullshit is that? If Barton is enemy number one, Baird is enemy number two."

I reached over and took Kim's hand. Smiling, I said, "Now *sweetheart*, Evelyn Baird has suggested another forum for my speech. For that kind of valuable information, I'd call her lovey dovey, pussycat, honey buns, or anything else."

Kim shrugged, threw up her hands, and exclaimed, "Oy vey, but *not* honey buns."

After I called Bill Vaughn, he immediately contacted Amos Toth, an old friend and the director of the Wesley Foundation. Bill phoned back with good news. "The foundation's hall is yours for Saturday night."

Kim and I then called Sue, Rachel, Pookie Loomis, Valerie, and other students asking them to alert the press and put up posters, on and off campus, indicating the new location. Also, circulars were to go into all faculty mailboxes the next morning for in-class announcements of the time and changed place for the speech.

Finally, almost two hours after we'd arrived at the cottage, Kim and I were able to warm up our Chinese food. I poured some wine, and we sat down for a late dinner.

"So, you and Evelyn Baird exchange information with one another," said Kim, crossing her legs. "What *else* do the two of you do?" With a sly smile, she ran her fingers through her dark hair.

I laughed. "You don't think that we . . ."

"Yuck! No, that's unthinkable."

"As you noticed," I said, pouring more wine, "the dean and I are on a first-name basis. She's a decent human being."

"That's news to me."

"Look, she just provided information that saved my Saturday speech. And you might have noticed that the dress code is no longer being enforced, and that there hasn't been a fake fire drill in the dorms for a couple of months. Evelyn Baird has changed."

Kim nodded skeptically, stood, and removed a container

from the refrigerator. "Happy birthday!" She placed a chocolate cake with twenty-eight yellow confectionary hearts on the table. In the center of the cake was a huge pair of red, candied, puckered lips. "Found it in Blacksburg this afternoon. The bakery added the hearts and lips."

We leaned across the table toward one another and kissed.

"It's beautiful," I said. "No candles to blow out?"

"Save your energy for me, honey." Kim beamed and kissed my cheek.

After a couple of slices of cake, we sat on the couch. Kim revealed that she'd applied to the PhD program in acoustical physics at the University of Illinois, and that John Manikas as well as a Virginia Tech professor had both written strong letters of recommendation. She also indicated, unsurprisingly, that she was dating "a couple of guys" at Tech, partly out of "curiosity," and partly because "you're not usually around when I want you." Kim continued, "Incidentally, who was that Marigold somebody you were with at the holiday dance?"

"She's a great dancer, but we don't date."

"Sure," Kim said with a smirk. "That's okay; you're fun. And a sexy rule-breaker." We kissed as she laid her hand in my lap. "We'll play together for as long as we play together."

Sex was, well, creative. Kim insisted on trying "something new." So, after twisting ourselves into multiple contortions, we finally fell asleep, dead tired.

The next morning, as I was driving us back to Traymore, Kim's hand was once again in my lap. Despite our gymnastics a few hours earlier, the embers of desire still glowed. "You're on-target," I said, trying desperately to hold the car in my lane.

"Oh," she giggled, "I thought that thing was the emergency brake."

Dropping her off at Third and Main, I said, "See you tomorrow night at the Wesley Foundation."

Kim took my hand. "I'll be there."

———

Shortly after my morning class, around noon, Bill Vaughn appeared in my office. "Dave . . ." Bill fiddled with his shirt sleeve. "Barton just threatened Amos Toth of the Wesley Foundation."

"Why am I not surprised?"

"Amos was called just minutes ago by the president. Amos said that Barton had 'reminded' him that the foundation and church would be responsible for any riot that broke out. He told me he apologized to President Barton for guffawing into the phone because the notion of rioting Traymore girls was about as probable as rampaging nuns."

"So, Amos Toth rebuffed Barton?"

"Yes. Amos and the foundation's other trustees will be present tomorrow night."

———

On Saturday evening, I arrived at the Wesley Foundation shortly before the scheduled time. The simple barn-like wooden building sat two hundred. It was completely full, with many people standing on the sides and at the back. I made my way through the crowd to get to the front of the hall.

Five trustees, including Amos Toth, were in the first row. They introduced themselves, and we shook hands. Bill Vaughn, in clerical collar, was with them. He patted me on the back. Pooky Loomis and Sue Ewal, the catalysts for the event, were also up front. I recognized and acknowledged two newspaper reporters. Evelyn was in the fourth row, trying without success to appear innocuous. A couple of rows behind her was Kim Sherman in a black wool sweater. I didn't see Valerie at first, but she stood up toward the back of the hall in her favorite pink dress and waved.

Students comprised most of the audience. The faculty was well-represented, although I didn't see my buddy John Manikas. There was also a smattering of others, including some members of the church. Notably absent, at least inside the building, were security personnel.

However, a few minutes before the event was to begin, loud voices came from the rear of the hall, by the main door. A uniformed fire marshal shouted, "Y'all listen up! To comply with the fire code, at least fifty of you must leave." When no one moved toward the door, the marshal and two associates escorted many of those who were standing out of the building. One of the foundation's trustees, an electrician, told me that he'd switch on a supplementary audio system that could project my remarks to those who were outside, where the temperature was near freezing.

Shortly after seven, Pooky walked up to the simple oak lectern. She adjusted her glasses and tapped the microphone. "Ladies and gentlemen." It took some time for the crowd to settle down. She tried again. "Ladies and gentlemen . . . It is gratifying to see such a huge turnout for a matter of supreme importance: nothing less than the future of Traymore College. This is *not* an overstatement. Unless the college treats its students as responsible young women instead of vulnerable innocents in need of so-called guidance from older males, Traymore has no future." Applause resounded throughout the hall. "It gives me great pleasure to now introduce President Barton's favorite faculty member—" Laughter. "—and someone who has done much to change Traymore for the better, Professor David Pritchard."

Pookie and Sue had asked that I deliver a rousing talk, "a clarion call" in Sue's words, a speech that would help legitimize and draw students to the forthcoming on-campus demonstration. I figured this required me to do three things. First, summarize and accentuate Traymore's profound problems, all of which related directly or indirectly to President Barton's governance of the school. Second, personalize them, so that everyone could understand the urgency of addressing these matters. Finally, encourage students and faculty to openly confront the administration. And I hoped to do this in under thirty minutes.

After thanking the Wesley Foundation, our "beloved" Professor Bill Vaughn, and "the many students who made this event possible," I began. "Bob Dylan sings, 'The times, they are a-changin'.' That song first appeared in 1964. In the intervening five or six years, a tidal wave of change has swept the country and college campuses. We are plop in the middle of the Vietnam Big Muddy. The pill has been out for ten years, although it's largely unavailable to single women in Southwest Virginia." Boos erupted from the audience. "Women today are no longer effectively limited to employment as school teachers, nurses, and clerical workers (as important as these professions are); African-Americans—who are virtually absent from this public college—have only begun to claim the equality they have long been due; and *in loco parentis* is dead or rapidly dying at respectable women's colleges."

A shout rang out, "Not at Traymore, Davey!"

I called back, "It wouldn't be the same without you, RJ." Laughter rippled through the audience as RJ, in jeans and a Liberate Traymore sweatshirt, stood and raised her arms in a 'V'.

"*You* know," I continued, "that times have changed. I know. But our overlord is either unaware of this or, more likely, he is resisting change to the bitter end. Either the president must adapt and act in the interest of Traymore students and faculty, or he will likely be ousted."

The audience leapt to its feet, stomping and chanting, "Barton must go! Barton must go!"

When the noise subsided, I continued. "To my knowledge, at least four faculty lawsuits have been filed against the college. Scores of outstanding professors are leaving Traymore after this semester. The media is following what is happening here, and the State Council on Higher Education might begin an investigation of the school." I looked at Bill Vaughn. "The first suit to be brought, and one that *will* succeed, was brought by Professor Vaughn."

Bill stood to tumultuous applause.

"Moreover, unless the president comes to his senses very soon—and that seems unlikely—one of *you* will likely file a lawsuit challenging Barton's refusal to accept a student chapter of the ACLU on campus. Kim Sherman, would you stand?"

Kim stood and was applauded.

"Incidentally, how many of you know that yesterday, President Barton called Amos Toth, Director of the Wesley Foundation, to threaten him and the church if tonight's event was held?"

Gasps and murmurs filled the hall. Amos, seated to my right, looked at me calmly, crossed his arms, and winked. This retired air force colonel and Korean War veteran was not about to be pushed around.

"Let me briefly refer to just two issue-areas relating to First Amendment freedoms of expression, both of which affect you directly—student demonstrations and publications. I have in my hand *The Traymore College Student Handbook, 1969-1970.* It states the following under 'Disruptive behavior': 'Students participating in or in attendance as a spectator at a disturbance disrupting the orderly function of the college will be subject to disciplinary action.'" Lifting the microphone off its stand, I stepped forward. "This provision is ambiguous and invites abuse. What is 'participation,' 'attendance,' a 'disturbance,' 'orderly,' or a 'spectator'? It is almost certainly an unconstitutionally vague prior restraint on dissent, such as the peaceful student demonstration you will soon have here at Traymore."

"Indeed," I said, loosening my tie, "courts have consistently held that if college regulations are vague, even students who grossly misbehave cannot be punished. The Fourth Circuit Court of Appeals, in ordering the reinstatement of a Virginia Tech student, recently stated that, 'A student's freedom to express peaceful dissent on campus is more than a privilege. . . . It is a basic right guaranteed by the First Amendment.' The First Amendment, of course, protects the right to assemble and to petition the government—that is, President Barton and Governor Holton. In short, *have* your demonstration, and enjoy it."

Almost everyone jumped to their feet and clapped.

"Finally, let me say a word about freedom of the press. The law is clear. Except for libel and obscenity, whatever that might be, a Traymore student may publish material in campus newspapers—or anywhere else—even if it is fiercely critical of the college. She cannot be punished by the institution in any way."

Turning toward the reporters sitting near me, I asked "the distinguished journalists" from the *Roanoke Times* and *Richmond Times Dispatch* to please raise their hands. Two frumpy middle-aged men smiled and waved. Applause.

"And Sue Ewal, would you stand?"

Sue shot out of her seat, pumping her fist as her peers whooped and hollered.

"Many of you know that, as editor of our newspaper, Sue has courageously protested the administration's persistent censorship. She, and those of you who write critical letters to the editor, have been chastised by deans and department heads. Autocrats never want a free press. One thing that especially infuriates them is adverse publicity." I was on a roll and loved it. I could feel the mood of the audience, and I exulted in the sensation—much as actors might revel in an awareness that they'd won over the house.

I walked up to the first row and raised my voice. "To close, Elzic Barton's oppressive practices *must* be criticized. They attract adverse publicity, and rightly so. Only when there is free expression in all its forms will Traymore College gain the respect that students, faculty, alumna, and the citizens of Virginia so richly deserve."

Now the entire audience was on its feet, even Evelyn, who was only a few yards from me. She, of course, didn't clap or join in the spontaneous chants of "Barton must go." Evelyn looked at me with watery, melancholy eyes and a languid half-smile. Neither the students nor the faculty knew how profoundly this strong, compassionate woman had changed. In her heart, and in practice, Evelyn was no longer the loyal agent of Elzic Barton. I felt a compelling urge to hug her.

Soon, I was encircled by students, faculty, reporters, foundation trustees, and others. I responded to various questions and comments until the crowd finally began to disperse. *Where is Valerie?* I wondered. Both she and Kim had apparently left the building.

Blue lights flashed from three of the sheriff department's patrol cars as I exited. John Manikas, who had been outside with many other people during the speech, ran up to me. He was breathing heavily, and, with a bloody nose, looked even more disheveled than usual.

John said that he'd encountered Aubrey Blount. "The fucker was photographing everyone." In John's version of events, he told Blount, "Get your ass out of here, now!" Blount had punched him in the face. Former paratrooper Big Bad John then leveled Blount. When Blount picked himself up, he gripped what John said appeared to be a Buck knife with a five-inch blade, "designed to gut deer, wild boar, and me." About that time, said Manikas, "The cops showed up, but Blount had vamoosed."

I rested my arm on his shoulders. "John, I only asked that my colleagues keep an eye out for the guy, not knock the crap out of him."

"Yeah," John said, kicking gravel, "couldn't help myself."

Sheriff Goetzke, who was standing behind Manikas, growled, "Lucky you weren't sliced and diced. Blount's a nasty cracker." Harley straightened his hat and turned toward me. "It's pretty damn clear what this means, David. Barton's still on your tail, and

Blount, like Barton, has almost certainly developed an intense personal grudge against you. I'd be *really* careful."

17

Thunder

After my Saturday night talk at the Wesley Foundation, I
headed home on I-81. It was a moonless night. I was thinking
about Sheriff Goetzke's warning when bolts of lightning streaked
to the ground. Rumbles of thunder followed. A high wind came
up, and driving rain and sleet pummeled the car. Visibility went
from poor to perilous. Turning off the interstate onto the narrow
road leading to the cottage, my speed fell to barely five miles per
hour. Debris flew across the now icy road, pinging the car with
sticks and gravel. At Piney Woods, my tires splashed through deep
puddles of slush. After parking, I sprinted the short distance to
the cottage, getting soaked in the process.

Xena performed her usual twirling dervish routine when I
opened the door, then rushed outside. Moments later, she yelped
to be let back in and shook herself upon entering, drenching
everything within a six-foot radius, including me. A deafening
thunderclap rattled the windows and sent her scurrying to the
bathroom, where she piddled on a bathmat and then wrapped
herself around the toilet. Flush to the tile floor with her rear legs
splayed, she wedged her snout between her front paws. Xena
feared no one, but thunder scared the piss out of her.

I was worn out after the long, tense day. So, in rapid succes-
sion, I dried myself off, mopped up after Xena, wolfed down a

peanut butter sandwich, brushed my teeth, and rolled into bed. The storm had not abated, and a crash of thunder sent Xena dashing into the bedroom seeking greater security. She curled up on the floor at the foot of the bed, where I'd spread a towel. Despite thunderous rumblings and the rank odor of wet dog, I soon fell fast asleep.

———

The raven looked unnaturally black that night. It was a blackness of the lost, the dead, the end of time. Other bits of my disjointed dream stood out. So, shockingly, one of the raven's eyes—only one—was a shimmering turquoise blue. Sparks spun off from the eye to vanish into the night.

And there I was, *inside* the eye. It wasn't a mirror-like reflection. Rather, I was drawn into the blueness, where I found myself backpacking in a forested and mountainous area. Xena was with me. She seemed content, sniffing bushes and chewing on a stick, but she hobbled along with a pronounced limp.

The raven was perched on a splintered branch of a naked pine; it stared down at me. When the bird melted away, there was a fleeting depiction of wanton destruction. A room or rooms were torn apart. The scene was isolated and without context. Blood and the smell of blood were everywhere.

This was followed by a bizarre parade of my most intimate allies. Evelyn led off, dressed smartly in a tailored gray suit. She smiled warmly as she looked my way: "I'm the president now. Please, won't you stay?"

A hugely pregnant, half naked RJ made an offer: "Davey, I have something you'll *really* like."

Kim Sherman came next. She was wearing—if that's the word—strategically placed red fox fur pelts. With a fuzzy black mortarboard hat on her head and a golden Phi Beta Kappa key as a necklace, she slowly ran her tongue along her upper lip and winked. "Let's play in the sunshine and dance in the rain."

The final vision was of Valerie. She stood demurely on the steps of an ivy-covered, stone church in a lime green sleeveless sundress. A single tear ran slowly down her cheek. "I love you," she said.

———

I awoke, unnerved, as the dream metamorphosed into an incoherent musing before evaporating altogether. No more visions of lovers, bloody destruction, and ravens.

The storm had passed. The morning sun filtered through my torn window shades and dappled the walls with splotches of light. Xena had crawled onto the bed during the night. One stern look, and she hopped off. Only beautiful women, not smelly dogs, shared my bed.

I let Xena outside, and, after breakfast, we walked up the muddy driveway to retrieve my Sunday *Roanoke Times*.

"David! Come on up." Mara Heath waved from her side porch, then ducked back into the house to escape the cold.

It had been six weeks since Caleb's death. I'd stopped by regularly to see how Mara was faring, and to furnish her with staples like canned Vienna sausages, fruit cocktail, eggs, and coffee. I'd also taken her to the pharmacy and to her doctor. Mara could drive Caleb's pickup truck, but she didn't like to, especially in inclement weather. I tucked the newspaper under my arm, stepped carefully up the slippery back stairs, and entered a kitchen made toasty warm by the wood-burning stove. Xena curled up on the porch.

Mara poured coffee into a burgundy and gold mug with a Washington Redskins logo, then handed it to me. The room still smelled of Caleb's chewing tobacco, as he often missed the spittoon. Dark brown spittle had seeped into the well-worn oak floor. "Sit down, dear. Tell me what's goin' on." Mara's frayed slippers might have been pink at one time. It was hard to tell. Her wrinkled cotton smock looked like she'd slept in it, which she probably had, and it was anyone's guess when she'd last washed her hair.

I sat with her at the kitchen table, which was covered by a red and white checked oilcloth. "Well," I said, taking a sip of coffee from the chipped Redskins cup, "I'll soon submit my resignation to the college."

"What's that mean?"

"That I'll be leaving here in June."

"Oh." Silence. Mara reached across the table and took my hand. "You're a good Christian and a good friend, David. I'm goin' to miss you."

"I'll miss you, too." Taking her hand in both of mine, I asked, "How are *you* doing?"

"Better. Reverend Grundy and the whole congregation have been wonderful. Praise the Lord. But it's been hard without Caleb." She cast her eyes upward. "I want to join him . . . with the angels." Leaning forward on her elbows, Mara said, "I do have some good news. My sister, Katie, and her husband, Lee, will move in with me next week. They lost their trailer home in a flood last month, and I need help lookin' after Piney Woods."

"That's great, Mara. I worry about you being up here alone." I got up to leave.

"Don't you fret none 'bout me," Mara said, standing to say goodbye. We hugged, and Xena and I headed back to the cottage.

As I walked down the driveway with Xena, I glanced at the front page of the newspaper. My photo—with tie askew and arms held high—was under the headline, "More Traymore Troubles." I stopped to read the story, despite the cold. Two sentences leapt off the page. "Professor Pritchard revealed that President Elzic Barton threatened the Forest Avenue Methodist Church and its Wesley Foundation if they allowed the professor to speak on their premises. This was confirmed by Amos Toth, director of the foundation."

"Yes!" I said out loud. Then, eyeing my furry companion, I chortled. "Xena, this'll spoil Barton's day." Both ears went up (that is, one and a half ears, thanks to Vincent Tavernetti). Xena tilted her head. "*Say again?*" she seemed to say.

The phone was ringing as I entered the cottage. "David!" said Valerie in a high voice. "We *must* have lunch today."

"Something wrong?"

"Yes—no—I mean . . . it's important . . . for us."

"Well, love, what is it?"

"I'll tell you in person."

Valerie was no RJ. She was older, more purposeful, far more mature, and dutiful about contraception. Nonetheless, I ventured a question, "You're not pregnant?"

"Oh, come *on!*"

"Okay, okay. Sorry for asking. Meet you at Bessie's in an hour?"

"Yes. Love you."

Valerie was at the restaurant when I arrived. I started to make my way toward her table when Bessie intercepted me. She grabbed me much like a three-hundred-pound defensive tackle might flatten a smaller running back. I was enfolded in her arms and crushed against her ample bosom. Glancing at Valerie, Bessie said, "Y'all been ignorin' ole Bessie? Ain't seen ya in weeks."

I struggled to find words that might free me from this woman's grip. "Oh no, Bessie," I stammered. "We . . . we adore you. . . . And your food is . . . divine."

"Well, now . . ." Bessie loosened her hold. "Guess you're forgiven. I just *love* that word, D-I-V-I-N-E. *Uh-huh!*" Valerie and other customers were laughing uncontrollably. Bessie shook her butt and waved at everyone with both hands. "That goes on my sign out front: Bessie's Restaurant—*Divine* Family Food. For that, David, lunch for you and Lady Love is on the house."

Having run the gauntlet, I finally made it over to Valerie. She'd stood up by this time and was still laughing. We kissed, sat down at the table, and gave our orders—two Sunday pot roast specials.

"So, what's up?" I asked.

Val pushed some hair out of her face, bent forward, and ran her fingertips along my arm. Her face was flushed. She had a pensive expression.

It must be important. She's wearing that Bellodgia perfume. "Something big has happened," I said. "A fatter fellowship from Johns Hopkins? A visitation from the Blessed Virgin?"

"It was a visitation, but from two Virginia state troopers." Valerie carefully folded a napkin in her lap and muttered, "I'm free." She closed her eyes and made a sign of the cross. Valerie said the police told her that her husband, Vincent Tavernetti, had been killed by another prisoner.

Valerie went quiet. She stared at me intensely. I didn't know whether to say, "You must be relieved," or to offer condolences. I inclined toward the former, but I was tongue-tied. Fortunately, the tension eased somewhat when Bessie brought our lunch.

I decided to ask, "Did the police say anything else?"

"Yes, but I was so overwhelmed that it didn't really register."

We were both aware of the elephant in the room. The thought of marriage had floated around formlessly, somewhere in the mists that enveloped us. But the M-word had never been mentioned. Indeed, while Vincent was in prison, the matter could be postponed because Valerie's divorce proceeding was still ongoing, and, at any rate, she and Vincent remained married in the eyes of the church. Now, everything changed. The marital ball had bounced, uninvited, into my court. I loved Val. But my future—professionally and otherwise—was clouded, to put it charitably. I was certainly not ready to pop the question.

"What shocking news," I managed to say after an awkwardly long pause.

"Yes. *We* don't have this hanging over *our* heads anymore," she said with a suggestive smile.

I returned her smile but steered the conversation toward other subjects. Normally, I would have invited her to come back to the cottage with me, but now the timing was clearly not right. So, after we finished our lunch, I grabbed her hand and we got up to leave. "Bye, Bessie," I hollered, laying some bills on the table.

Bessie waved goodbye. "Y'all come back, ya hear?"

Once outside, we kissed and agreed to get together soon.

———

I was surprised to see Evelyn at my office door early Tuesday morning before class. Senior administrators never visited faculty offices. When meetings were necessary, protocol required faculty members to go to rooms or offices designated by the Grand High Poohbahs.

"What a rare honor," I said as she quickly slipped in, closed the door, and sat down.

Evelyn glanced at her watch and clutched her purse tightly. "I shouldn't be here." She shifted uneasily in the chair. "I have five minutes."

"Must be serious."

"I couldn't reach you on the phone, but that's okay." Evelyn closed her eyes and took a deep breath. "I'm so afraid that I want to tell you this in person."

"Oh-oh. You have my full attention."

"President Barton called an emergency meeting yesterday with Ned Thompson and me. Carla attended, of course. He's drafting letters to the editors of the Roanoke and Richmond papers highlighting the disturbance that occurred outside the Wesley Foundation building where you spoke. He blames you."

I clenched my jaw and crossed my arms. "Naturally. But his paid thug, Aubrey Ray Blount, caused the fracas."

Evelyn's hand went to her throat. "Really? The president said nothing about that."

"Of course not. Blount punched John Manikas. When John retaliated, Blount pulled a knife."

Evelyn gasped and shook her head. "The president did say

that Professor Manikas would receive a letter of reprimand for his involvement in the incident."

I swiveled my desk chair around and kicked the wastepaper basket across the room. "The SOB."

"I'm here because of something else President Barton said about you." Evelyn spoke rapidly and in a breathy voice.

"I'm getting a raise?"

Evelyn was not amused. She gave me an anguished stare. "I was frightened by what he said and by his vicious tone." She swallowed hard. "He said, and I quote, 'Pritchard is dangerous. He is turning everyone against me. He threatens everything I've done for Traymore. I *know* that you all agree.'" Evelyn pressed a trembling hand to her cheek. Her voice fell to a whisper. "Then he said, 'I assure you that, within the next two or three months, Pritchard *will* be dealt with.' And what made my heart stop was that he concluded with, 'Something could happen to him.'"

Evelyn jumped up, almost losing her balance. "I've got to go. I'm worried about you." Her hands were still shaking.

I stood, walked around the desk, and took both of her hands in mine. "Thank you." She gave me a quick kiss on the cheek and left the office.

———

That evening, I called Evelyn from the cottage. "Tell Barton, especially if you think someone might have seen you enter or leave my office, that you just learned from me that there will be an on-campus student demonstration on Friday, February 13."

"Sounds unlucky."

"Only for Barton, should he attempt to impede it. Be sure to also inform him that two lawyers will be on hand—one from the ACLU, another who is volunteering his time *pro bono*.

"You're *good*, Pritchard."

"And you, my dear dean, are lovely. I'm sorry to have caused you so much distress."

18

Demonstration

It would be more than two weeks before I again saw Valerie—a longer period apart than any time since we'd first met. We spoke on the phone, but that was it.

I missed her, really missed her. Our relationship had evolved from friendship quite rapidly to affection, and then well beyond that. We both knew this and addressed one another with endearments, but we had never explicitly acknowledged it, let alone solidified this mutual sentiment in a formal engagement.

The time that we were apart afforded Val some space after the shock of Vincent's death and allowed her to meet with her attorney and sign various documents. Meanwhile, I focused on my personal mission, one that was now as intense as my love for Valerie: kicking Barton's butt.

Since Mary Jo Shifflet had been expelled—"shipped"—in September shortly after I'd arrived at Traymore, I'd waged a systematic, escalating campaign to topple Elzic Barton. In the process, I'd acquired important, sometimes intimate, allies. Which, circuitously, brings me to another reason why Val and I hadn't seen each other for so long—Kim Sherman.

Kim was a key ally and co-leader, along with Sue Ewal, of the forthcoming demonstration. And with Kim, there was another consideration: lust. Fervent and often imaginative sex.

For two full days, Kim and I met at the cottage to plan the February student demonstration. Who would lead and advise the demonstrators? Who could participate, and what behavior should be avoided? Where and how would they demonstrate? What to do, and who to contact, should the administration interfere? What to print on placards and how to effectively deal with the press? Etc., etc. All the while, our planning was interspersed with periodic lovemaking as Simon and Garfunkle's "Cecelia" often played in the background.

———

Despite President Barton's repeated threats to punish "disruptive behavior," which everyone understood to mean *any* opposition to his policies and practices, the demonstration on the thirteenth went off without a hitch. This would not have happened without our careful planning, my very public assurance to students at the Wesley Foundation event that they could not be punished, widespread media coverage, and the watchful on-site presence of two attorneys.

A central purpose of the protest was stated succinctly on several of the placards: "Demonstrate for the Right to Demonstrate." But placards also referred to other grievances. "Men Don't Have Curfews," "I Need an Education, Not a Babysitter," "Education, Not Repression," and simply, "Ship Barton!"

More than 450 students marched around the campus in below freezing weather chanting, "Free Traymore!" Hundreds of others watched from grassy areas, porches, and dormitory rooftops and windows.

About three dozen faculty, including me and the attorneys,

braved the cold to observe the long, slow moving line of students. At the far end of the campus, several department chairs and senior administrators could be seen monitoring the protest.

Evelyn was standing among those who, in varying degrees, remained Barton loyalists. Only I knew that Dean Evelyn Baird, who was still universally disliked—even despised—by the students, was genuinely devoted to these young women. She had changed so profoundly over the past several months, from Barton's faithful agent to clandestine opponent of the very administration of which she was such an integral part. I hoped and expected that our peculiar friendship would last a lifetime.

It occurred to me that the women about whom I truly cared were right here, right now. They were all courageous, but they differed radically from one another. The stunningly attractive RJ would always be RJ: too hot to handle, too electric to ignore. I was at ease with Kim, a fellow New Yorker. Kim was comfort food, pepperoni pizza with loads of red chili pepper. She was bright, highly organized, doggedly determined, and almost professional in her demeanor. Indeed, in bed . . . well . . . there she *was* a pro.

But Valerie was The One. We were a duet, humming and harmonizing together. Our affinity for one another was instinctive and involuntary, like inhaling and exhaling. We were so emotionally intertwined that we often anticipated what the other would say. Indeed, we could communicate without saying a word.

Evelyn, RJ, Kim, and Valerie were my recent past and present. Valerie, I hoped, would also be my future. But in a few months, she would enroll at Johns Hopkins and I would be . . . Where would I be?

Kim and Sue led the line of protestors as they twice circled the periphery of the campus. Both women waved as they passed by the faculty. Shortly thereafter, RJ broke from the pack with her placard ("Scrap Bullshit Rules") and raced over to me. Whacking me accidentally with her sign, she kissed me on the cheek, shouted, "Thank you, Davey!" and rejoined the demonstration, but not before gamboling around the assembled faculty while shouting, "Free Traymore!" Faculty and students broke out in laughter, and ACLU attorney Ron Cohen asked me, "What kind of cologne do you use, David?"

Five minutes later, another student left the line of protesters, ran over to me, and asked whether I remembered her.

I hesitated for an awkward moment. This young brunette with bell bottoms and a navy-blue pea jacket was not one of my students, but she looked awfully familiar.

"Bea!" she announced.

"I apologize, Bea. Of course, I remember you. You're Bea McNally."

"You saved me," said the former president of the Young Democrats.

"How are you doing?"

"Very well, thanks. I'm back in school now." Bea gave me a tender hug and rejoined the protest.

Toward the end of the procession, in a fire engine red wool coat, Valerie appeared. We smiled and waved at each other. Her placard was heart shaped. In red letters, it said, "Love One Another." Which (intentionally?) reminded me that tomorrow was Valentine's Day. We needed to reconnect.

———

That night, following the demonstration, and after stopping at a florist on the way home, I called Valerie. When she arrived at the cottage the next morning, I presented her with a dozen pink roses. "You're so sweet," she said. Xena greeted Val with customary zeal, knocking a box of Russell Stover chocolates from her hand onto the floor. Thankfully, the box was still sealed. I retrieved this high value offering and kissed her. Val and I settled into a long weekend together.

When not in bed or eating, bathing, walking by the lake, or visiting Mara Heath, Val was on the phone, especially with her mother. "No, Mom, we didn't make it to church this morning. . . . I know, I know. . . . Maybe next Sunday. . . . Well, it might *not* be a Catholic church. . . . You still there, Mom? . . . Yes, he remembered. David is so thoughtful. He gave me roses. . . . No, Mother, they were not red. . . . Yes, and I love him, too."

While Val was on the phone, I did something that I'd been planning to do since September. I wrote a resignation letter to President Barton, effective in June. The opening paragraph challenged his view of the role and purpose of a public women's college in the year 1970 and denounced his disdain for civil liberties, repression of academic freedom, and arbitrary treatment of faculty. The rest of the two-page letter detailed these criticisms.

I read the draft to Val while she was in the kitchen preparing our Sunday dinner. "Not bad," she said, removing a meatloaf from the oven. "It certainly burns your bridges."

"Bridges were burned even before you and I met. Traymore's a career-killer." We sat down to dinner. "Wow! Your meatloaf and mashed potatoes sure beat the lousy spaghetti I subjected you to. What's your secret?"

Valerie gave a half shrug. "Oh, ground beef and pork, egg yolk, breadcrumbs. I add salt and pepper, lemon juice, onion, parsley, thyme, and garlic." Val reached across the table and took my hand. "And the most vital ingredient: love."

"Does love explain the ketchup and bacon strips on top?" I asked.

She gave me a smile while, under the table, her bare feet rubbed against my legs.

Xena barked to be let out. She darted into the night as a heavy snow began to fall.

We finished dinner, and I did the dishes, but Xena had not returned. I wasn't too concerned. She was hardy and knew every inch of the area. Maybe she'd rousted some critter. Nonetheless, I put on my coat and rubber boots. "Be back soon, Val. I'm retrieving my dog."

"Wait for me. I'm worried about Xena being out for so long in this weather."

"Stay here. You don't have boots."

She gave me the Look, extracted a pair of sneakers from her bag, and threw open the door. "Let's go."

We headed toward the lake with flashlights. Except for the barely audible sounds that icy snowflakes made when they hit frozen ground, there was only silence. No wind, no geese, no dog—just the sounds of our feet crunching the snow and softly falling flakes.

At the lakeshore, I shouted, "Xena!" No response. To the west and directly ahead, visibility was near zero. The cottage lights behind us winked dimly through the darkness. But far to the east, a peculiar turquoise radiance frosted the crest of the mountains in a jagged line. The aptly named Blue Ridge Mountains were largely obscured, except that through the blackness and falling snow, a thin bluish-green streak silhouetted the highest peaks. And, not unlike calving glacial ice, a single luminescent blue slash tumbled vertically down from a mountaintop only to vanish in a splash of brilliant sparks.

"Mother of God." Valerie crossed herself. "What's happening?"

I shivered, but not from the cold. The sight brought back my disturbing dream and the blue haze that hung over the Heath's house the night Caleb died. "Let's go back inside," I said.

As we turned toward the cottage, we heard what sounded like heavy breathing. Something large was heading our way, and it was coming fast. Poised to meet an attacker, I assumed my high school wrestling stance, but to no avail. I was knocked on my back into two inches of snow. Panting, Xena licked my face. Shaken but unhurt, I got up slowly. Xena led us—actually, shepherded us—to the cottage's front door.

Valerie and I pillow-talked about the strange light on the mountaintops until we fell asleep. The following morning, we continued our conversation over breakfast. "It *was* God's hand," Val said with conviction. She said, "Hail Mary, full of grace . . ." while crossing herself repeatedly.

I was less moved than perplexed by what we had witnessed. Oddly, however, I recalled with a chuckle something that was both frivolous and wholly unrelated that Valerie had once told me about her parochial school dances. When couples danced too closely, the nuns would admonish them with, "Leave room for the Holy Ghost." I, too, left room for the Holy Ghost. There are occurrences that neither science nor logic can explain.

———

That Monday morning, I submitted my resignation. Less than three hours later, Carla Pogue appeared in my office. "President Barton asked me to deliver this." She handed me an envelope and left quickly. The president's letter contained a single line. "Your resignation from the Faculty of Traymore College is hereby accepted, effective at the end of this academic year." I exhaled deeply and bowed my head.

The phone jolted me from my brief reverie. "David," said Ron Cohen of the ACLU, "could you inform Kim Sherman that today we filed her suit concerning the student ACLU chapter? It's such a clear violation of freedom of assembly that the federal district court could issue a directed verdict in a few weeks."

"Ha!" I slapped my thigh. "Thanks, Ron." I called Kim to relay the news. Barton was not rid of me yet.

19

Marvin Ott

Two days later, a lanky young man knocked on my office door. He looked to be somewhere between eighteen and twenty years old, and he evinced a pronounced uneasiness. "Sir." He cleared his throat and tried again. "Sir . . . could I—may I sp-sp-speak with you? That is, if . . . you're not too busy."

"Sure, come in. What can I do for you?"

He took two tentative steps into the office, froze, and looked everywhere around the room except at me. "Sorry for bothering you, sir." He clutched his arms tightly behind his back.

"No problem. Have a seat. What's up?"

He sat uneasily on the edge of the chair and rubbed his razor-nicked chin. "Dean Evelyn Baird said you might help."

"How's that?"

Finally looking at me, the young man replied, "Well, sir, I'm local. Dad works at the Arsenal. We're not too well off, but I figure I can probably afford Traymore's tuition. I can walk here from home, as I did today. Dad says he pays lots of taxes to Richmond, that it's not fair for a state college supported by taxpayers to admit only women."

Eureka! God answers prayer. Here's what Barton most fears. The Dougs and Peters and Georges of the world would surely remind the president of the Virginia Tech student who impregnated his daughter. I grinned, and leaned across my desk toward the nervous young guy sitting across from me. I could've hugged him. "Damn straight! It *is* unfair, and almost certainly illegal. Oh, I apologize for not asking sooner: What's your name?"

"Matt Yancey, sir." He put his hands on his knees and bent forward. "My application to Traymore was rejected." Matt retrieved a crumpled letter with the Traymore letterhead from his back pocket and handed it to me.

I read it aloud. "Dear Mr. Yancey: You are extremely well-qualified, but I regret to inform you that Traymore College admits only women. We recommend that you consider applying to Virginia Tech. Sincerely, Marvin Ott, Dean of Admissions."

Matt looked down dejectedly. He stopped rubbing his chin and repeated what he'd already said: "Dean Baird said you might help."

"How did you happen to meet Dean Baird?"

"When I came to campus today, I asked the first student I met where the dean's office was. She was very nice, but took me to the Dean of Students instead of the Dean of Admissions. Dean Baird was really understanding, though."

"Yes, Dean Baird is a welcoming and understanding person." I stood, walked over to Matt, and sat on the edge of my desk. I reached over and shook his hand. "Matt, it might take a year, two at most, but we *will* get you into Traymore."

Matt's Adam's apple bobbed up and down as he gazed at me with open mouth and wide eyes. "Wow. What should I do?"

"Not much. Give me your phone number and address. Hold onto that letter from Dean Ott, and keep a copy of your application to the college. I'll call an attorney I know. He will probably contact you within a week."

Matt teared up. "Dad won't believe this." He stood and shook his head. "Thank you so much, Professor Pritchard."

"Thank *you*, Matt. It took courage to do what you've done." I put an arm loosely around his shoulders, then walked with him out of the office and down the hall. "Matt, generations of young men may be indebted to you."

When I called Ron Cohen in Roanoke, we cried "Bingo!" simultaneously and laughed. I gave him Matt Yancey's phone number.

"I'll call Arnold Thieleman tomorrow at the ACLU's Richmond office," said Ron. "It's a slam-dunk, legally, but it could take a while before Traymore actually sees its first male student."

"That's what I told Matt, Ron. After you speak with Thieleman, could you tell Matt that the legal action won't cost him a cent?"

"Will do."

———

Early the following week, Kim Sherman called. "Have you heard about Sue, Dave?"

"No."

"She's been screwed by the administration for demonstrating."

"Have *you* been threatened?"

"No, but Sue needs support. Please call her."

"I'll call right now."

"Speaking of calling, why haven't you called *me*? We play well together."

"Uh-huh, we do. I plead gross negligence."

Sue's voice broke when she answered the phone. "Sorry, professor; I'm pretty freaked." She related that on the day of the demonstration, unbeknownst to her, Dean Marvin Ott had inserted a disparaging confidential letter of non-recommendation into her file. Shortly thereafter, she had a job interview in Roanoke with a prospective employer.

"The interviewer," Sue said, "was vice president of the company. He told me that the inclusion of a disparaging letter in a file like mine, without my consent, was improper and highly unusual. Therefore, he felt compelled to ignore confidentiality. He made a copy and handed it to me."

"What did it say?"

"It accused me of having . . ." Sue giggled. "Get this, of having a 'disruptive attitude' and of being 'a radical and rebel.'"

I guffawed and almost dropped the phone. "Sue, those are some of your most endearing qualities."

"And guess what? The vice president offered me a job."

"That's great, but others will view that unsolicited and wholly inappropriate letter quite differently. You want it out of your file."

"Oh, yes. I am very concerned about it."

"I'll talk with Dean Ott tomorrow."

"Thank you, professor."

I didn't know Marvin Ott too well. He did not have a particularly malign reputation. Rather, he was a timid, "go along to get along" kind of guy, a compliant Barton toady.

Early the following morning, I waited for Ott in his outer office. He was a heavy, jowly, mostly bald man in his mid-forties who seemed always to be perspiring, even in February. I heard his footsteps as he toddled down the hallway toward his office.

When Ott saw me, his face turned ashen. He stammered, "Pr-Pr-Pritchard, what brings you here?"

As we walked into his office together, I said, "Sue Ewal, Marvin."

"Oh, damn." Marvin collapsed into a large, sweat-stained leather chair. "I asked President Barton to leave her alone, but he dictated that letter and ordered me to place it in her file. What could I do?"

I was still standing, looking down at a fidgeting Dean Ott. His breathing was labored, and his hands trembled. Beads of perspiration formed on his upper lip.

"Marvin, you could have told Barton to go screw himself. Do you know how many lawsuits have been brought against Traymore in the last few months?" Ott twitched, yanked a wrinkled handkerchief from his pocket, and wiped his face. "Purge Ms. Ewal's file of that defamatory letter and any similar items. Do it today. You wouldn't want your name in the press as a defendant in a defamation of character suit, would you?"

"Pritchard . . . David, I didn't want to do it."

"I know, Marvin. Just clean up Ms. Ewal's file by five o'clock this afternoon, and everything will be fine."

"Okay, okay, I'll try."

"Don't fucking *try*—DO IT!" I turned and walked out.

———

Marvin Ott called an hour later. "The Ewal file is clean, David. Nothing to worry about."

"Marvin, would you phone Ms. Ewal to apologize? Oh, and send her a short letter of apology as well."

"Umm. I don't know. . . ."

I was quiet for several seconds before saying, "*Marvin*. . . ." It wasn't necessary to finish the sentence.

"Yes, yes, of course."

"Thanks, Marvin."

20

Invasion

A week later, I was lecturing in my afternoon American Government course when a secretary opened the classroom door. "Professor Pritchard, could I speak with you?"

Classes were never interrupted, except for emergencies. I walked out into the hallway where the secretary said, "Mara Heath at Piney Woods Cottages called. She was very upset and wanted you to call immediately."

I raced down the hall to my office and called Mara. "It's horrible, David," she said.

"What's horrible?"

"Xena is at the vet, in town. She's in a bad way."

"What happened?"

Mara said that Xena had come to her back porch whining sometime after I'd left for work. She opened her door and found Xena lying on her side, covered in blood. She followed a trail of blood to my cottage, then called the sheriff. "Your place is trashed, David, just *trashed*. Blood's everywhere."

"Who took Xena to the vet?"

"One of Sheriff Goetzke's deputies. The sheriff and other officers are here."

"I'm off to the vet, then Piney Woods." I stuck my head back into the classroom long enough to cancel my class, then jumped in the car.

———

The same veterinarian who had treated Xena when Vincent Tavernetti shot off half of her ear was in the clinic. This time, however, he had a graver prognosis. "She might not make it. Blood loss is considerable. Her injuries look like knife wounds. A deep puncture wound in her upper left shoulder, a lesser one to the neck, and a long gash—perhaps fifteen inches—along her left side."

I winced.

Xena's tongue lolled out as she laid on a stainless-steel dolly. An IV had been inserted into a vein in her leg, and her dressings were blood-stained. I bent over, gently stroked her head, and whispered, "I'm here, girl." The tip of Xena's tail flopped once, her only acknowledgement of my presence.

"She needs to be taken to Virginia Tech's veterinary school immediately," said the vet. "If she survives the trip to Blacksburg, her odds might rise to fifty-fifty."

"Do it," I said. "I'll cover transportation costs."

"Treatment at Tech will be expensive, maybe as high as fifteen hundred dollars."

I winced again. This was more than my monthly salary. "That's okay."

The vet patted my shoulder. "I understand. My assistant will wheel her out to our van. She'll be on her way in ten minutes. I'll call ahead."

I stayed with Xena until the van left for Blacksburg.

———

A state trooper stopped me as I pulled into Piney Woods. "Crime scene, sir. Can't come in here."

"It's my place, officer. Mara Heath called me. Sheriff Goetzke's a friend."

"Leave your car here. Don't go in the cabin."

Several officers were scouring the ground, and others were inside the cottage. As I approached, Harley Goetzke waved. "I'd ask who you pissed off this time, David, but I'm pretty sure I know."

I was not permitted inside, but I peered through the open door. Furniture was broken, clothes were strewn haphazardly, food was thrown about, and my papers and several books were ripped apart. Most shocking was the blood. It was splattered even on the ceiling. And there were distinctive bloody boot prints, about size twelve I'd guess. Xena had fought with everything she had. My best friend, defender, and ever-loyal companion was butchered. Feeling nauseous, I clenched my fists.

"Aubrey Ray Blount," I said.

"Yup," said Goetzke matter-of-factly. "We have his blood type and fingerprints on file, so we'll be able to confirm that." He spat in the grass. Resting a hand on his sidearm, he added with a satisfied smile, "The forensic guys already reckon that not all the blood is the dawg's. She must've chomped down on him *real* good." He stepped toward the door. "Sam," he shouted, "could you hand me that plastic bag with the note?"

With latex gloves, Sheriff Goetzke carefully removed a rumpled, bloodied sheet of paper from the bag and held it up by one corner. "Don't touch. Read it."

Fuck Face—

*Missed you. Will try again. Good news. Your
damn dog is dead.*

Rage and fear were companion emotions. "That's a morale-
booster," I remarked sardonically, biting my lower lip.

"Wish I could say we'll soon track down the bastard," said
Harley, "but after the incident at the Wesley Foundation last
month, the sheriff over in Giles County told me that Blount
had moved his trailer out of Pearisburg." Harley removed his hat
and scratched his head. "He could be anywhere, maybe in West
Virginia or somewhere in the hundreds of square miles of the
Jefferson National Forest, an area he knows well."

I started to head back to the car, but couldn't resist the
impulse to kick my garbage can, and kick it hard. It bounced
off the back of the cottage and flipped over, deeply dented. My
mind was not focused on Christian forgiveness as I walked up
the driveway to where Mara was waiting.

Mara hugged me. "I'm so sorry, David. How can I help?
How's our poor Xena?"

I kneaded my forehead and looked away. "She's been taken
to Blacksburg. It'll be a close call. . . . Can I use your phone,
Mara?"

"Of course, honey."

The technician at Virginia Tech confirmed that Xena had
arrived and was still hanging on. "She's in intensive care."

I made three other calls, first to Cob and Polly Maplewood
to see if I could stay with them for a few days. "Sure," said Polly,
"come on over."

Then to Malcom Todd, the bank president who owned Piney Woods. He was surprisingly agreeable to my proposal to stay on in the cottage when I told him, "There's no structural damage. I'll pay for all repairs, cleaning, and painting."

Finally, to Valerie, who wanted me to stay with her in Christiansburg. I declined her offer. "That's really generous, love, but I don't want to put you in danger."

The police finished their work at the cottage two days later. Sheriff Goetzke called. "David, we've confirmed that the fingerprints and blood type are Blount's." He said that Blount's whereabouts remain unknown, but a warrant for his arrest had been issued. I was then permitted to return to the cottage.

Xena was still in recovery. Her prognosis had been upgraded from "poor" to "fair." One day, when I entered the clinic in Blacksburg, I was surprised to see Virginia Tech Professor Henry Buchanan seated in the waiting room across from me. He had been my fierce opponent on the Vietnam Panel last fall, but subsequently, he had been a welcoming parishioner at Christ Church Episcopal when Val and I had attended a service.

"Henry, what brings you here?"

He looked up from his newspaper, revealing dark circles under his eyes. "Well, if it isn't Pritchard. I read about Xena and the invasion of your cottage. She's probably the most famous German shepherd since Rin Tin Tin. Is Xena here at the clinic?"

I nodded. "She's mending, but slowly. Do you have a pet here?"

"My Jack Russell terrier got into it with a black bear. Not smart, but typical of the breed. Nipper is alive—just barely."

Men who are neither related nor close friends don't commonly confide in one another. Henry Buchanan and I didn't know each other that well, but a shared concern for our dogs paved the way for conversation.

Buchanan volunteered, "Nipper is my closest companion."

"Do you have family?" I asked.

"Lost my wife three years ago when her car skidded off the road. Afraid I haven't adjusted too well."

"I'm so sorry."

"I am active in the church, and Reverend Greenway has been a blessing. Still, when I return home from the campus, even with my little Nipper there, it can get pretty..." He hesitated and gazed at the far wall. "Well, you know, after twenty-five years of marriage . . ."

Henry couldn't finish his sentences. That's when it struck me. Evelyn! She was my dear friend, but I knew with certainty that only Valerie could be a long-term romantic partner. So, I figured, why not toss a lure into the pond and see what happens?

I stood up, walked across the room, and took a seat next to Buchanan. "Henry, are you seeing anyone?"

Buchanan's eyes narrowed suspiciously. He crossed his legs and looked at his watch. "Why do you ask?"

"Her name is Evelyn Baird. Single, thirty-eight, attractive, a churchgoer, and a fantastic cook. Evelyn is Traymore's Dean of Students. I know her well."

Henry tilted his head and raised an eyebrow. "I don't know. . . . She may think that a fifty-two-year-old widower is too damn old and tell me to piss off."

"What if she says yes?"

We exchanged phone numbers. After leaving the clinic, I

called Evelyn from my office and filled her in on Buchanan.

"What if he's a dud?"

"What if he's great? Can I give him your number?"

Silence. "I guess."

I called Henry with her number and wished him good luck.

Buchanan paused for a moment. "Thanks, I think."

21

Transformation

In early February, I'd written to a branch of the National Education Association requesting an investigation of Traymore. My letter to the NEA cited six blatant violations of academic freedom in addition to the current and prospective lawsuits against the college. I asked that my letter and all future communications be kept in the strictest confidence and signed it *David Pritchard, JD, PhD, Associate Professor of Political Science.*

To my surprise, I received a call just four days later from Steven Browning, the NEA's deputy director and an attorney. "Professor Pritchard," he said, "because of our involvement in representing Professor Bill Vaughn in his suit against the college, we are familiar with some of the abuses you cited in your letter. Our board voted unanimously this morning to send me to Traymore to investigate the situation. What about early next week?"

Browning and I agreed he would interview representative faculty members from all departments of the college, these discussions would be confidential, and his presence at Traymore would be kept secret until all meetings were completed. Had Browning met openly and transparently with the faculty, there would have been certain and severe retribution from Barton.

The following week, Browning and his legal assistant made

daily visits to Traymore from their hotel in Blacksburg. Through the good offices of Bill Vaughn and Amos Toth, meetings were held at the Wesley Foundation with fifty-one faculty members. All interviews were recorded, and Browning's presence in town went undetected by the administration.

At the end of the week, I had dinner in Blacksburg with Browning and his assistant. "We already knew a good deal about the situation at Traymore," said Browning. "But what we learned this week is simply stunning."

I shook my head. "Yes, it is."

"You will hear from us soon."

The NEA sent its investigative report to the State Council on Higher Education, President Barton, the press, and me in mid-March. The report called for the dismissal of President Barton for, among other things, "wrongfully interfering in faculty matters, harassing and denying salary increments to those faculty who speak out, and instituting arbitrary internal procedures especially concerning the evaluation of faculty." The report stated that "at least 10 faculty members had grievances that could be subject to litigation."

"Home run!" I shouted when I read the report. I ran off dozens of copies of the report's conclusions and distributed them to colleagues throughout the campus. The investigation certainly hadn't sealed Barton's fate, but it drove the first hard nail into what might become his coffin. The headline on the front page of *The Roanoke Times* the following day read, "Traymore Prober Asks Dismissal of Barton." Of course, Millard Truse, Chairman of Traymore's Board of Visitors and close friend of Elzic Barton, denounced the report as baseless, and Barton, in a classic case of the pot calling the kettle black, protested the secrecy of the investigation and the absence of an open hearing.

————

My UVA friend Phil Johnston and I had planned to get together for lunch the next weekend in Lexington, a town located about midway between Traymore and Charlottesville. Since Rachel Sherman had been dating Phil on a fairly regular basis and would be with him, I asked Kim to accompany me.

Phil and I had spoken on the phone, but we hadn't actually seen one another in several months. My tip to Phil in November had been instrumental in securing him a tenure track position at Miami of Ohio University. Meanwhile, I still faced unemployment.

Phil and Rachel were sitting at a circular table near the bar of the Southern Inn restaurant when we arrived on a cold Saturday afternoon. They were laughing and holding hands, so they didn't notice us until I touched Phil's shoulder. A tipsy Rachel jumped up and gave me a hug that was a bit too cozy, while Kim and Phil, who had never met, were more discrete. Phil and I shook hands warmly, and we all moved to a larger table in an adjoining room, where a waitress took our order from a menu that featured the Inn's homemade pecan pie and its popular southern style fried chicken and okra.

Relaxed and happy, Phil leaned back in his chair and looked at me. "My orals are scheduled for mid-May, then graduation, and after that Oxford, Ohio, in late July. I'll see you in Charlottesville for our graduation, but what are your plans after that?"

I grimaced. "Maybe I'll sell chestnuts on Wall Street out of a pushcart."

"What! You *still* don't have a position?" Phil gave me an incredulous stare. "Good God, man, you must be scared shitless."

"I am," I admitted. "May have to return to New York and practice law."

Kim spoke up, "Why don't you come with me to Champaign-Urbana?" I smiled and winked.

"Well," said Phil, swallowing hard, "normally I wouldn't even mention this, but I was called last week by a former professor of mine in Florida who is now at American University's School of International Service. She asked if I'd like to be considered for assistant dean of undergraduate studies. Naturally, I turned her down, but would you be interested?"

"I have zero interest in administrative work, but a drowning man grabs for whatever keeps him afloat."

Kim touched my arm. "Take it. Doors will open up once you're there."

"Indeed," I agreed. "That can happen."

"I'll call her Monday," said Phil.

After lunch, the four of us visited the tombs of Robert E. Lee and Stonewall Jackson. Kim and I then returned to my cottage.

As I drove Kim back to the college on Sunday afternoon, she said, "*Fiddler on the Roof* is at the Roanoke Convention Center on Friday. I could get tickets."

"That'd be nice." I dropped her off several of blocks from campus so we would not be seen together.

———

I had been regularly checking in on Xena, and early Tuesday morning, she was finally ready to leave the veterinary clinic in

Blacksburg. "It was touch and go," said the vet, "but now we can hardly contain her. She's raring to leave." When Xena was brought to the reception area, she yipped, did a triple pirouette, and crashed into my legs, nearly knocking me over. I dropped to the floor to hug her and was instantly covered in dog slobber. *What would I do without my best girl?*

Later that morning, I received a phone call from Washington, D.C.: "Professor Pritchard?"

"Speaking."

"Jack Petrovsky, Dean of American University's School of International Service."

"Oh, yes. Thank you for calling."

"I understand from one of my colleagues that you might be interested in applying for the position of assistant dean of under-graduate studies."

"Yes, that's correct, Dean Petrovsky."

"What about March thirty-first? It'd be a full day of meetings and interviews, starting with coffee and pastries at eight in the morning."

"That's fine. I'll put my CV and some other things in the mail tomorrow."

"Great. Look forward to meeting you."

———

Late Friday afternoon, shortly before picking up Kim for *Fiddler on the Roof*, I received more good news. The local radio station announced that the federal district court in Roanoke had ruled for Kim and the ACLU. Traymore's refusal to permit an on-campus student chapter, the court held, was a clear violation of the First Amendment's guarantee of freedom of assembly. Of several suits that had been filed against the college, this was the first to come to trial. Coming so soon after the damning NEA report, the court had delivered another blow to Barton.

Our seats for the musical were in the first row of the mezzanine. As people poured into the theater before the curtain went up, Kim leaned over the rail and stared. Pointing to the front of the orchestra section below us, she said excitedly, "It's him." Indeed, the bald, bulbous head gave him away—President Barton with his wife. Kim and I stood and raised our arms in a V for victory. He looked in our direction but didn't seem to recognize us.

At the intermission, Kim and I walked down to the main floor. I excused myself to use the men's room. As I was about to enter, the door swung open and out came Elzic Barton. We both spun around. He stared at me, bug-eyed and mouth agape, as if he had encountered the Grim Reaper. "You—you . . ." he said, unable to articulate his shock and anger.

I smiled and said nothing.

"I swear—I swear that I'll . . ." Barton thrust his finger in my face without finishing the sentence. He then turned and bulled his way through the crowd until he was out of sight.

I told Kim what had happened as we returned to our seats in the mezzanine. "Be careful, Dave. He's wounded and probably feels besieged. Barton wants your head." For whatever reason, the Bartons did not return to their seats after the intermission.

Kim and I enjoyed the remainder of the musical. When the final curtain came down, we held hands, raised them high, and gamboled in the aisle singing, "If I were a rich man—ya ba dibba dibba dibba dum—all day long I'd biddy biddy bum. . . ."

An elderly couple sitting next to us were laughing. The woman, probably in her eighties, said to Kim, "Oh, to be young again, dear. You two make such a lovely couple."

Kim stopped frolicking for a moment and gently took the woman's hand. "Thank you. You are so sweet."

Then, as the woman's husband (who walked with a cane) looked on, Kim did a little twirl in the aisle with the lady, whose face lit up. This strong-willed ally of mine who could bite off Barton's ear had a bottomless reservoir of warmth and caring.

As the crowd filed out of the Convention Center, Kim clutched my hand and, with a naughty grin, said, "Let's forget Traymore and find a motel off of I-81. We can fuck our brains out and then drive to Washington tomorrow."

"I especially like the 'fuck our brains out' part," I said.

We zigzagged out of the Convention Center to the car, arms wrapped around one another. We were happy in our victory, happy in the moment, and happy in the thrill of anticipation. Once in the car, Kim slid over next to me and dropped her hand on my lap. We made it to a Holiday Inn by the narrowest of margins.

Kim and I were in the Washington area by early afternoon on Saturday. We checked into a motel in nearby Arlington, Virginia, not far from where I'd lived when working summers at the CIA. From there, we drove across the Key Bridge, down M Street through Georgetown, and eventually to the National Mall.

I knew Washington well, but it was all new to Kim. She wanted to see the Lincoln Memorial and, to my surprise, pursue her hidden passion for Asian art. So, after paying our respects to Honest Abe, we spent two hours in the Freer Gallery of Art. We didn't have time for one of my favorite places, the Jefferson Memorial, but we agreed to visit the Tidal Basin after dinner to honor the founder of the University of Virginia, commonly referred to by UVA students as Mr. Jefferson, or simply TJ.

Back at the motel in Arlington—and after calling to check on Xena, who was staying with Mara Heath—Kim extracted a dime bag of marijuana from her purse.

I protested, "Weed fuzzes my mind."

"Oh, loosen up, Dave." She nuzzled my neck. "This is *our* weekend. In a few months, I'll be at the University of Illinois, and you'll be . . . well, maybe right here in D.C. Let's go for it."

Kim rolled and lit a joint, inhaled deeply, held her breath, and passed it to me. The possession of any amount of grass was a serious offense in the Commonwealth of Virginia. *But what the hell?* I took a toke.

With Jefferson Airplane blaring on the radio, we drove very carefully to the Orleans House restaurant in Rosslyn for dinner. Of course, we had wine with the meal. Then, while sharing yet another joint, we drove on to the Jefferson Memorial.

The cherry blossoms weren't out yet, but they soon would be. Thomas Jefferson's nineteen-foot bronze statue was bathed in light as we wandered along the Tidal Basin, wobbled up the steps of the Memorial, passed through the white neoclassical columns, and entered Jefferson's D.C. Rotunda.

It was well after dark. Except for one sleepy park ranger, who waved and walked away, we had Mr. Jefferson to ourselves. Inscribed on the walls were passages from some of his renowned contributions to Virginia and American history, none greater than the Declaration of Independence. Holding Kim's hand high, I read, "We hold these truths to be self-evident, that all men are created equal . . ."

"And women," Kim yelled.

"They're *more* than equal," I replied, my voice echoing off the marble walls. I continued: ". . . that they are endowed by their Creator with certain inalienable Rights, that among these are Life, Liberty and the pursuit of Happiness. . . ."

Kim pulled me close and whispered in my ear, "Let's pursue happiness."

Whether it was her prompt, the weed and wine, the aura of the evening, or the glory of the venue—I don't know. But I responded with, "Let's get married."

"Yes!" she said. "Let's get married."

Circling Mr. Jefferson, giddy and hand-in-hand, we kissed and kissed again before finally waving good-bye to our third president, stumbling down his stairs, and trying desperately not to splash into the Tidal Basin. The relatively uncluttered roads facilitated our *very* cautious, deliberate drive across the Potomac to our Arlington motel.

Kim was exhausted. Her head rested on my shoulder as I drove. I could scarcely keep my own eyes open as I half-carried her into our room. Sleep was instant and deep. No lovemaking, no brushing of teeth. Only our shoes came off.

Late the next morning, a knock on our door startled me. *Cops! Did someone report the lingering stench of marijuana smoke?*

"Maid!" came a voice.

I exhaled, leaned over, picked a shoe off the floor, and flung it sideways at the door. "Go away," I grumbled. I rolled over, and—*Oh, Hell!*—I remembered what I'd done. Damn weed.

Kim stirred. "Coffee."

I stumbled in and out of the bathroom before tending to the coffee. My offering of bitter black coffee was accepted stoically by Kim, who was now sitting on the edge of the bed yawning.

I sat down next to her and asked, "Did we do what I think we did last night?"

"We smoked some joints."

"Anything else?" I asked, hoping maybe she wouldn't recall.

"Uh-huh."

Caught. "Did I. . . . ?"

"You did."

"Did you accept?"

"Uh-huh."

I gently massaged her neck. "Were we of sound mind?"

Kim poked me in the ribs. "You gotta be kiddin', sweet cheeks."

I rested my hand on her knee. "We're a blue-ribbon team under the covers, Kimmy, but do we *really* want to do this?"

Laying her hand on mine, Kim said with a slow smile, "Mom wants me to marry a nice Jewish boy."

Thank God for Jewish mothers, I thought before saying, "But Kimmy, I'm circumcised. Isn't that close enough?" We dissolved into laughter and hugged one another tightly before collapsing onto the bed.

Our drive back to Southwest Virginia that Sunday was relaxed. No awkwardness, no prolonged silences, plenty of Janis Joplin and Creedence Clearwater Revival, and lots of banter. It was as though nothing consequential had happened.

But it had. Kim and Evelyn were Wonder Women whom I hoped to know forever. They were vital allies in our campaign to change Traymore. But for months I'd known that Valerie was the One. Val would now be my only *intimate* ally.

———

Evelyn was animated when we met for lunch at the faculty club. She exhibited an odd blend of exuberance and anxiety. Her facial expressions alternated between smiles and frowns. Her index finger tapped nervously on the table, yet her voice was bubbly, even lilting. Something was up. Evelyn was not being Evelyn, let alone dean-like.

"You seem, uh . . . different, *Dean* Baird," I said, raising an eyebrow. "Are you okay? Did Henry Buchanan ever call?"

"Henry called, and I'm fine, but I need to tell you something."

"First, tell me about Henry."

Evelyn leaned back and sighed. "*Such* a gentleman."

"Unlike me?"

"No, I didn't mean it that way. He's *so* mature and worldly."

"Unlike me?"

She kicked my ankle under the table. "Pritchard! Can I tell you about Professor Buchanan?"

"Sorry."

Evelyn was clearly charmed by Buchanan, even swept away. She said that, in less than three weeks, they'd been on two dinner dates, and last Sunday, they'd attended a service at his church in Blacksburg—Christ Church Episcopal. "Henry introduced me to Reverend Matthew Greenway. What a pleasant man."

"Yes, he is." I winked. "I take it things are working out?"

Nodding and, with a radiant smile, Evelyn lifted her water glass in a toast. "Here's to my favorite matchmaker. Thank you."

"That's terrific!" I raised my glass. "And to my favorite dean. But a few moments ago, you seemed to have had some kind of reservation."

"Oh, not about Henry. It's a completely different and troubling matter."

Evelyn skootched her chair closer to mine and fingered the gold cross on her neck. She lowered her voice, although no one was within earshot. "Carla came to the house last night. She'd come across something and wanted to talk."

"Oh?" I asked, putting my fork down and crossing my arms. "Sounds important."

"As Carla told it," continued Evelyn, "President Barton had given her his expense reports to send to Richmond for reimbursement. She was alarmed by two items. First, the president wanted repayment from the state for what he claimed were his personal expenditures to that Roanoke investigation firm 'for emergency campus security.'"

"That is," I interjected, "Barton wanted to be repaid for his own payments to the outfit that hired the felon who trashed my cottage, almost killed my dog, and remains at large?"

"Yes. But the president did not provide Carla with canceled checks or any other evidence that his purported campus security expenses were, in fact, personal expenditures. Nonetheless, the state reimbursed him within three days."

Evelyn ran her fingers through her hair. "The second item that Carla noticed was an unexplained transfer of funds from the library's account to the Office of the President. The amount transferred was exactly equal to the president's requested reimbursement from the state." Clearing her throat, Evelyn continued: "Carla said she went immediately to the president, who told her brusquely to 'just submit the damn reimbursement; don't get down into the weeds.'"

"I see," I said, raising an eyebrow.

"She complied," said Evelyn, taking a deep breath, "but not before making a copy of the signed and completed reimbursement form and of the books showing diversion of funds from the library to the president's office. Carla said she also keeps meticulous written records of what occurs in the office and what the president says."

"This confirms the concerns we had some time ago about how Barton would pay the investigation firm," I said, shaking my head. "Barton gets paid for so-called personal expenditures he never made. It's win-win for him. His office pays the investigator out of funds quietly diverted from the library. Then the SOB falsely claims to have paid the investigation firm out of his own pocket. What gall to ask for reimbursement from the state, that is, the taxpayers! Fraud, pure and simple . . . and stupid."

Evelyn lowered her head. "The president can be arbitrary and vengeful. But, until now, I never thought he would do something like this. Neither did Carla. Her faith in the president has been shattered."

"He's hardly the first to mishandle public funds. The state's auditors won't be unemployed any time soon." I pushed my chair back, stood, and lingered for a moment. "I've got to go." My fingertips brushed Evelyn's shoulder. "I'm delighted you and Henry are hitting it off. . . . Tell Carla to put those documents in a safe place. I have a couple of phone calls to make."

The first call was to the NEA's Steven Browning, and the other was to the ACLU's Arnold Thieleman in Richmond. Both men reacted identically: "Holy shit!" They agreed to contact Carla Pogue, and then perhaps go to the attorney general's office and the State Council on Higher Education.

Thieleman cautioned, "This is damning. If the alleged criminality pans out, it'll be fatal to Barton. But he'll pull out all the stops. It could take months, maybe much longer, before this is resolved. You may be gone by then."

"That's okay. It will be mission accomplished."

―――――

About the time I'd written to the NEA in February requesting that it investigate Traymore, I had signed a petition with three dozen other faculty members that went to the college's Board of Visitors. We asked for an impartial study by an independent body whose members would be appointed by the State Council of Higher Education. Serious turmoil at Traymore was now widely acknowledged throughout Virginia's higher education system. Scarcely a week went by without the media reporting on yet another troubling incident, demonstration, lawsuit, or investigation—not to mention the attacks on me, my cottage, and the now-famous Xena. Despite the public attention to Traymore's troubles, I was skeptical that our petition would be well-received by the board because of the close friendship between President Barton and board chairman, Millard Truse. I was wrong.

Even before the ACLU and NEA were able to confirm Carla Pogue's recent revelation about Barton's apparent misuse of public funds, the lead story in *The Roanoke Times* on March twenty-sixth was headlined, "Traymore Probe to Be Opened Soon." *The Times* reported that, well before the faculty's petition in February, a majority of the Board of Visitors had become "gravely concerned about deteriorating conditions at Traymore."

Within days of receiving the petition last month, the *Times* story said, the board had requested that the State Council on Higher Education appoint an independent study commission to examine the situation at the college. The newspaper further reported that the commission appointed by the State Council of Higher Education to investigate faculty unrest at Traymore College would hold its initial meeting the following week, shortly before Traymore's annual spring break.

22

Deliverance

I was exuberant when I called Valerie. "Don't see how Barton can survive, babe."

"You started it all, way back in September."

"Let's do something different this weekend," I said.

"Practice chastity?"

"Not *that* different. Let's climb Mount Rogers. Virginia's highest mountain is only an hour or so drive from the cottage."

Val wasn't much of an outdoors person, but she agreed. I, on the other hand, had been a hiker since I'd been a Cub Scout. While attending college, I'd backpacked the Long Trail in Vermont, the Northfield-Lake Placid Trail through the Adirondacks, and several sections of the Appalachian Trail from Virginia to Maine.

Our climb up the 5,729-foot Mount Rogers would only be a nine-mile roundtrip day hike, starting from Grayson Highlands State Park. The trek, however, involved a substantial change in elevation.

We left the cottage at dawn and were on the trail to Mount Rogers by eight in the morning. The first mile went well, but then Val slowed to a crawl. We brought Xena, who, because of the violence inflicted on her by Aubrey Blount, now walked with a pronounced limp. But she trotted right along, happy to be with us.

This late March day was clear and cold. We were greeted by some early-blooming bloodroot with their white petals and yellow stamens, but spring was still only a hope in the mountains. Except at lower elevations, no leaves were yet on the trees. When we finally reached the rock outcroppings on the summit early that afternoon, we were buffeted by a fierce wind. The views were spectacular, but because Val's teeth were chattering, we ducked behind a boulder to escape the wind. She devoured the tuna sandwich and Snickers bars we'd brought for lunch, while I wrapped her in my windbreaker. Two of her toes were blistered, so I dug around in my pack for moleskins and, between wind gusts, gently applied them to her aching feet.

"I'm really sorry. I shouldn't have subjected you to this."

"Th-th-that's okay," she stammered.

I removed my wool pullover hat, drew it down over her head and ears, and put my arm around her.

"Where were you last weekend?" she asked, still shivering. "You didn't answer the phone when I called."

Uh, oh. Think fast, Pritchard. I kissed her cold cheek. "I was in Washington."

"But you're going up there on Tuesday for the interview at American University."

"That's part of the reason I went to D.C., to see the campus. It's on Ward Circle."

"What else did you do?"

Why doesn't Val concentrate on keeping warm and nursing her blisters instead of asking perfectly reasonable questions? "I visited a friend I knew when I was at the CIA last summer. He's invited me to stay with him Monday night before the interview."

Val nodded. This was followed by a long pause. "That's nice."

We started back down the mountain. No more questions. Perhaps pain preempted her curiosity.

I felt a little guilty about lying, but only a little. Last weekend's romp in D.C. with Kim was off-the-wall risky. In retrospect, however, it might also have been a necessary, self-inflicted slap upside the head. Now, I was where I belonged—with Val.

The sun had set by the time we got back to the car. Val had hung onto me for most of the descent. We were famished, so we headed straight for the Hungry Mother Cafe in aptly named Rural Retreat. The over-cooked hamburgers were gristly, but we wolfed them down along with milkshakes and greasy fries before finally returning to Piney Woods and collapsing into bed.

It was not until late the next morning that my lovely, if aching, partner showed any sign of life. She was flat out. Xena and I were up at sunrise. We let Val sleep and took a long walk in Claytor Lake State Park, had coffee with Mara Heath and her sister, then returned to the cottage with the Sunday newspaper.

"Aargh. . . ." Milady stirred.

I tip-toed into the bedroom. "Awake?" I whispered.

"Aargh." Val rolled over on her side, swept tangled hair out of her eyes, and peered at me with a strained smile. "No more mountains."

"Okay, love." Returning her smile and kneeling beside the bed, I offered to kiss whatever hurt.

"*Everything* hurts."

"Yum." I kissed her maimed toes and started an upward journey. My ascent up her shins was soon interrupted—"First, coffee."

After complying with her request, the remainder of the

morning and early afternoon was spent recovering from our ordeal. As we reclined on the bed, Val said, with her head on my chest, "Take the job at American. It's only a short drive from Johns Hopkins."

"Let's hope I get an offer."

Val returned to Christiansburg later that afternoon, and I started to think seriously about practicing law if the interview did not work out.

———

My last shot at an academic position was really the quasi-academic job of assistant dean for undergraduate studies at American University's School of International Service. It was an administrative role, something that most faculty try to avoid. I'd be largely removed from research and teaching, but I would be in Washington, which was the place to be for someone with my interests.

I arrived at the campus early, well before the agreed meeting time, and poked around inside the boxy, architecturally unremarkable building. A bronze plaque on the wall stated that SIS had been inaugurated by President Dwight D. Eisenhower in 1958, only twelve years ago. When I returned to the entrance, a distinguished gray-haired woman of perhaps sixty was standing, leafing through a manila folder. With a ruffled white blouse and tailored navy-blue suit, she was clearly someone of consequence.

I introduced myself. "Good morning. I'm David Pritchard. I'm here for . . ."

"Oh, yes." We shook hands. "I'm Elizabeth English, chair of the search committee. I was just browsing through your CV and the other materials you sent us. I'm the one who contacted your friend at UVA, Phil Johnston." Smiling warmly, Professor English said that Phil had been one of her outstanding undergraduate students when she had taught at the University of Florida.

We chatted amiably as she led me down well-worn steps, flanked by institutional cinderblock walls, to a large, ground-level classroom where coffee and pastries were set out on a table. "Six of us are on the search committee," she said, "including a graduate student and an undergraduate student."

"That's remarkable. Students at Traymore College have no input on faculty hiring or anything else."

"So I gather. Your letter to Dean Petrovsky and the newspaper clippings you enclosed are startling. *The Washington Post* occasionally reports on the situation at Traymore in its Metro section. I think I even recall a photograph of your dog."

"How about that," I chuckled. "Xena's quite a dog."

Professor English—who had co-authored a widely assigned undergraduate textbook on U.S. diplomatic history—introduced me to the others on the committee as they entered the room. We exchanged pleasantries with one another and then retired to a nearby seminar room, where we sat around an oval table. The committee members included a bright young assistant professor of political theory, a pony-tailed associate professor of Latin American studies wearing sandals and blue jeans, a forty-something professor of comparative politics whose outstanding article in *World Politics* I had (thank God) read, a willowy undergraduate coed majoring in international development, and a red-haired doctoral student in East Asian studies who was about my age and a Vietnam veteran.

I spoke about my background, my professional interests, and the reasons I was applying for the position. For the next two hours, we discussed my aspirations, various interests and concerns of the committee, and several substantive foreign policy matters.

I had anticipated many of the issues that came up. *Why would anyone teach at Traymore College?* ("It was the only place I could get an academic position on very short notice.") *Have you been sued?* ("No.") *Why did you switch your professional focus from the law to international relations?* ("I like the law, but I love international relations—and the two are interrelated.") *Why did you work summers at the CIA?* ("To be grounded in the real world, and the pay was good.")

But some questions took me by surprise. For instance, the young assistant professor said, "I also have a German shepherd. How's Xena?"

And the coed drifted into sensitive territory: "I understand that there are four thousand women at Traymore. Are you married?" This drew an immediate frown and reproachful stare from Elizabeth English and an equally instant apology from the student: "Sorry, I shouldn't have asked."

I smiled. "That's okay. I'm not married."

Professor English ended the session and escorted me into the dean's office. Dean Petrovsky was a specialist in the Soviet Union. The burgundy and gold Washington Redskins pennant on his wall hung next to an old, discolored photograph of Lenin. We shook hands, and Jack Petrovsky welcomed me to the school. But he politely walked me to the front door and said, "I know you're going to lunch now, so I won't hold you up. We will talk later in the day."

Professor English was waiting outside the door. We walked across campus to the faculty club, where we joined the rest of the search committee, who were seated at a reserved table. Lunch was buffet style, and we served ourselves. Elizabeth English and the other senior professor on the committee, whose *World Politics* article I made a point of praising, reiterated what they'd told me during the morning session: namely, that their primary concern was my lack of scholarly publications. "But," said Professor English, "you only passed your PhD orals a few months ago, and we fully understand the horrendous conditions at Traymore. Your commitment to research seems sincere, and, of course, the position you are applying for is primarily administrative in nature." I assured them, once again, that research and writing were among my foremost objectives.

The graduate student had asked few questions in the morning, and he remained quiet. He was my major concern. So, I took the initiative: "What's your dissertation topic?"

He frowned. "You wouldn't know the subject. Frankly, I don't understand why I'm here. The position you're applying for concerns undergraduates."

"Try me."

The student scowled, as if I'd crossed some line. After clasping his arms, he said tersely, "It concerns the role of China's People's Liberation Army, or PLA, in North Vietnam."

I looked him in the eye. "The Chinese operate most of the anti-aircraft batteries in the north. It will be a difficult topic to address without access to classified information unless you place the study in a broad historical context. History affects everything in Vietnam's relations with China." I removed my jacket and loosened my tie. "You should also factor in escalating Sino-Soviet tensions and weigh heavily the critical importance of Soviet, not just Chinese, aid to Hanoi."

Bingo! The graduate student's face lit up. I had his attention. "What did you do at the CIA?" he asked.

"I'm not at liberty to answer your question with any specificity, but it concerned Vietnam. China was one of my fields of study at the University of Virginia. I wrote two papers on the PLA, and I'd be happy to share them with you." I grinned. "The analyst sitting behind me at Langley had a photo of a World War I biplane on his desk which he labeled 'China's Air Force.'"

My new-found ally asked, "How should I proceed?"

"Well, three things come to mind. The forthcoming issue of *Orbis* has an article you'll want to read carefully, including the footnotes. I know the author and reviewed her draft."

The grad student pulled out a pad of yellow paper and started taking notes.

"Second, I'll introduce you to an analyst at the American Enterprise Institute who can be helpful. He was in military intelligence and works with some beltway bandits. Third, I can put you in touch with a foreign service officer at State. He's a China specialist who served in Saigon. Like you, he's a Vietnam vet." I thought for a moment. "Oh, yes. And I know Henry Buchanan at Virginia Tech."

"Wow!" The grad student took a deep breath and rubbed his hands together. I relaxed, feeling confident that I'd won him over.

After lunch, I was the focus of an open forum for the entire SIS community, both faculty and students. In earlier meetings with the search committee, I'd addressed most of the issues that came up in this gathering of about fifty people. Some questions were off-the-wall, including yet another one about Xena. One questioner wondered whether I might someday write a book about my experience at Traymore. I burst out laughing. "Yes, but it'll be a novel."

The final question came from a cute, dark-haired girl who might have been Amerasian. She had startlingly bright green eyes, a slight New York accent, and a multicolored suede mini-skirt. "Professor, what do you think about our involvement in Vietnam?"

"Miss, I could give you a detailed and comprehensive response. But let me be succinct. This may sound unprofessional, but it *is* my considered opinion." I took a slight step in her direction. "If we take every dollar the U.S. has spent on this war, and the billions more we will continue to waste, pile it high on the National Mall and light it on fire . . . that would be a wiser expenditure of taxpayers' money."

She shot her fist in the air. "Yes!" Except for two or three older faculty members, the audience applauded enthusiastically.

Afterward, the search committee met with me briefly once again. I thanked the members for their time and hospitality.

Professor English turned to me. "You are certainly qualified for the administrative position, but, if you had your choice, what would you *really* like to do?"

"That's easy." I shifted forward in my chair. "Teach and write in my field, U.S. defense and foreign policy."

The graduate student spoke up. "The professor who taught national security policy retired last year."

Before I could comment, the Latin Americanist on the

committee chimed in, "Yes, I was thinking the same thing."

Elizabeth English added, "Me too. Maybe we should consider you for *that* position." All heads nodded, including my own.

Toward the end of the day, as Professor English was taking me to Dean Petrovsky's office, I commented that both of the students on the committee were impressive.

"Our students are full participants in the school's governance," Professor English explained. "All SIS committees, including Rank and Tenure, have student representation—and they vote."

"How refreshing for the consumers of education to have a say in the quality of the education that they receive and pay for."

Dean Petrovsky was standing outside his office when we arrived. He touched my arm and offered an apology. "Please forgive me, but I'm in a bit of a hurry today. The provost is waiting. But you and I will speak again soon." Before leaving, he asked, "Did you get a good feel for the school?"

"It's welcoming and incredibly democratic."

"We like to think so." Then, abruptly changing the subject, he said, "Elizabeth tells me you might be interested in the national security position."

"Yes. That's my area."

Jack Petrovsky placed his hand lightly on my back and guided me from his office door into the hallway. "I absolutely must leave, but you should know that the feedback from Elizabeth is positive. The committee meets tomorrow morning. I'll call you in the afternoon."

We shook hands, and he rushed out to see the provost. I was about to exit the building when a beaming Professor English came up to shake my hand. "David, thank you for coming all this way.

It went well. We'll be in touch with you very soon."

I floated down the steps. The usually tedious drive to Traymore flew by. Xena greeted me with her customary acrobatics. I petted her head. "We're on a roll, girl." Then, I called my other best girl. "Val, looks like I'll be in D.C."

"Whoopee!" she shouted. "I'm coming right over to give you a big kiss." She did come right over. She delivered a big kiss and more.

The Call came late Wednesday afternoon. "David, Jack Petrovsky. The committee's decision was unanimous, and I concur. We are offering you the position of assistant professor of international relations to teach U.S. defense and foreign policy. Salary is twelve thousand five hundred."

This was slightly higher than what Traymore was paying me, but I would have accepted an even lower salary. "That's great news. Thank you. I accept."

"You'll soon receive a contract. We look forward to having you as a colleague."

With that call, everything appeared to be changing for the better—or so I thought.

23

Confession

Appalachia's hills were splashed with pink and white dogwood blossoms. And life was good. Regime change at Traymore appeared imminent, and Val would be in nearby Baltimore when I was in Washington. As I approached the ARSE-N-ALL Bar in early April for what was likely to be my final POF meeting, I could not have known that a grave crisis awaited.

John Manikas was holding forth at the faculty table when I walked in. He stood on a wobbly metal folding chair, holding a can of Old Horsey in each hand. Clearly more sloshed than usual, he was admonishing his colleagues, several of whom had already submitted their resignations. "You guys are fleeing the battlefield before the war is over. Barton's on the ropes."

As I neared the table, littered as always with crushed beer cans and smelling of spilled beer, John blurted out, "Well, shit. . . . Look what the cat dragged in. Boat Rocker. Rather, Boat Sinker."

I laid my hand on John's shoulder. "Gonna' miss ya', old fart."

John—more bluster than action—sat down, raised a leg, and pointed his prosthesis at me. "You're leaving this peg-legged soldier high and dry, Pritchard."

"Don't know about the dry part," I said, "but you're sure as hell high."

We all proceeded to exchange information about lawsuits,

job offers, student demonstrations, the prominent press coverage, and the Council on Higher Education's investigation. Despite our amiable banter, the mood was subdued. We knew that we might never meet again, at least as a group. So, when it was time to adjourn, we all stood and, with Merle Haggard, payed homage one last time to the "Okie from Muskogee," raising our voices with Merle's as he sang, "We like livin' right and bein' free. . . ."

———

An opportunity to hike on the Appalachian Trail arose when Val announced that she would be with her parents in Baltimore over the college's spring break. Hiking had always been my passion. It was a physical challenge, an emotional high, and—on rare occasion—almost a transcendental experience. Hiking was a pressure valve. Despite multiple demands on my time at Traymore, I walked regularly in the nearby state park with Xena, I'd hiked Mt. Rogers with Val, and my brother and I had hiked the Peaks of Otter in the fall. Immersing myself in nature—whether alone, with others, or with my dog—was crucial to my corporal and spiritual well-being.

Meeting the unpredictable challenges of traversing remote areas on-foot reaffirmed my self-confidence, which was precisely the kind of assurance needed to confront Elzic Barton.

I inventoried my equipment: well-used boots, backpack, mini-stove and fuel, down sleeping bag, slightly frayed nylon tent, ground mat, rain gear, and many other items. I borrowed a five-year-old Appalachian Trail guidebook for Virginia from the library, included food for Xena, and purchased snacks and dinners for five days at the army-navy surplus store in Roanoke. Val agreed to follow me to where I would park my car and then take me to the trailhead.

We dropped my car off on US 460 in Pearisburg, which was about twenty miles from Traymore and near the West Virginia border. Valerie then drove me and Xena north to just outside of Roanoke, where the trail touched Virginia Highway 624 close to the small town of Catawba.

On the drive Valerie said, "Remember when we climbed Mount Rogers, and I asked where you'd been the prior weekend?"

Uh-oh, I thought. *The past has not passed.* "Uh-huh," I said warily. "I was in Washington."

"Right." Valerie glanced at me. "I saw Kim Sherman at the honor society meeting this week. She mentioned that she was in D.C. at the same time you were."

"Oh?"

"When I told Kim that you were in Washington that weekend, she said that she'd seen you at the Jefferson Memorial. What a coincidence." Val clutched the steering wheel with both hands as she passed a large tank truck on I-81. She looked over at me again. "I've always loved that memorial."

Curve ball. I hesitated before responding. "Yes, my friend and I did see her there."

"Funny. She didn't say anything about your friend."

My face and ears felt hot. I crossed my arms and stared out the window. After an awkward silence, I said in a cracked voice, "Val, I . . . love you, and . . ."

"And?"

"This is really awful. It was a stupid thing to do. Kim and I *were* in Washington together that weekend. I flat-out lied to you."

Valerie clenched her jaw and stared straight ahead. She was deathly quiet. A tear ran down her cheek. I struggled to find the right words, but there were no right words. "It was a terrible mistake," I said. "You are everything to me. I won't see Kim again."

The silence was suffocating. My mind raced back more than two decades to when I was a five-year-old kindergartener. The teacher, a disciplinarian about whom I remember little, lifted me onto a stool and forced a too-tight scarlet dunce hat down on my head. It had hurt. I'd apparently violated one of her many rules. Can't remember which one. Maybe it was for kissing a girl. I vividly recall the humiliation. She sternly warned the children not to speak to me. An hour or so passed, and I timidly raised my hand to go to the bathroom. Ms. Gestapo stormed across the room, glowered at me, and said nothing whatsoever when I pleaded for permission to go to the bathroom. She'd smirked, shook her head, turned, and stomped away. I peed in my pants.

Valerie gave a disbelieving head shake. "How *could* you?"

As we pulled up to where the trail intersected with Highway 624, I reached over to touch her. She pushed my hand away.

"Val, please. . . . We've been through so much together."

Val glared at me and said nothing. I didn't pee in my pants, but I was deeply pained and embarrassed.

Xena and I hopped out of the car onto a narrow asphalt road riddled with potholes. Valerie got out, dropped down on one knee, and wrapped her arms around Xena. "Be careful, pretty girl." Xena's tail twitched as she licked Val's face. Turning to me, Valerie scowled and snapped, "Don't you let anything happen to her."

"We'll be fine. Xena's in great shape now." I tried to give Val a hug, but she backed away and jumped into her car. She didn't roll down her window or wave as she swung her 1965 red Ford Mustang back toward I-81 to resume her trip north.

What had been a much-anticipated venture into the mountains was suddenly something darker, more ominous. Everything was colored by the enormity of loss that I had brought upon myself. As I stood at the trailhead watching Val drive away, I sensed that the next few days might reveal, or maybe seal, my fate.

24

Trail Trials: Days One and Two

I had chosen this sixty-three-mile section of the Appalachian Trail—universally known as the AT—for its proximity to Traymore, and because Valerie could easily shuttle me to where I would start hiking south. I was acutely aware of what Sheriff Goetzke had said a couple of months earlier—that Aubrey Ray Blount had removed his trailer from Pearisburg to avoid arrest, and his whereabouts was unknown. Although this was unsettling news, the likelihood of encountering him on a trail in the rugged mountains of western Virginia seemed remote. Blount was overweight and clearly not a hiker.

My backpack was heavier than usual, a price I paid for carrying Xena's food. On this clear, mostly sunny day with the temperature in the mid-sixties, I stepped onto the trail and started out. I patted Xena's rump. "It's just you and me, babe."

The white-blazed AT left Virginia 624 and ascended steeply via several switchbacks. I paused for a moment to take in a view of Cove Mountain to my right. A small brown bird landed on a nearby bush. She quickly flew away in surprise with an offended chirp.

My guidebook indicated that the trail would ascend to a rocky rim known as Rawie Rest in another mile. Half an hour later, I stood on a narrow, knife-like ridge. Continuing to climb along the sharp crest, I reached Devil's Seat, a rock outcropping with a sweeping view of the valley below. It was time for a handful of gorp (mostly M&Ms, peanuts, almonds, and raisins) and a dog biscuit for Xena. Despite the permanent limp inflicted by Blount, Xena's tail wagged, and she flashed her German shepherd smile. She trotted several yards in front of me, but not out of sight, occasionally rousting a chipmunk, box turtle, or some other critter.

It was four o'clock, and I was getting a bit concerned about the time. My destination for today was the Pickle Branch Shelter, which was another five miles away and an additional half mile on a blue-blazed side trail. But the weather was splendid, hardly weather at all. The Appalachian spring hummed to the chords of life, very much like Aaron Copeland's orchestral suite.

Two deer darted in front of us. Then a turkey narrowly eluded Xena's hot pursuit; its flapping wings sounded like a rug being whacked. Wildflowers bejeweled the forest and lined portions of the trail. Purple-crested iris with their dashes of yellow welcomed us, as did scarlet Indian paintbrush, Virginia bluebells, and my favorite—the tri-petaled white and pale pink trillium, the first of the season.

Another strenuous mile over rocky slopes and ridges brought us to Dragon's Tooth Overlook, a soaring quartzite monolith. From there, I could see McAfee Knob, which the guidebook described as "one of the most spectacular, panoramic views." Also visible was the Catawba Valley, and far to the east were the Peaks of Otter. I was grateful for my five-foot-long bamboo hiking stick; this "third leg" afforded added stability on the steep slopes.

Dragon's Tooth was popular with day hikers because of its vistas. A short side trail provided easy access to the pinnacle. That afternoon, however, Xena and I had it to ourselves. I drank from one of my liter canteens and poured water into a metal Sierra cup for Xena. We pushed on, crossing over the 3,050-foot summit of Cove Mountain.

The sun had begun to sink in the west, and a chill was in the air. We picked up our pace, descending precipitously on a stony trail with sharp drop-offs to the right. By about five-thirty, we'd reached the blue-blazed trail that led to Pickle Branch Shelter. Twelve minutes later, we arrived at a typical six-person shelter with its fire ring of rocks in front and a grease-stained picnic table on which Peter had carved his "eternal love" for Dee. I rubbed my eyes and thought of Valerie.

We hadn't seen anyone all day, not even a day hiker. There could have been section hikers this time of year, who like me, only had time to backpack a portion of the AT for a few days or for a week or two. April was still a little early to encounter most through-hikers, those who aim to complete the entire twenty-two hundred miles of the AT from Springer Mountain, Georgia, to Mt. Katahdin, Maine. Ninety percent of through-hikers go from south to north. These hardy, sometimes foolhardy, souls—the vast majority of whom never make it—usually begin heading north from Springer between mid-March and early April. However, a few able and determined young hikers who start out early, average twenty miles or more a day, and have a high tolerance for pain from blisters, muscle pulls, bee stings, giardia, dehydration, and multiple other afflictions might now be in Central Virginia.

The shelter was empty. An orange, dog-eared, ringed notebook—a log, like those found in most shelters—indicated that a speedy north-bound through-hiker from Wisconsin had spent the night here three days ago. Sprinter (his trail name) had written: "Damned mice! Lots of wildlife. Beware of an iffy area north of Pearisburg."

With a pencil, I scrawled, "Val, I'm so sorry."

Mouse droppings dotted the warped planked floor, a common sight in these trail shelters. In the past, mice had chewed through my pack in search of food even when I'd hung it by a nylon cord from a shelter's main rafter.

Rather than combat rodents, I found a relatively level spot some distance away near a thick patch of mountain laurel bushes, where I set up my tent and its fly. A clear cold creek flowed by the shelter. I boiled water on my trail stove, poured it into a plastic bag of dehydrated chili, and *voila!* dinner. Well, the reddish mush smelled vaguely like chili.

Xena devoured two cups of dry dog food and begged for more. "That's all, girl," I said. She dropped to the ground, whining. With her head between her paws, she gave me a pitiful look: *Aren't I your best girl?*

"Come to think of it," I said out loud, "with Val gone, you are my only best girl." I gave Xena another cup.

I cleaned up, brushed my teeth, spread out the ground mat and sleeping bag in the tent, and took Xena down to the creek for a drink. She chased off a raccoon that was hunting for crayfish. It was dark at eight o'clock, and time to turn in.

The tent was large enough to accommodate Xena. However, except in a hard rain, she preferred to sleep outside but close by. I'd just dozed off when her low growl jarred me awake. Sporadic muffled sounds came from the direction of the shelter. Another hiker had arrived, late. I sat up, unzipped the front flap, and stroked Xena. "It's okay, girl." She settled down. We were soon both fast asleep.

I awoke before sunrise and reluctantly rolled out of the warm sleeping bag into a frigid morning. My down jacket felt good. A light frost coated the ground. Standing barefoot in the cold, I stretched, scratched my head, and inhaled the scent and embrace of the brisk darkness. As I struggled to lace up my boots, Xena leaned hard against me as if to say, *Let's go—let's go—let's go!*

My trail breakfasts were uncreative: instant coffee and oatmeal. After cleaning up, I broke camp, hoisted a slightly lighter pack, and made my way toward the shelter to connect with the blue-blazed trail that led up to the AT.

By now, the sun had started to rise in the east. At the shelter, I walked down to the creek to fill my two canteens. When I returned, an older man who looked to be in his mid-sixties was sitting up in his sleeping bag. He smelled of wood smoke, insect repellent, and of course, body odor. A hiker.

"Thought I was alone," he said.

"Heard you come in. I was tenting with my dog."

We shook hands. "Horace is the name. Gramps is my trail name."

Gramps revealed that he'd section-hiked the trail all the way up from Georgia over the past three years. "Last night," he said, "mice ran across my face, but I was too pooped to set up a tent in the dark."

As he talked on, Xena hopped into the shelter, tail wagging, and laid down beside him. "Good dog," he said, gently stroking her head. "Miss my two Labs."

We chatted for a few minutes, exchanging intelligence about

the trail ahead. Gramps was heading north, while I was going south. "You'll find that water is not always reliable," he said, "and the last fifteen miles before reaching 460 is sketchy."

"So I understand from reading the log. How so?"

"Didn't trust a couple of guys I ran into. They weren't hikers. Might've hung out in one of the rusty trailers wedged into the hollows that the trail passes through. Probably towed them up into the hills on fire roads or old logging paths."

I thanked Gramps for this information and had a fleeting thought of Aubrey Blount. We shook hands once more before Xena and I headed up to the trail for our second day.

More than fourteen miles had to be covered before we'd reach our next destination, Sarver Shelter. We'd slept well, and were dry. A moleskin covered my one small blister.

The Appalachian Trail dropped down to a creek before it crossed Virginia Highway 620 and ascended along the side of Brush Mountain. The elevation changed little over the next six miles as the trail snaked across dry streambeds, low ridges, and gullies.

Xena and I took a water and snack break by a muddy pond where the trail entered an old apple orchard before descending to Virginia Highway 621. Suddenly, Xena plunged into the pond and thrust her head under water. The source of her excitement? Big tadpoles, none of which were in any danger from their would-be canine predator.

The first cold raindrop struck my hand after we crossed 621. The sun disappeared behind gray clouds as a breeze came up.

Thirty minutes later, we arrived at the Niday Shelter, which afforded a brief respite from what was by then a steady spring shower. I put a waterproof cover on my pack and donned a poncho.

We were about halfway to Sarver Shelter. A two-mile gradual ascent to the crest of Sinking Creek Mountain brought us to an intersection with a side trail. It was here that we encountered Noche, the name I gave to a heavy coal-black dog with a scarred, mud-splattered coat and short stumpy legs. Noche blocked our path and snarled. He was of no identifiable breed, but pit bull must have been somewhere in the mix.

Xena was beside herself with rage. Her hair shot up like quills on a porcupine. "Come, Xena." I took her by the collar and pulled her away from Noche.

"Sit!"

Xena sat, reluctantly. Panting heavily, her eyes locked on this ostensible challenger.

"Stay!" I commanded.

Noche hadn't budged. I walked toward him slowly, trying not to show fear or look him squarely in the eye. "Such a good doggie, Noche. Bet you're lonely up here on this wet mountain. Poor baby. Noche want a cookie?" I pulled a dog biscuit from my pocket. He was *very* interested.

Xena, however, was furious. She growled and scooched forward several feet.

"Xena, STAY!" I repeated, this time more forcefully. She whined but remained in place.

Noche's little stub of a tail was all out of proportion to his chunky body. It started to wiggle. As I stepped to within a few feet of him and held out the biscuit, he shuffled over and gently took it from my hand. He then ambled to the side of the trail and laid down as if to say, 'Toll paid. You may pass.'

I told Xena to come. She did, but I had to intercept her in mid-stride as she lunged for Noche. Still savoring his biscuit, he ignored her. Noche meandered along after us for a while before eventually veering off into the woods.

The trail continued along the ridgeline of Sinking Creek Mountain, crossing several slanting rock ledges. The views to the west were probably spectacular, but they were obscured by the mist and what was now a light drizzle.

———

I heard them before I saw them. Hoarse sounds. *Krruck!* Then, *Krruck! Krruck! Krruck!* Ravens. Some of the birds were strutting, wings outstretched, cawing in shrill, harsh voices. Others pecked at a dead animal, plucking off fragments of flesh and vying with one another for what little remained. With bits of fur and bones scattered over the forest floor, it was hard to identify the creature. I guessed opossum or feral cat.

We continued on, but two of the ravens followed us for a while with their characteristic penguin-like struts. A brilliant shaft of light from the west pierced the mist and filtered through the oak trees. On cue, a glimmering rainbow appeared. The ray of light proceeded to accompany us while we hiked along the trail. Goosebumps covered my arms, and I found myself inexplicably humming Beethoven's "Ode to Joy."

The ravens vanished, but the beam of light stayed with us, as if by design, until we reached Sarver Shelter. The experience affected me deeply. The light was a dazzling white, but the emotional effect was similar to what I'd experienced from the blue glow that had enveloped the Heaths' house the night Caleb died.

Two young men who appeared to be slightly younger than me were at the shelter when we arrived in the late afternoon. Coon Dog, a carpenter from North Carolina and a Marine Corps veteran, said he was hiking the entire trail "to forget shit that happened in Nam." Pilgrim was a recent graduate of Williams College who'd postponed medical school to hike the trail. "We've been hiking together since Damascus," said Pilgrim.

"How far did you come today?" I asked.

"From Pine Swamp Shelter, twenty-three miles to the south," said Coon Dog. The two men were fleet footed. I didn't plan to arrive at Pine Swamp Shelter until the day after tomorrow.

Sarver Shelter was relatively new. No sign of mice. I set out my sleeping bag and mat next to the other men's and introduced Xena, who eyed them suspiciously.

Coon Dog greeted her. "Hi there, sweetheart. I'm Coon Dog."

Pilgrim followed suit. "Pleased to meet you, Ms. Xena."

After Xena swished her tail and hopped into the shelter next to me, I asked about the stretch north of Pearisburg about which others had been apprehensive.

"Yeah, that's right," said Coon Dog. "We double-timed it through that section. One guy hobbled out of a run-down trailer and wanted to sell us a pint of white lightening. He said, 'It's *really* good; taste it,' and we did."

"How was it?"

"Tasted like distilled piss," said Coon Dog. "Spat it out. Said it came from his cousin's still."

We talked through dinner and, as the light faded, we continued to talk until turning in around eight o'clock. Behind Sarver

Shelter stood a stone chimney, the last remnant of the old Sarver Cabin. Pilgrim said that the cabin was rumored to be haunted. "A guy we met at the hostel in Damascus was writing a history of Appalachian Trail shelters. He claimed that hikers often avoid Sarver. Some who do stay here leave in the middle of the night when they hear voices. Henry Sarver's brother, who helped him build the cabin, apparently died at Gettysburg in Pickett's charge."

"I'm not superstitious," I said. However, before falling asleep, I related my experience with the ravens, the rainbow, and the extraordinary ray of light that had accompanied me to the shelter. "It's just too coincidental to be without some kind of meaning."

Coon Dog turned toward me in his sleeping bag. "The Lord works in mysterious ways, but I *know* that my Redeemer liveth."

Pilgrim flicked off his flashlight and ended the evening's conversation with, "Liveth? Sounds like George Frederick Handel's *Messiah*. He's no longer around. Haven't seen the Redeemer recently either."

25

Trail Trials: Days Three and Four

No apparitions were seen, nor tormented voices heard. I slept soundly until awakened by the stirrings of Coon Dog and Pilgrim, who were hitting the trail early. We exchanged high-fives. They petted Xena and hiked off into the dark.

After breakfast, I filled the canteens at a nearby spring. Before heading off on this sparkling April day, I added my name to the shelter's log and wrote, "No ghosts, unless we're all ghosts." I thought of Valerie. No ghost there.

Shortly after leaving the shelter, the Appalachian Trail passed through an overgrown field with a few arthritic apple trees. The trail went under a power line, descended from the crest of Sinking Creek Mountain, and crossed over a sulfurous smelling rivulet that even my cow pie-eating dog avoided.

Xena and I walked across a dirt road, climbed over a stile into another field—this one with patches of woods—and arrived at paved Virginia Highway 42. Hikers detest road walking, and not only because it reminds us of what we're trying to get away from. Walking on asphalt with a heavy pack, often in the direct sun, drains energy, brutalizes the feet, and jars every bone and joint in the body. However, we had no alternative but to follow the AT's white blazes, telephone pole to telephone pole, for a half mile until it eventually veered off into a pasture.

We forded Laurel Creek and ascended three miles to Kelly Knob, at an elevation of thirty-five hundred feet. The temperature had risen to the mid-seventies on this humid day, and one of my canteens was emptied even before we reached the summit.

After climbing over Kelly Knob and continuing on toward Big Pond Shelter, we encountered a four-foot-long blacksnake sunning itself on a lichen-covered ledge. As with others of the kind, I treated this snake as a reincarnation of my childhood companion, Cecil. Xena sniffed it and turned away, uninterested. Good place for a break—gorp for me, biscuit for Xena.

"What's it all mean, girl?" I asked aloud.

Xena's one-and-a-half ears shot up, and she tilted her head. I poured some of our diminishing supply of water into a Sierra cup for my goofy-looking dog. As irrational as it sounds, I'd found that coming across a blacksnake or a raven was often followed by a significant event. It didn't take long.

We continued on to the shelter, where I was shocked to discover no water source. As I drank from a nearly empty canteen, Xena heard something rustle in the bushes. She darted behind the shelter. Seconds later, legs churning and tail between her legs, she barreled past me with an *Oh shit, what did I do?* look in her eyes. Something crawled in my hair. I slapped it—yellow jacket. Killed the bugger before it stung, but another one got me on the leg.

I shot down the trail after my dog, both of us running like hell. When we'd gone a hundred yards or so I screamed, "Xena! Xena, stay!" She skidded into a moss-covered log like a ball player sliding into second base and gnawed at her tail as if she wanted to chew it off. I zapped two wasps on her ears and crushed two more on her tail and coat. After that, no more yellow jackets.

For the first time on our hike, I thought of RJ and Kim. Those two beautiful and steadfast allies, each in her own way, were also yellow jackets, albeit strikingly alluring ones. RJ was a firecracker, and with Kim, I'd stepped squarely on the hornet's nest. I waited much too long in both instances to flee down the trail. Stings were inevitable.

Another mile brought us to a rocky high point where a fire tower once stood. Still nursing our wounds, we crossed a primitive, largely overgrown dirt road and descended steadily past huge cliffs. When the trail leveled off and we had passed into a stand of pines, I froze.

The skeleton of a deer was impaled high on one of the rusted iron spikes that encircled a small graveyard. Virginia creeper covered most of the rough-hewn tombstones, only four of which still stood more or less upright. Hunters or, more likely, a pack of dogs must have been chasing the deer when it attempted to jump over the spiked fence. The skull's jaw was locked in an eternal scream.

I entered through an opening where an iron gate had long ago fallen off its hinges. Xena stared at the skeleton, whined, and refused to follow me into the graveyard. I ripped vines from two of the standing stones. Hand-chiseled into the tombstones were the words: WILMA MAY BLOUNT—BORN 1908/DIED 1946, and WAYMON RAY BLOUNT—BORN 1901/DIED 1944.

Good God. I pulled vines from several more gravestones. One was too weather-worn to make out, but in all, I found five Blounts. A family graveyard, long forsaken.

Xena pawed the ground anxiously. I started to leave, but noticed another vine-covered headstone lying at an angle against the iron fence. It was further obscured by a tree branch that had fallen. Something about this mostly hidden stone drew me to it. Large black ants scurried away as I tore at the vines and lifted the dead branch.

"Wow!" I shouted. The name read: ELIZA BARTON BLOUNT—BORN 1879/DIED 1919. *Could Elzic Barton be related somehow to Aubrey Ray Blount?*

———

The guidebook had said nothing about the cemetery. It did indicate that we would come to a stream in another half mile, and we soon came to a barely flowing rill that ran through a rhododendron thicket. I decided to pitch camp nearby for the night. No telling where the next water source might be.

It was three o'clock. We'd covered twelve miles. I set up the tent and boiled the musty smelling water. With time on my hands, I ambled a couple of hundred yards down the trail and was surprised to find a U.S. Forest Service road that was unmentioned by the guidebook. I followed the white blazes across the road to an overgrown field where the AT entered the woods and started to ascend. That's where I stopped to lean against a huge, long-ago-fallen chestnut tree.

Xena's hair shot up, and she positioned herself defensively in the middle of the trail. Soon, I heard the crunch of hiking boots coming toward me.

She was Moon Glow; he identified himself as FUBAR ("Fucked Up Beyond Any Recognition"), another Vietnam vet. They were up from Georgia and had spent a day south of Damascus with Coon Dog. One glance told me that they were in a bad way.

"We're heading for Big Pond Shelter," said FUBAR.

"No water there." I pointed down the trail. "Get water from the small flow where I'm tenting. Should be boiled."

"Used up our fuel long ago, but we still have some iodine tablets," FUBAR said.

Hikers smell, but these two reeked. I stepped back, but Xena, attracted by the odor, sniffed FUBAR's pants a bit too zealously. I yanked her collar. "Sorry about that." FUBAR's gamy smelling green T-shirt was torn, and mice had chewed through his pack in at least two places. He looked to be about my age.

Moon Glow was much younger—disturbingly so, not more than fifteen. She was hurting. Her cheap boots were so ripped up that her bare, blistered toes were exposed. "Wore out my socks long ago," she said. Her matted hair was bound tightly by a red bandana she'd apparently found in a shelter, and her arms and face were scratched and insect bitten.

Moon Glow's rumpled state reminded me to caution them, "Don't go *behind* Big Pond Shelter. Yellow Jackets."

Xena and I walked with them back toward our tent site. On the way, they disclosed a little about themselves. Moon Glow had run away from an abusive stepfather in Houston. FUBAR, like Coon Dog, was trying to get his "head straight after Nam." He and Moon Glow started hiking together by sheer chance when they first encountered one another on Springer Mountain during their initial day on the Appalachian Trail. "Been together ever since," FUBAR said.

When we reached my campsite, Moon Glow fixated on my tent. "Nice. Wish we had one." This was shocking to hear, particularly from aspiring through-hikers. Hypothermia was a real threat. Shelters are often full, too far apart, dilapidated, or rodent infested.

"Why don't you?" I asked.

In unison, they replied, "Can't afford one."

"It's amazing you've made it this far."

"We started early from Springer," said FUBAR, "too early—March second. Deep snow in the Smokies stranded us in a shelter for days. Almost ran out of food."

"How are you doin' now for food?"

"Noodles and peanut butter."

They filled their canteens, dropped an iodine tablet into each one, and were about to begin the long ascent to Big Pond Shelter. I reached into my pack, extracted two Snickers bars, and handed one to each of them. "Good luck, guys."

Moon Glow dropped her pack and gave me a foul-smelling bear hug.

Maybe that's what softened me up. The teenager had "RJ" written all over her. She was innocent, unrestrained, and vulnerable. I waved her over to me, "I want to tell you something." I assured FUBAR, who was chomping on his candy bar, "Don't worry; we'll only be a minute."

He was unconcerned. "No problem, take your time."

Moon Glow and I walked behind a fifteen-foot tall rhododendron. Whether FUBAR and Moon Glow were an item or not was neither my concern nor my business. They were clearly comfortable together, and I liked him. Still, I felt uneasy about her.

"Listen," I said. "If things get really tough while you're still in Virginia, I want you to call Dean Evelyn Baird at Traymore College." I gave her Evelyn's home phone number from memory.

"Can you remember that number?"

"Think so." She repeated it.

I wrote it down for her. "Tell Dean Baird that I asked you to call her and that we met on the AT. Evelyn's a really nice person. She'll help."

"Okay," said Moon Glow in a neutral tone of voice, neither grateful nor offended.

I extracted almost all the money I had in my wallet, one hundred and thirty dollars, and gave it to Moon Glow. "Get a good pair of boots in Roanoke and a goddamn tent as well."

Her mouth dropped open. "I can't take it."

"You *will* take it. Get on the trail. It's late."

Moon Glow hopped over to me, kissed my cheek, and— RJ-like—squealed, "Thank you! Thank you!" She then skipped out from behind the bushes to rejoin her trail-mate. Her radiant face was my reward. I shook hands with FUBAR and was kissed again by Moon Glow as her bemused companion looked on. And away they went.

Two minutes later, FUBAR returned. He handed me his Zippo lighter. "For you." Back up the trail he went.

Engraved on this very personal gift was:

NAM 68-69

WE THE

UNWILLING

LED BY THE

UNQUALIFIED

TO KILL THE UNFORTUNATE

DIE FOR THE

UNGRATEFUL

I fed Xena and ate some gray lumpy slop that the makers of this packaged dinner had the balls to label beef stroganoff. After washing up in the brook and brushing my teeth, I slipped into my sleeping bag while Xena assumed her usual watch in front of the tent. My thoughts once again turned to Valerie and how much I missed her as I drifted off to sleep.

———

After breakfast the next day, I refilled the canteens, fed Xena, and broke camp. I adjusted my noticeably lighter pack, and we resumed our southward journey on a cool overcast morning. Pine Swamp Branch Shelter was today's destination, fourteen miles away.

Xena and I soon passed by an empty War Spur Shelter and ascended steeply for two miles to the wooded crest of Salt Pond Mountain. Deer were everywhere, forcing me to leash my hyper-excited dog for a while. We crossed the summit of Potts Mountain an hour later and began a long, gradual descent. Halfway down the mountain, heading toward Bailey Gap in a light drizzle, we came to a dramatic protrusion of overhanging rock ledges that formed a protective shelter from the elements.

Near the innermost fold of this huge rock cavity was a distinct glow. I took two steps in the direction of the light, but stopped when a sharp voice commanded, "Touch me not!"

Xena dropped onto her belly, ears erect, eyes fixed on the dim silhouette of a figure at the rear of the chamber. Oddly, Xena's fur was not raised, nor did she growl. She was alert yet remarkably calm.

I removed my pack, told Xena to stay, and focused on the

shimmering light that appeared to come from the shadow or silhouette. "Sorry to disturb you," I said. "We're just taking a short break."

"I was expecting you," came the booming voice.

What the hell is this all about? Then I heard movement, followed by the sound of sandals slapping on rock as a figure loomed and became clearer.

I retreated a couple of steps but remained just inside of the overhanging ledge. Xena stayed put but piddled on the rocks. My bladder held, but my heart pounded.

A tall, imposing man with a biblical-like appearance and demeanor in the mold of an Elijah or John the Baptist emerged from the darkness. True to form—and I swear to God Almighty that this is the truth—he gripped a carved oak staff that curled at the top. It dwarfed my puny bamboo hiking stick. He was not wearing a shoulder-to-toe heavy monk-like robe, but was instead dressed in what looked like a handmade broadcloth cloak or serape with loose-fitting pants of the same material. Of course, his hair and beard were long and mostly white, with flecks of gray and hints of red. I guessed his age to be somewhere around fifty-five or sixty.

What stood out above all else, shockingly so, was his face. *This* was the light that had shone out from the dim inner cavity. His face shined, literally glowed, even in the daylight. Its shimmering brightness reminded me of the luminescence of lightning bugs, except more so. The radiance was silvery and constant.

"You were . . . uh . . . expecting me?" I asked. He inhaled deeply and closed his eyes. A distinctive smell of cedar filled the air. He was definitely not a hiker.

He neither gave his name nor explained why I had been expected. What did flow from his mouth were unnerving quotations from the Bible. "'And the light shineth in darkness; and the darkness comprehended it not.'"

I froze. Xena didn't budge.

Stepping out into the drizzle from under the ledge, the man raised his arms high in the air, staff in hand, and recited from memory passages from Exodus and Luke. "'Moses . . . came down from the mountain. . . . His face shone because he had been talking with God.'" He waved his staff as if transporting himself from the Old to the New Testament. "'Jesus went up on the mountain to pray. And while he was praying, the appearance of his face changed.'"

Finally, the man turned and approached to within five feet of where I stood. I saw two striking cerulean blue scars, not tattoos, on his forehead over each eye. One was shaped like an anchor; the other (strangely enough) resembled a pelican. He looked at me—or rather, through me—as he quoted from the Gospel of John: "'I have yet many things to say to you, but you cannot bear them now.'"

I stiffened and took a step backwards. My neck and arms tingled, and I couldn't return his piercing stare. Hoisting my pack, I called Xena and fled down the trail toward Bailey Gap. I was freaked out. This formidable prophet-like figure had accomplished what Elzic Barton never had—he terrified me.

Racing double-time toward Bailey Gap with my mind fixed on the encounter, I tripped on a root and tumbled onto the trail, skinning a knee. "Damn!" A concerned Xena licked my face as I lay in the dirt. "It's okay, girl." I patted her head. But it wasn't okay. Something was out there. The threat was undefined, but I sure felt it. *Why did that weirdo think I couldn't bear to hear the many things he supposedly could tell me?*

We reached Bailey Gap and soon thereafter crossed two rural roads. Another unremarkable three miles of hiking in the Jefferson National Forest brought us to Pine Swamp Branch Shelter, which was located much too close to paved Virginia Highway 635. Because of the shelter's proximity to the road, at least twenty-five people from what appeared to be a family reunion or church group were milling around in the picnic area.

I was physically and emotionally drained. Only one very long day and part of another remained before we'd arrive at my car in Pearisburg. I hiked past the shelter for perhaps another mile until I came to a large spring. The area was muddy and rocky, with dense patches of nettles. A lousy campsite. But the water was decent, and dusk was near.

So, I pitched the tent on this inhospitable spot where no hikers or prophets were likely to intrude. I quickly prepared dinner, fed Xena, brushed my teeth, and crawled into the sleeping bag. Neither ravens nor prophets tormented my dreams. Rather, Bessie's pot roast and a hot shower with beautiful Valerie got center stage.

26

Rattlesnake Spur

The next morning, a dark cloud of no-see-ums forced me to break camp in a hurry, without breakfast. Hundreds of tiny black flies swarmed my head, and two kamikaze flies drowned in my eyes. Their preferred target, though, was Xena. My fingers were bloodied from squishing dozens of the little tormentors feasting on her ears.

We fled up the trail until we'd outrun what the Scottish Bard, Robert Burns, called the "wee beasties." When we reached a laurel and rhododendron thicket, I paused to give Xena her breakfast while I settled for a handful of gorp and my last Snicker's bar.

Continuing on, we crested a mountaintop and dropped down to Dickinson Gap, where the AT straddled a ridge until it entered an open grassy area called Symms Gap Meadow. The trail, still in Virginia, now followed a little-used dirt access road with sweeping views of West Virginia's high mountain terrain.

The primitive track through the meadow was squishy, gutted, and crisscrossed by cow paths. Several cows grazed nearby as I stepped gingerly around their flops. In a few minutes, I came to a ramshackle hovel, where chickens pecked in the ooze of what once might have been a front yard. Honeysuckle vines ran up the side of the shack onto a crumbling roof that seemed about to collapse at any moment.

I hadn't replenished the canteens that morning because of the no-see-um crisis, and, having already hiked six miles, we had an urgent need for potable water. So, hoping for relief, I waded through the muck, the chickens, and the chicken shit to the sagging front porch, where I knocked on a warped door with its faded red, white, and blue "Jesus Saves" sticker.

No one answered. Peering through a cracked dirt-stained window held together by frayed duct tape, I saw a bent-over old man shuffling toward the door with a cane. He wound his way through mountainous stacks of what appeared to be magazines and newspapers. He skirted a potbelly stove, passed under a drooping, water-stained ceiling, and finally—with an "oof" — shoved open the door.

The odor was nauseating. His faded blue jeans were splattered with brown flecks of manure, and his grayish T-shirt gave no hint of ever having been washed.

"Water?" he said, stepping onto the porch.

"Yes, sir. How'd you know?"

"Hikers 'bout only folks I see these days. Always want water. Pump's out back, but don't want no dog goin' for my chickens."

"No, sir." I clicked a leash on Xena.

I pumped cold spring water into the canteens, gave Xena some, and returned to the front porch, where I'd left my backpack.

"Braxton Fields' the name." The grizzled good Samaritan only now introduced himself as he extended his hand. He looked to be well into his eighties and had settled himself precariously on a wobbly three-legged stool.

We shook hands. "David Pritchard. Glad to meet you." Since I would soon enter the section of the trail hikers had warned me about, I asked Mr. Fields about something that had been on my mind. "Would you know anything at all, sir, about an Aubrey Ray Blount?"

Braxton looked down at his shoes, twisted his mouth into a grimace, and shook his head. He crossed his arms and spat at a hen that, with an indignant cackle, darted deftly out of range. "Blounts' place 'bout eight to ten miles from here on Peters Mountain. Never knew 'em well. Never *wanted* to. They died long ago. Fire burnt the place to the ground. Heard their boy, Aubrey, in trouble with the law."

"Yes, sir." I swung the pack onto my shoulders.

"Know him?"

"Only by reputation." I thanked Braxton Fields for the water. Xena and I walked to the far end of the meadow and entered the woods.

———

Over the next two miles, the trail crossed under a power line, briefly followed red blazes that marked the boundary between the Jefferson National Forest and private land, and passed over a pipeline right-of-way before merging onto a jeep road. I heard the crack of a rifle, not uncommon in rural Virginia.

These incursions along the Appalachian Trail—road, power line, pipeline, and gunshot—annoyed me. Forests and mountains are healthy in spirit only when their core is wilderness. Thoreau universalized what lovers of nature know to be true: "In wildness is the preservation of the world."

The jeep road I was following dead-ended at an even larger pipeline right-of-way, where four young men with camouflage jackets, rifles, and pickup trucks were dressing a deer, obviously poached. Deer hunting season was in November. Xena's hair went up. I grabbed her collar, exchanged "up-yours" glances with the poachers, and continued along the AT as it forked uphill into the forest.

Twenty minutes later, the trail crossed an overgrown logging road where a dilapidated trailer was wedged between two dead locust trees. Another trailer was partially visible further down the trackway. I smelled smoke and heard someone chopping wood.

I passed several moss-covered old trailers over the next half mile. Those with busted-out windows, flat tires, and fallen tree branches straddling their roofs were long-abandoned. A deer bounded in front of us. Xena gave chase. She pursued the doe down an unmaintained, poison ivy-infested forest road until it leapt over a creek that flowed by yet another trailer. A man appeared. He shouted, shook his fist, and went back inside.

"Come, Xena," I called. She ran back to me. The distance was too great for me to see clearly, but I made out a rusted piece-of-crap pickup truck.

In another thirty minutes, we came upon two springs close to a level patch of ground just inside the national forest. The well-worn area, directly on the trail, was obviously a popular campsite. But that was a problem. Snakes, biting insects, and precipitous cliffs were to be expected, but I was most wary of the locals, many of whom were hostile to hikers.

So, after filling the canteens with spring water, I walked up the AT about a hundred yards, swerved off to the left, and bush-whacked through the brush until coming to a large lichen covered boulder. Here I pitched my tent. The ground was lumpy, and the tent slanted downhill, which would not be good if it rained. However, I was well-hidden.

The sun was beginning to set, and my pooch and I were tired. I boiled water on my mini-stove and poured it into the last dehydrated dinner pouch, labeled "Shepherd's Pie." A millipede meandered over my boot as I willed a few spoonfuls of the salty grayish mush down my throat. Xena eagerly lapped up the remainder before we turned in for the night.

———

Xena's deep growl jarred me awake a couple of hours later. I unzipped the tent's front flap. "Come, Xena." She came into the tent. "No, girl. Hush." She softened her growl to a pissed-off grumble.

I had heard nothing. Then a stick snapped some distance away, followed by what sounded like a muffled groan. Shafts of scattered light refracted through the forest from the direction of the camping area near the springs. This continued for a few minutes until silence and darkness returned. *A hiker probably arrived late and pitched his tent.* I kept Xena in the tent and fell back to sleep.

———

Early the next morning, I broke camp quickly and quietly, once again without breakfast. We made our way through the brush back to the AT, where I whispered, "Sit. Stay." Xena tilted her head and sat. Leaving my pack with her, I took a measured and vigilant walk down to the campsite in the faint morning light. It was vacant. No tent. No hiker.

I took a flashlight from my pocket to examine the ground. No tent stakes had been driven; no campfire had been set. By the two springs, however, was a fresh gouge in the wet moss where someone might have slipped and fallen. More revealing were recent boot prints in the moist sandy soil. A visitor had been there last night. The prints bore some resemblance in size and impression to the bloody ones that were on my cottage floor in February when Blount slashed Xena. But that didn't make sense. *Why would he be way out here, and in the nighttime?* Still, it seemed prudent to assume the worst. I could well be in Blount country.

"Xena, come!" I shouted. She ran to me, tail wagging. She sniffed the ground obsessively as the hair on her back rose. Xena and I were now both on alert.

The trail guide indicated we had one last rigorous ascent to a prominent knob on Rattlesnake Spur. From there, it was all downhill to where I'd parked the car. In bold letters, the guide warned: "Use extreme caution here. Timber rattlesnake den. Hikers have been bitten."

Before resuming the hike, I retrieved my pack, topped off the canteens, gave Xena a drink, and boiled water for coffee. The sun was rising into a cloudless, robin's egg blue sky. It promised to be a warm spring day. I hoisted the pack onto my back, and we headed out.

Ascending toward Rattlesnake Spur, I stopped. More than a dozen large, jet-black birds had gathered—often called a "conspiracy" or "unkindness" of ravens. Most were patrolling the ground, but some perched on low branches. They were feeding, or trying to feed, on a small dead blacksnake. Next to the dead snake was a larger, coiled, combative blacksnake that struck at the ravens as they darted in to peck off flesh. It was a losing battle for the outnumbered blacksnake. Yet he persevered, perhaps because the smaller snake was his mate, offspring, or sibling.

It was a deadly struggle, savage and tenacious. Ravens eat carrion and about everything else, including snakes. How extraordinary for a blacksnake to defend one of its own against impossible odds, especially when his companion has already expired.

The tense ordeal had clearly lasted for some time, as much of the smaller snake's body was torn away. Still, the larger blacksnake continued to lunge at the birds. *Krruck, krruck, krruck* echoed through the forest. A formidable raven with a glistening saber-like beak then dropped from a branch and delivered a fierce blow to "Cecil." The snake twisted in agony. Another bird followed suit.

Glaring and abusive power imbalances infuriated me. Although this was a classic interspecies Darwinian struggle, something inside me snapped.

"Enough, you bastards!" I shouted, swinging my hiking stick. Xena joined in the fray, barking frantically and chasing the birds. The gang backed off, cursing us. *Krruck, krruck, krruck.*

I knelt by Cecil, who was coiled tightly. He'd suffered two pinkish colored lacerations near his head. "It's over, fella. Let's get you away from here." I gently lifted him onto my hiking stick and carried him to a nearby rock pile, where he slipped away to safety.

With Xena leading the way, we arrived at Rattlesnake Spur sometime before noon. We started to scramble up the layered rocky ledges until, about halfway up, I stopped to remove my pack and take in the panoramic views to the west. Ridge after ridge of mountains, dressed in the delicate yellow green of early spring, rolled on to the horizon. My car was located somewhere below us, only about three miles south of where we stood.

Woof! An unusual singular bark was muffled and cautionary. Xena crouched down low, ears pinned back. She drew away from something that had frightened her. She'd long ago learned to avoid skunks. I didn't smell one, but I wanted her away from possible trouble.

"Come."

Xena trotted over to me, panting heavily in the hot sun. She sat a few feet off the trail in the shade of azalea bushes whose buds were about to burst into brilliant, aromatic orange blossoms.

"Stay!" I commanded.

I was on alert for venomous snakes. A rattler can strike its target only at close range—usually about half the length of its body. With that in mind, I cautiously approached whatever had spooked Xena with my bamboo hiking stick extended in front of me.

Sure enough, a rattlesnake laid uncoiled on a rock ledge. It looked at least five feet long and as thick around as my arm. This rattler was the biggest I'd ever seen, and I'd seen many. When I was a teenager, I killed them just to collect the rattles.

The snake's eyes, with their vertical black pupils, were locked onto me, but its rattles weren't buzzing the classic warning, at least not yet. The rattler was yellow tan with dark brown bands. It had probably emerged this morning from its den to lounge on a warm ledge.

I'd walked to within ten feet of the snake when, from a higher ledge to my right came a guttural voice. "Knew it was you, shithead. Missed you last night."

Aubrey Ray Blount was top-heavy, all shoulders with a barrel chest and square head. Rivulets of sweat ran down his flushed, deeply pitted face. Even from fifty feet away, he smelled like last week's garbage. He was unshaven, he swayed like a drunkard, his barn door fly was wide open, and his unbuttoned Army green shirt revealed a bulging fish-belly white abdomen.

"Where's that fuckin' dog? Bitch should be dead," said Blount with a smirk. "Know she's here somewhere. Ran past my trailer after a deer." He clutched a large hunting knife, probably the same one he'd pulled on John Manikas in January and later used on Xena when he trashed my cottage.

"And where's the girlfriend? She's real nice."

I didn't budge or say a word as Blount slowly edged toward me along his ledge. My eyes flicked back and forth between Blount to my right and the snake in front of me. I gripped the hiking stick tightly with both hands as if anticipating a fast ball from the pitcher.

Xena was a hundred feet or so behind me, out of sight under the bushes. She'd obeyed my "stay" command, but I heard her low grumble. In dog-speak, she was saying, *Let me at him.* One "okay" from me, and Xena would be on Blount. She probably recognized his voice and definitely his foul odor.

Unsteady on his feet, Blount tripped on his rock ledge and fell, tearing his pants—but he managed to hold onto the knife. When he stood up, blood seeped through the fabric.

I could see the rattlesnake, which blended perfectly into the moss-covered rock, as it began to coil. The large diamond-shaped head swung from side to side as its tongue flicked out and tail twitched. But still no warning buzz.

Blount was now directly across from me. His eyes were fixed on me, not the snake. He stood about four feet above and somewhat behind the snake. Blount leapt down onto my ledge and landed squarely on the huge rattler. He slipped on the reptile's body and fell backwards, slamming his head on the rock. The snake whipped around and sank its fangs into Blount's face. He screamed in terror. He panicked, staggered to get up, and was bitten again, this time in the left hand. Once again, he fell, hitting his neck and head before struggling to his feet and spitting out a tooth.

Now standing, Blount still managed to clutch the knife in his right hand, albeit with bloody knuckles. Although thoroughly disoriented, he lunged at me, slashing wildly. I stepped back and swung, whacking his arm and head so hard that my hiking stick splintered.

"Okay, Xena!" I cried.

Xena bounded onto Blount, eager for vengeance. His knife fell to the ground as Xena knocked him off balance and then tore at his leg. Blood splattered on the rocks, and this time it wasn't Xena's.

With Xena clamped onto his leg and me pummeling him with my fists, Blount tried to retreat to the higher ledges. Just then, Xena let out a high-pitched yelp and released her hold on Blount. The snake had struck her on a hind leg. Although crazed by the snakebites, Blount started to scramble up toward the ridgeline. The snake, seeing an opening, slithered into a crevice.

Xena yowled in pain and licked her leg obsessively. I gripped her by the collar and led her away from the rocks to a shady area under some dogwoods. Except for the pain, she looked pretty normal, but I feared a severe delayed reaction. "Stay, girl. I'll be right back."

By this time, Blount had ascended almost to the ridgeline, but I could see that he was confused. I kicked his hunting knife to the side and, without handling it, carefully covered it with a heavy, flat stone. I followed Blount, warily and at some distance, while keeping him in sight.

Before long, I was standing much closer to him. He was clearly deranged and wholly unaware of his surroundings or my presence. The venom had taken hold, his face was red and swollen. He stumbled along an ever-narrower ridge, falling repeatedly. Blount then tripped over a stone, lost his balance, screamed, and plummeted to the rocks below. I crawled along the ridge on my hands and knees to where he'd disappeared from sight. His body was sprawled chest-down on boulders, but his head and neck were so grotesquely wrenched that his eyes stared up at me. Blood oozed from his mouth and ears onto the rocks.

27

Love, Indeed

I made my way down from the high ridge and ran over to Xena. She was lying on her side, whimpering and panting irregularly. Her tongue lolled out, and her hind quarters were severely swollen. She flinched at even the gentlest touch. Beneath Xena's fur, the skin was turning a dark plum color. How was I to carry an eighty-pound dog and my backpack down the trail?

Dropping my pack directly on the trail, I took a slug of water from the canteen and got down on my knees. "I won't leave you, girl." My arms went under Xena, and, lifting her, I rose up on one knee. Bending forward, and with considerable effort, I swung her torso across my shoulders in a fireman's carry and stood straight up.

I trudged down the trail about a hundred yards until I tripped on a tree root and fell, snapping a sapling and dumping us both onto the ground. "Sorry, girl." Another grueling fireman's carry was followed by another nasty fall. After an hour of this, we'd covered less than a half mile. I was bone-tired, bruised, and badly scratched. The canteen was empty.

My shirt was drenched in perspiration. Dog urine and diarrhea dribbled down my chest and legs. Xena was limp, but still breathing.

When I crumpled to the ground one last time, I leaned against a bank of red dirt, not noticing or caring whether I was sitting on a wasp's nest, a poison ivy patch, or Aladdin's magic carpet. My mind was fuzzy; everything hurt.

I was alone, all alone. Twisting, falling, being transported to . . . somewhere. The muted chords of a moving J.S. Bach chorale prelude sounded as visions of Blount's shattered body, parading ravens, the deer skull, Caleb Heath, the strange prophet, and a wounded Cecil funneled up, spinning tornado-like, only to whiz off into an ethereal cosmos.

What I saw, or imagined I saw, in my delirium was filtered through a faint blueish mist. Valerie stood on a sunlit college campus wearing a peach-colored jumper. A gentle breeze caught her long, sandy hair and swept it across her face. She smiled. Kim, in a revealing little black dress with plunging neckline, held Val's hand. They hugged. Kim whispered something in Val's ear, winked at me, and gradually melted away into a dense haze. Now standing alone and beaming, Val blew me a kiss.

———

"Hey, you okay?" Someone shook my shoulder. "Looks like you wrestled a bear and lost."

Another male voice asked, "What happened to your dog? Where's your backpack?"

I heard them but saw only blurry images and wondered where Valerie had gone.

"Drink this," said a third voice.

Water! I emptied his canteen. The mystical aura dissipated, and three young men came into focus.

"Snakebite," I muttered.

"Pearisburg's just down the hill," said a tall, lean guy with a dark mustache that begged to be trimmed. "We'll get you there."

"No, it's my dog."

My head was still pretty foggy. They probably revealed who they were and where they were from, but all I could recall when the mental fog began to lift was the lavender t-shirt that one was wearing with the words, "The journey is the destination."

A few minutes later, when my mind was clearer, a wiry guy with runners' legs zipped up the trail to retrieve my pack from where I'd told him it was. The other two men lashed together sturdy, seven-foot-long tree limbs with nylon cord to form a crude litter. This took only thirty minutes, by which time the runner had returned with my backpack.

We eased my comatose dog onto the litter, secured her with the cord, and headed down the trail. Every few minutes, we took turns dragging or carrying Xena until we reached US 460 and my parked car. I lifted her gently into the backseat.

"How can I possibly thank you?"

"We're glad to help," said the one with the mustache. He chuckled. "Maybe send a dollar or two to the Sierra Club."

"Will do." I hugged each of them. They petted Xena, wished her well, and swiftly disappeared into the forest.

I did not tell them what had happened on Rattlesnake Spur. I wanted the authorities to be the first on the scene, and there was no reason to alarm them. Fortunately, Blount's body was out of sight, and the AT was more than a hundred feet away from the blood-splattered rocks and hidden knife.

I quickly changed shirts, then drove the twenty-five miles from Pearisburg to the Virginia Tech veterinary clinic in record time. Xena was admitted immediately and given an IV with anti-venom.

The admitting veterinarian was glum: "Her abdomen is distended, and there's blood in her nose. That's not good. We'll have to hold her here for several days."

I rubbed away tears with my sleeve and muttered, "Okay. Whatever is best for Xena. "

"My God!" the vet exclaimed when he realized my dog had returned to the clinic. "Xena." He put his hand on my shoulder. "We'll do *everything* we can. She's famous. Should we inform the press?"

"Don't know. Maybe."

By now, the sun was beginning to set. I left Xena in the hands of the vet and drove on to Traymore, where I stopped at the sheriff's office. For more than an hour, I related my story to Sheriff Goetzke, answered his many questions, and told him where Blount's body and knife could be found.

It was pitch dark by the time I pulled up to my cottage. I opened the door, flicked on the lights, and turned up the heat. No Xena. No Valerie, either. Alone and dead tired, I fell onto the bed without washing up or eating.

———

Three days later, at the college, a voice at my office door said, "Hi, love." Dressed exquisitely in a gray skirt, powder blue blouse, and coral necklace, Valerie sauntered in, sat down, and stunned me with, "My turn to apologize. Yes, you made a poor decision with Kim, and it hurt. But I made an even worse one in marrying Vincent." She slid to the edge of the chair and leaned her elbows on my desk. "You never abandoned me, even after he almost killed you."

I rose, skirted the desk, and kissed her while she sat in the chair. "Have I *ever* missed you," I confessed.

Val stood and we kissed again. The office door was wide open, but I didn't give a damn. I'd soon be gone.

"But," said Val, raising an index finger, "I still *do* have a bone to pick with you." She reached into her book bag, extracted the *Roanoke Times*, and spread the front page out on the desk. The headline read, "Xena Does It Again!" Flashing a sly smile with hands on her hips and an elevated eyebrow, Val admonished me: "You promised to protect Xena."

I nodded. "Xena came to my defense, not the other way around."

Over the next week, with the end of the academic year in sight, Val and I moved her things from Christiansburg to my Piney Woods cottage. My spirits, and certainly my meals, improved dramatically. We often had Mara Heath to dinner, and we paid daily visits to Xena at the clinic. And the media reported on May twenty-eighth that the independent study commission had unanimously recommended to the State Council on Higher Education that President Elzic Barton be immediately removed from his position as president of Traymore College.

28

I Was There

Like an exquisite wine, fine gems have a presence that says, "I am here."

Like a lover's embrace, finer gems have a presence that says, "Remember this."

But like God's grace, priceless gems have a presence that says, "I was there."

———

The regime of intimidation was collapsing. I was there as Traymore College moved from repression and disrepute toward openness and respectability. Change was palpable. It was irreversible and accelerating. The few remaining days of the academic year raced toward the college's June sixth graduation.

President Barton hung on bitterly as forces beyond his control gathered momentum. For most students and many faculty members, as well as outside investigators, the press, civil libertarians, the State Council on Higher Education, and even Traymore's own calcified Board of Visitors—Elzic Barton had become a costly and insufferable liability.

The independent study commission's recommendation that the already grievously weakened president be removed had been anticipated by the media for weeks. Two days before the commission's determination was publicly released, I had a final, bizarre encounter with Barton.

Evelyn and I were having our last lunch together in the faculty dining room. Our mood was beyond convivial; it was celebratory. I'd secured a new faculty appointment, and Evelyn's ring finger featured a sparkling diamond engagement ring from Henry Buchanan. We laughed and spoke more freely than in the past, giving little heed to what others might think.

Everything suddenly went mausoleum quiet as President Barton, who always ate lunch in his office, entered the faculty dining room. All eyes were on him. He walked briskly to our table. Color drained from Evelyn's face, and she instinctively clutched my arm. I touched her hand before standing to face a disheveled Barton. His tie was loose, he was without a jacket, his eyes were bloodshot, and he obviously hadn't shaved in two or three days.

Standing intimidatingly close to Evelyn, who remained seated, and thrusting a finger in her face, Barton spat out, "Judas!"

Evelyn gasped, covered her face with both hands, and doubled over in her seat.

Turning to me and shaking a fist, an irate Barton could only stammer, "You . . . you . . . murderer."

I thought of Aubrey Blount and the vine-covered tombstone of Eliza Barton Blount, but kept quiet. The president then turned around and stormed out of the dining room, knocking into a student waitress and splattering tomato soup on her blouse and onto the floor. He didn't pause to apologize.

———

Barton was ousted a week later on June first, 1970. The next year, Traymore went coed. To widespread acclaim, and with an expectation that the temporary appointment would become permanent, Dean Evelyn Baird was named Acting President of Traymore College. Attorneys for Professor Bill Vaughn were always confident that his case against the college, filed in 1969, would succeed. Sure enough, the court rendered a major decision in Bill's favor in 1971, faulting Barton for gross infringement of Professor Vaughn's First Amendment rights and awarding him two hundred and fifty thousand dollars.

And Xena? Well, she survived her third brush with death. She leapt into my arms, sending me butt-first onto the Virginia Tech veterinary clinic's linoleum floor. Once again, the media throughout the State of Virginia lavished attention on her. Xena made the cover of *Boy's Life* and even rode with Miss Virginia in Roanoke's Memorial Day parade. For the press, my dog *was* the story. I was a minor footnote.

––––––––––

Earlier in May, on what has been the symbolic center of the University of Virginia since its founding in 1819, the Lawn, I was formally awarded the PhD degree. The academic procession was led by a grand marshal who carried an ebony and silver mace crafted by Patek Philippe. The warm day was made warmer by my long black gown with its three doctoral velvet bars on each sleeve, a fuzzy black mortarboard hat and gold tassel, and an orange and blue silk hood that hung down the back of the gown. With the Rotunda to the north, the graduates proceeded in a long line down the Lawn, past parallel colonnaded brick pavilions that reflected Mr. Jefferson's preference for Palladian and neoclassical architecture.

Valerie's dazzling carnation pink dress caught my eye and everyone else's. When she saw me approaching, Val, in a flagrant contravention of protocol, left my parents (who had driven down from New York) and hundreds of other spectators observing the procession, and sprinted barefoot across the grass in my direction. She tugged on the sleeve of my gown and planted a wet kiss on my cheek. With the scent of Bellogia, she handed me a single yellow rose before dashing back to the sidelines to the applause of onlookers.

"Lucky guy," said a male voice behind me.

After receiving the degree and putting in a brief appearance at the reception for graduates, Val and I started to make our way across campus to my car. When we were only steps away from what had once been Edgar Allan Poe's room, we heard a familiar harsh crackling sound: *Krruck, krruck.* A solitary raven stared down at us from a nearby white oak tree. I recalled a line from the last stanza of *The Raven*: "And the Raven, never flitting, still is sitting, *still* is sitting."

———

Traymore's graduation in early June was bittersweet. I was there, adorned in my newly acquired academic plumage. It was both a celebration and a last hurrah for battle-hardened students and faculty. In full view of everyone, I kissed Evelyn on both cheeks and said, "I'll miss you, Madam President." We had succeeded in upsetting the status quo, but at a cost. Barton had threatened everyone, bludgeoned many, and ruined the careers of some.

Several of my closest student allies in our protracted campaign against the administration were graduating, including Sue Ewal, Kim Sherman, and Valerie. Sue was entering the corporate world, while Kim and Val were going on to graduate school. On that day, we knew each other in ways we never would again.

Late that afternoon, Valerie and I returned to Piney Woods to get Xena. We first stopped to say goodbye to Mara Heath because, while I knew that Val would not disappear from my world, Mara surely would. She was a teetotaler, but I handed her a precious possession—my last bottle of St. Julien Bordeaux. "Do with this as you like, my dear."

"Oh, David," she said, surprising me by snatching the bottle out of my hand. "Let's open it. God will forgive me."

I uncorked the bottle, she produced three juice glasses, and I poured each of us a smidgen of the glorious wine.

I raised my glass to "the Lady of the Lake."

Clicking our glasses together, Mara said, "May the Lord bless you and keep you." We toasted, but I doubt she swallowed even a drop.

When we hugged for the last time, Mara's tears dampened my shirt. Here was a simple, compassionate woman who lived the Golden Rule and walked in the ways of the Lord. A better person than I, by far.

———

Val and I drove on down to the cottage, where Xena greeted us with anxious exuberance. The empty cottage told Xena that change was in the air. Then—with Val beside me, an alert Xena by the front seat window, a trailer in tow, and the back seat and trunk jammed with boxes—I paused to look back at Claytor Lake.

Some memories would remain forever, like Vincent Tavernetti's attack on the cottage, Evelyn's courage and integrity, my face-to-face confrontation with Barton, battling Aubrey Ray Blount, and Valerie's love. As we drove away, we knew that this leg of our journey together was over, but we had grown in ways that would forever bind us to one another.

Acknowledgments

This book would not have been written except for the influence of two strong and talented women. My lovely wife, law professor Ann H. Clarke, read every line. Brilliant writer Roxan McDonald lit the fire that made a professor her eager student.

I am indebted to Christina Clarke, Deborah Fitzgerald, Nancy Hildebrand, Gordon May, William Niesh, Diane Rosolowsky, and Bill Rosolowsky for their critical commentaries and professional expertise as—respectively—dermatologist, retired federal employee, priest, emeritus professor, editor, librarian, and veterinarian.

Finally, I am grateful for the skill and dedication of my editor at Brandylane, Christina Kann.

Duncan L. Clarke is Professor Emeritus of International Relations and former Director of the United States Foreign Policy Field at American University's School of International Service, Washington, D.C. He was Visiting Professor of Politics at the University of California, Santa Cruz, and Professor of National Security at the National War College. He has served in the intelligence community and authored numerous articles and five books on U.S. defense and foreign policy. Clarke lived and taught in Washington, D.C., for many years before moving to the Central Coast of California. He earned his BA at Clark University, JD at Cornell University, and PhD at the University of Virginia. *A Little Rebellion Is a Good Thing* was inspired by his experience in 1969-1970 at Radford College, which was then a public women's college in Southwest Virginia. Clarke is writing a second novel about a serial murderer on the Appalachian Trail. He has twice hiked the entire Appalachian Trail.